D1187459

So This Is Love

A Twisted Tale

ELIZABETH LIM

Disney · HYPERION
Los Angeles • New York

Printed in the United States of America
First Hardcover Edition, April 2020
3 5 7 9 10 8 6 4 2
FAC-020093-20191
Library of Congress Control Number: 2019940034
ISBN 978-1-368-01382-6

Visit disneybooks.com

SUSTAINABLE FORESTRY INITIATIVE
Certified Sourcing
www.sfiprogram.org
SFI-00993
Logo Applies to Text Stock Only

To Charlotte,
for teaching me a mother's love
—E.L.

Chapter One

It was the event of the season—a royal ball in King George's palace that every eligible maiden had been invited to attend.

And Cinderella couldn't believe she was going.

One dance, she promised herself, watching the palace draw near from within her carriage. *If I just have one dance . . . even if it's by myself, I'll be happy. I just want to remember what it's like to be free, to spin round and round under the moonlight.*

The palace was tremendous, a city within itself; Cinderella could have spent the entire evening simply exploring the courtyard where her carriage dropped her off.

But she'd arrived hours late, so late that there was no one at the entrance to greet her. Even the halls inside were empty but for the dozens of unsmiling guards standing against the walls. She didn't have an invitation, so as she wandered up the grand staircase in search of the ballroom, she didn't dare ask a guard for directions, lest they ask her to leave.

If not for the charming young man who found her searching for the king's party, she might have spent the entire night happily lost in the palace.

"The ballroom is this way, miss," he said, gently tapping her hand.

Flustered, she whirled to face him. She'd expected him to be one of the guards, but to her relief, he was a guest at the ball—like herself. "Oh, so it is. Thank you!"

Her cheeks were already warm, flushed from climbing the endless staircase, but they seemed to grow hotter still. How foolish she must look. Why hadn't she simply followed the music? She could hear the strains of the orchestra not far, and the low, dense murmuring of the king's guests.

But the young man made no indication that he thought her a fool. Maybe he was simply being polite; that would explain his squared shoulders and stiff posture. Yet his eyes were warm and kind, and as he bowed to her, something unfamiliar but wonderful fluttered in her stomach.

"Thank you," she said again, instinctively curtsying.

"Would you . . . would you like to dance?"

Cinderella blinked. "Did you read my mind?" she said with a soft laugh. "All I wished for tonight was a dance . . . it's been so long I worried I've forgotten how."

At that, the young man chuckled, and he seemed to relax, breaking the formality between them. A smile as warm as his eyes spread across his face and he offered her his arm. "Then allow me to remind you."

The next few minutes were a blur. A beautiful, rapturous blur, yet Cinderella knew she'd never forget the waltz that stirred the hall, its lilting melody singing its way deep into her heart.

Nor would she forget the way her companion looked at her—as if there were no one else in the ballroom. Every now and then, he parted his lips as if he wanted to speak to her, but the music was so overwhelming he must have thought better of it. It was a miracle they hadn't collided with anyone else dancing, or were they the only ones on the floor? Cinderella hardly noticed.

When the waltz ended, Cinderella braced herself to wake from the most beautiful dream. Murmurs of conversation replaced the orchestra's lush music, a potpourri of perfumes thickened the air, and the chandeliers seemed to glow dizzyingly bright.

She half expected her dance partner to make an excuse to leave, but instead he leaned in to whisper, "Do you want to walk outside for a short while? I'd love to show you the gardens."

Again, he'd read her mind. Or were they simply of one mind? Her father used to say that about himself and her mother, that from the moment they'd met it had felt like they'd known each other forever.

Or maybe I feel that way because it's been so long since I've made a friend, she thought as they left the palace. A cool breeze tickled her nape, and she inhaled, relishing the garden's freshness.

"It's so peaceful," she said, brushing her fingers across the finely pruned hedges. "Would it be awful if I told you I preferred it out here to the ballroom?"

"And why is that?"

She hesitated, wondering what he'd think of the truth. "I think I'm more comfortable around the flowers and the trees. I haven't been around so many people in a long time," she admitted shyly. "I wouldn't even know what to say to most of them."

"You didn't come to the ball to meet the . . . to meet new people?"

"I came to the ball mostly to watch. To listen to the music and see the palace. But I have to say, it's even more beautiful out here than it is in there."

"It's certainly not as stuffy."

They laughed together, and Cinderella felt that flutter in her stomach again.

"I want to remember everything about tonight," she said. "The waltz, the flowers, the fountains—"

"And me?" her companion teased.

She smiled, but she was too shy to answer. Yes, she wanted to remember everything about him. The way he held her hand, gentle yet firm—as if he never wanted to let go. The way his shoulders lifted when she smiled at him, the tenderness in his voice when he spoke to her.

But she didn't even know his name. She should have asked when they first met, except her mind had been—and *still* was—in such a whirlwind. Besides, now that they had danced together and escaped the ballroom to this beautiful garden, it felt like they had gone on a grand adventure together, and she didn't want to take a step back with pleasantries.

And, if she was honest, she was also afraid he would ask where she was from.

"What's on your mind?" he asked, sensing her thoughts had escaped the present.

"Simply that I don't want tonight to end," she replied.

He leaned closer, and Cinderella tilted her head, waiting for him to say something. But he closed his lips and cleared his throat, an odd flush coming over his cheeks.

"I don't, either." He hesitated. "I've been away from Valors for years. Didn't think I wanted to come home, but now I'm starting to change my mind."

"Oh? Where were you?"

He blinked, as if surprised she didn't know the answer, but he quickly recovered. "Away at school. It's not a very interesting story. Come, would you like to walk more?"

She nodded. "I love it out here. Strange that there aren't more people in the gardens. Are we the only ones?"

"Everyone's inside," he responded.

"Dancing?"

"That . . . or looking to meet the prince."

"I see. Well, I'm glad to be out here. We used to keep a garden . . . not as magnificent as this, of course, but . . . oh!" Cinderella spied a path of rosebushes not far ahead.

"You like roses?"

"Who doesn't?" Cinderella knelt, careful that her skirts did not snag on the thorns. "My mother used to grow roses in her garden. We'd pick them together every morning."

She fell silent, remembering how she'd carried on the tradition with her papa after her mother died. One by one they'd cut the flowers, each still so fresh that dew glistened on its petals and trickled down her trembling fingers.

"Eight pink roses, seven white ones, and three sprigs of myrtle," she murmured, pointing at the pink and white roses in the line of bushes.

"What is that?"

"It's what I would always bring Mama—the same arrangement my father presented to her when he'd asked her to marry him."

The story of their courtship had been her favorite, one Papa had told her over and over. She'd never tired of it, never stopped asking him to tell it to her.

Before her mother had died, he'd always ended the story with a smile, saying, "Your mother is my true love."

Once she was gone, his expression became solemn, shadows sinking into the lines of his brow, his teeth clenched tight to keep from grimacing. Then he would say, "Your mother *was* my true love."

So Cinderella had learned how one word could change everything. And she had stopped asking her father for the story.

"I'd nearly forgotten about it," she said softly, a strain in her voice. "It's been so long. . . ."

"Eight pink roses, seven white ones, and three sprigs of myrtle," he repeated. "I'll help you remember."

She looked up at him, a rush of warmth flooding her heart. How could it be that someone she'd known for only a handful of hours could already feel so dear to her?

By the time they had strolled across the gardens, past the marble pavilions and sparkling ponds, taking a rest by the stairs—she'd completely lost track of time.

"There's a part of the garden you haven't seen that I know will make you smile. It's a little far—are you tired?"

"No, not at all."

He started to lead her toward it, but as she followed, Cinderella glanced behind her. "Wait, I want to take a moment to admire how beautiful this is."

He tilted his head. "What is there to admire?"

"Everything. The towers, the trees, the scraps of curtain peeking out from the windows. Even the clouds." Cinderella clasped her hands to her chest and turned toward Valors, watching the city sparkling below. "And if we look this way, what a view."

"I'd never appreciated it much."

"I see the palace every day from my window, but seeing it from this angle is another story entirely," Cinderella said. She leaned against the railing, admiring the glittering white palace and the garden skimming beneath it. "I don't know the next time I'll be back."

Then she sat on one of the steps, moving the folds of her gown to hug her knees close. "I used to dream about coming here. Strange to think I don't have to do that anymore."

He knelt beside her, taking the lower step. "What other dreams do you have?"

Cinderella paused. Before coming to the ball, she'd had

so many dreams. But they'd been simply that—dreams. Wishes, really, if she wanted to be honest about it; wishes about living a different life. She hadn't even dared leave home, not until tonight.

But she couldn't tell him that.

"I'd like to see more of the world," she said slowly, "and I want to help people—"

She stopped. She hadn't given it much more thought than that. She didn't even know what it meant to help people—besides, how *could* she, when she was trapped in her stepmother's house?

"Anything else?"

Cinderella pursed her lips. After the ball, she might never get a chance to discuss such things with someone again. She'd go back to working for Lady Tremaine and her stepsisters, to being forgotten.

"I'd like to remember what it's like to be loved," she finally confessed, staring at her hands. As soon as she said it, she wished she could take it back. It sounded miserable, even to her ears. But she couldn't remember the last time anyone had said anything kind to her, let alone held her hand and spent time getting to know her.

To have to go back to mistreatment and neglect—it was the last thing Cinderella wanted to think about. She wished this night could last forever.

"You must think I'm hopeless," she said quickly, before her companion could respond.

"No. Not at all."

She didn't dare look up at him, but he shifted closer to her so their fingertips nearly touched.

"I can understand. Sometimes, I wish that for myself, too." He drew a deep breath. "My mother used to tell me that there are many kinds of love. Unconditional love, self-love, love for your family, love for your friends . . . romantic love." He paused, seeming to search for the right words. "That all are important in fulfilling the heart. You say you haven't been around people in a long time. For me, it's the opposite. I'm surrounded by people, but few see past my . . . my . . ."

"Your heart?" Cinderella asked.

His mouth bent into an unreadable smile. "Yes, my heart," he said softly. Then he kissed her.

She'd never been kissed before, never been in love. Yet when his lips touched hers, something inside her bloomed, coming alive for the first time in years. In that moment, all her worries and troubles grew wings, leaving her with a rush of joy she hadn't felt in a long time.

Out of nowhere, a clock chimed, and her fairy godmother's warning came rushing into her memory:

At the stroke of twelve, the spell will be broken—and everything will be as it was before.

Cinderella jolted, ending the kiss. "Oh my goodness!"

"What's the matter?"

"It's midnight."

"Yes, so it is." When she started to rise, he caught her hand. "But why—"

Cinderella faltered. A hundred explanations spun in her head, but the only thing she could say was: "Goodbye."

"No, no, wait. You can't go now, it's only—"

"Oh, I must." Cinderella disentangled herself from his arms. "Please. Please, I must."

"But why?"

The clock chimed again, overpowering her sense. What could she say? "Well, I . . . oh, the prince! I haven't met the prince."

"The prince?" His brows drew together.

"Goodbye."

She ran as fast as she could through the gardens and the ballroom, stopping only briefly to wave goodbye to the guards waiting in the halls. Everyone seemed to want her to stay longer, but Cinderella ignored their cries. Even when she left her glass slipper on the staircase, she thought better of retrieving it.

There was no time.

Once she was in the carriage, it sped out of the palace, spiraling down the hill into Valors. It was the longest minute of her life. Little by little, her sparkling ball gown sparkled no more, and when the clock finished blaring midnight, she was back in her rags, sitting on a pumpkin, surrounded by Bruno, her dog, and Major, her horse.

She lurched, spying an oncoming coach speeding their way. As she bolted off the road, it trundled past, smashing her pumpkin under its horses' hooves.

Once it was out of sight, she caught her breath and knelt to pick up the mice that had served as her elegant horses.

Her head swam, reliving the last few moments at the ball. She wished she could have stayed longer with that handsome stranger she'd met; oh, what a silly excuse she'd made to him. What did she care about meeting the prince? She shook her head, simmering with embarrassment.

For better or worse, she didn't think she would ever see him again.

Despite all that, what a wonderful time she'd had. To finally see the palace, with its glistening chandeliers, and all the beautiful gowns and the gardens. To drink in the ball's romantic music.

In the shadows, a glass slipper shimmered on her foot. She bent to pick it up.

Strange, that everything should disappear except her glass slipper.

She hugged it to her chest. Before this night, she hadn't

thought magic would ever touch her life. None of this would have been possible without her fairy godmother.

She gazed at the stars twinkling above her. Somehow, she knew her godmother was listening. "Thank you so much . . . for everything."

Carefully, she tucked her glass slipper into her pocket. At least she would have it to remind her of what a beautiful night it had been.

Her fairy godmother's spell had been broken. Tomorrow, everything would go back to the way it was before. Her stepmother would go back to ordering her around the chateau, her stepsisters, Anastasia and Drizella, to tormenting her over every one of their needs, but she'd caught a glimpse of happiness, something she hadn't felt in many years.

Her eyes had opened to the possibility of leaving home, of dreaming dreams that might actually come true. But she wasn't brave enough to chase them—not yet. Not so soon, anyway, after such a magnificent night.

What she didn't realize was—she might not have a choice.

Chapter Two

Threads of dawn embossed the sky, rays of pinkish light stretching over the opalescent clouds to brighten the city beneath it.

Many of the young ladies who had traveled from afar to attend the ball were only now arriving home, their feet swollen from dancing all night and their spirits deflated from failing to catch even a single glance from Prince Charles.

For Cinderella, the morning was like any other, though she woke in better spirits than usual, and she hummed to herself while she prepared breakfast for her stepmother and stepsisters.

Anastasia and Drizella weren't awake yet, at least not when she ascended the staircase to deliver their meals. But once she reached the top, she heard her stepmother barging into her daughters' rooms, urging them to get dressed.

"Everyone's talking about it," Lady Tremaine said while Cinderella brought a breakfast tray into Anastasia's room, where everyone had gathered. "The whole kingdom. Hurry now, he'll be here any minute."

"Who will?" asked Drizella.

"The Grand Duke. He's been hunting all night."

"Hunting?" her stepsister repeated.

"For that girl—the one who lost her slipper at the ball last night. They say he's madly in love with her."

Anastasia yawned. "The duke is?"

"No, no, no. The prince!"

Cinderella gasped and dropped the trays. *The prince?* She couldn't believe it. The last thing she would have guessed was that the young man she'd spent the evening with was Prince Charles himself.

Then again, she'd never expected to see him again, much less learn the next day that the heir to the throne of Aurelais was looking for *her.*

"Pick that up, you clumsy fool."

Obediently, Cinderella knelt, but her attention was far from the shards of broken porcelain on the floor. She clung to her stepmother's every next word.

"The glass slipper is their only clue," Lady Tremaine

continued. "The duke has been ordered to try it on every girl in the kingdom. And if one can be found whom the slipper fits, then, by the king's command, that girl shall be the prince's bride."

His bride.

The word made Cinderella's head reel. Everything blurred, and she forgot her stepmother and her stepsisters—even where she was. If the prince wanted her to be his bride—that meant he . . . he *loved* her. It meant she'd no longer have to work as her stepmother's servant, or live in the attic alone. She'd be free.

Without thinking, she began humming the song she and her companion—the *prince*—had danced to. An imaginary orchestra accompanied her: strings swelling with a lush harmony, a harp tinkling a luxurious sweep at the cadence, and flutes singing the dulcet countermelody. She swayed with every step as she made her way back to her room to make herself presentable for the duke's arrival. It just would not do to see the Grand Duke with dust in her hair and crumbs all over her apron.

She was numb with anticipation. How long had it been since she'd allowed herself to feel such hope?

Cinderella reached for the comb beside her mirror and ran it through her hair, a thrilling tingle shooting up her spine with each stroke. From the window, she could see the king's castle gleaming in the distance, its towers and spires glittering white as pearls. Graceful as a swan, it sat on a cloud of green: a glorious garden, with endless rows of elm and spruce trees so verdant that emeralds were dull in comparison.

Was the prince inside now, looking out from one of those tall arched windows and wondering where she was? Would he really marry her once he found out she possessed the other glass slipper? She didn't know what would happen when they reunited, but that didn't matter. In fact, it thrilled her. For once the future would bring more than her quotidian chores, her stepmother's rebukes, her stepsisters' spite. Her life was going to change. Finally.

Leaning closer to the mirror, she studied herself, wishing she had something nicer than her work dress to wear.

Setting down her comb, she glanced out the window reflected on her mirror. No sign of the Grand Duke yet. How she hoped he would arrive soon; she didn't know how much longer she could wait. She hugged herself, feeling her anticipation building inside.

So deep in a daze was she that she didn't realize Lady Tremaine had followed her up the winding stairway to her tiny garret room in the attic, not until it was too late.

"No," she whispered, finally seeing her stepmother appear behind her, her dark silhouette filling the mirror.

Her horror grew as Lady Tremaine's fingers slid across the wooden door. Cinderella turned, but her stepmother seized the key and slammed the door shut.

"No!" Cinderella raced across the room and pounded her fists against the door. "You can't keep me in here! Please! You can't. You just can't."

But Lady Tremaine's footsteps were already fading, quickly descending from the tower. Cinderella crumpled against the door.

It was no use; her stepmother wasn't coming back. She was trapped.

Below, the gates outside creaked open. Horses nickered, and the heavy wheels of a carriage trundled onto the driveway.

The Grand Duke had arrived.

A burst of hope swelled in her chest. Picking herself up, she rushed to the window, frantically trying to get the duke's attention.

"Your Grace!" she shouted, waving. "Over here! Please, help me!"

Below, the footman helped the Grand Duke out of the carriage. He cast an odd shadow, thin but for the paunch at his belly, with an egg-shaped head. A tall blue hat capped his black hair, its bright red feather matching the sash around his torso. As Lady Tremaine greeted him outside, he walked briskly to the door, giving what seemed like only the most obligatory of greetings.

"Your Grace!" Cinderella tried again. Louder, this time.

But the duke disappeared into the house.

He hadn't heard her. No one had, and no one would. After all, she was locked up in the chateau's tower, so high she was peering down at the tops of the trees. It was no use shouting.

Anger bubbled at the back of Cinderella's throat, but she pushed it away. She never used to question her stepmother's cruelty. Over the years, she'd toughened her heart, forgiving Lady Tremaine and her daughters every night for the unkindness they seemed to enjoy meting out to her.

But today, her stepmother had taken a dream Cinderella had only just begun to have faith might actually come true— and shattered it. And Cinderella was more trapped than ever.

Mice scurried out of their hiding places inside the walls and nibbled at the hem of her skirts. Another day, seeing them might have made her smile, but blinking back tears, Cinderella turned away from them.

"I just want to be alone," she told them softly.

Not understanding, the mice circled her, their little paws tapping against the wooden floor.

For so long the mice had been her only company, besides

Bruno. They were certainly preferable to the company of her stepsisters. Until the previous night, she hadn't spoken with anyone outside her father's house in weeks, likely even months.

An ache stirred in her heart as she remembered her easy conversation—with Charles, the prince. If only she'd known.

What would it have changed? I would still have run off at midnight, wouldn't I?

Unsure of the answer, she sighed and watched the mice finally scurry off, disappearing back into the wall. She wished *she* could escape her room as easily, but no one was coming to save her, least of all the mice.

She inhaled a ragged breath and steadied herself. She used to spend hours every night wondering what she'd done to make her stepmother hate her so much. Her attempts to swallow her pride and obey Lady Tremaine so she might feel some affection for her seemed to only infuriate her stepmother more. As Cinderella grew older, she gave up and simply focused on making each day as bearable as possible.

Time crawled forward. Cinderella didn't know how long she sat there, drying her tears and trying to convince herself that everything would turn out all right. After what seemed a very long time, the gates outside closed once more.

She rose and went to the window, leaning against the

wooden sill as she watched the Grand Duke's carriage curve out of her father's manor and disappear beyond the oak trees lining the road. Her stepmother did not see the duke out, which could only mean that neither Anastasia nor Drizella had fit the glass slipper.

No surprise there, yet Cinderella felt no satisfaction. Only relief.

Maybe now everything will go back to the way it was.

She pursed her lips; only a fool would believe that was true.

Things couldn't go back to the way they were. Besides, now that she'd tasted the possibility of a new life—for the first time since her father's death—could she fathom returning to being her stepmother and stepsisters' servant?

Stifling a sigh, she bunched up the folds of her apron in her fist, squeezing tight.

Not everything is lost, she reasoned. *I still have the other glass slipper.*

But what good would that do her here? Storm clouds brewed in the distance, a bitter breeze gusting into her room. Cinderella shut the window, but her hand lingered on the pane.

Her father's chateau had been her home ever since she was born. It had been beautiful, once. Towering oak trees had surrounded the estate, ivy crawling over the gray-painted bricks; Cinderella's favorite part had been the garden, where she'd spent countless hours with her mother on a swing richly covered with flowers.

The swing was no more, long since taken down. Aside from her memories, this place was all she had left of her mother and father—Lady Tremaine had sold most of her parents' belongings years ago: their portraits and paintings, their books, their furniture, their clothes. And their letters, she had burned.

For so long, Cinderella had ignored the tug in her heart to leave. How could she go when this place was all she knew—when it was all she had left of her loving parents? How did she know that life out there would be any better than the one she suffered here? Not to mention the fact that she had nowhere to go, no plan for how to support herself. There weren't a lot of options for a penniless orphan.

Besides, Lady Tremaine and her daughters were the only family she had left. So whatever bitterness she felt toward them for making her a servant in her own home, she swallowed. *Papa would have wanted me to help take care of them,* she would tell herself.

But for the first time, she was beginning to question whether that was true.

For the first time, she saw that Lady Tremaine would never want what was best for her, that any time Cinderella came close to feeling a spark of happiness, she would try to smother it.

As though she'd summoned her, Cinderella heard her stepmother's footsteps again, steadily ascending the tower's stairwell. Except this time, Lady Tremaine would not visit alone.

"Can you believe the nerve of that man?" Anastasia huffed. "That was clearly my slipper. My slipper!"

"*Your* slipper?" said Drizella. "That's rich."

Their mother rebuked them. "Girls! Some dignity."

Cinderella's stepsisters quieted, but not for long.

Anastasia was the first to complain again. Slightly breathless, she said, "Why do we have to go all the way up here? It's so dusty."

"I thought I heard a mouse," Drizella added. "Mother, can't we just have her come down? Why are we going to her? That's so—"

"Quiet, you two," Lady Tremaine said sharply. "Enough complaining."

Cinderella steeled herself. From the sound of it, her stepmother was not in a good mood. But Cinderella wasn't afraid—what more could she do to her? The Grand Duke had already left, and he wasn't coming back. He was off to find another girl who'd fit the glass slipper and who would marry the prince—a girl who wasn't her.

The footsteps were getting closer. "It's time you saw her true colors," Lady Tremaine said. "She expressly disobeyed my orders and stole her way to the ball."

Cinderella froze. How did her stepmother know she had gone to the ball?

She'd gotten home well before they had, and in the morning everything had seemed normal enough, at least until she'd heard the news and—

The song she'd been humming—it was from the waltz at the ball. A chill twisted down Cinderella's spine. Could her stepmother have heard her?

If so, Lady Tremaine would know that Cinderella was the girl with the glass slipper—the girl the prince was searching for.

Following her up to her room and locking her in the attic without any explanation—suddenly it made sense. But the Grand Duke had gone, so what would happen to her now?

I will not apologize, Cinderella told herself staunchly, *not for going to the ball.*

As the key clicked into the lock and the doorknob began to turn, Cinderella took a deep breath, gathering her nerves—

—and fearing that she was just as trapped as ever.

Chapter Three

What a debacle!

Ferdinand, the Grand Duke of Malloy, leaned back against the carriage's plush velvet cushion, wishing he were anywhere but there.

Unfortunately, according to the rolled-up list by his side, its pages slightly crumpled at the bottom corners, he still had nearly a hundred households to visit.

He closed his eyes, knowing that the moment he fell asleep they would arrive at the next house on the list. All he could hope was the next family wouldn't be as dreadful as the last.

Simply recalling Lady Tremaine's awful daughters made him shudder. It'd been shameful how the two young women had thrown themselves at the glass slipper.

"Why, it's my slipper!" they had cried at each other. "It's my glass slipper!"

If Ferdinand heard those four words again today, he would go mad. Indeed, it wouldn't surprise him if tomorrow he woke to find all his black hairs had gone gray.

The indignity of it all!

Sunlight streamed in through the folds of the carriage's curtains, the bright light making the duke wince. He opened an eye, stealing a glimpse outside. They were about to pass the statue of his father in one of the city's finer squares. It was his favorite part of Valors, and as a boy, Ferdinand could never get enough of boasting to his friends about how important his father was, to have such a dignified and heroic likeness in the center of the city.

"One day, I, too, will have a statue," he'd declared.

So imagine his horror to see pigeons perched on his father's head, the stone facade of which clearly hadn't been scrubbed clean in weeks! And dogs were relieving themselves among the flower beds surrounding the statue!

If he hadn't been on such a tight schedule, he would have barged out of his carriage, shooed away the pigeons, and demanded the utterly disrespectful commoners take their canine brutes elsewhere.

"Disgraceful," muttered the duke with a scowl. And after all his family had done for Aurelais! He made a mental note to have the filth-ridden state of his father's statue addressed as soon as possible.

How times had changed. When he was a child, people had *respect* for nobility. The sheer idea of the prince marrying a lesser noble would have sent tongues wagging. What's more, a commoner of undistinguished background would have been unheard of!

His father, the previous grand duke, certainly would have advised the king against it, as Ferdinand had tried.

His father had overseen the rebuilding of Aurelais after the Seventeen Years' War. This magnificent statue in Valors's main square now honored him for facilitating the exile of all magical beings—namely fairies who'd held far too much sway in politics, what with that ridiculous tradition of blessing and cursing princes and princesses—from the kingdom. Ferdinand was not going to get any statue for finding Prince Charles's so-called true love.

What had he done to deserve such a fate? To be volleyed around the kingdom like some common messenger boy? He'd spent all night and all morning reciting a silly proclamation about a glass slipper instead of working on critical laws and budget plans to share with the council.

Yes, Aurelais had been at peace for over half a century, but there were important treaties still to be negotiated, great minds to meet. Why, just the other day Ferdinand had read about an inventor who traveled the world on a flying balloon. And he could even take passengers in it! Other nations were chartering ships to circumnavigate the world, establishing important trade routes and discovering new lands.

But here he was, the right-hand man to the king of Aurelais, dispatched to each corner of the realm to find the owner of—a shoe.

Ferdinand stared at the glass slipper sitting on his lap, hating the very sight of it. He had half a mind to throw it out the window.

He blamed the prince.

"You frightened her," Prince Charles had accused him late the night before. "If you hadn't sent your men after her, she might have come back."

The youth was delusional. And it had taken all of Ferdinand's restraint to bite his tongue and not tell him exactly that.

The king hadn't been much help. It'd been *his* idea to have every maiden in the kingdom try the slipper, an idea Ferdinand had agreed to. In fact, Ferdinand had happily penned the proclamation:

It is upon this day decreed that a quest be instituted throughout the length and breadth of our domain.

The sole and express purpose of such quest is to be as follows: that every maid throughout the kingdom, without prearranged exception, shall try on her foot this slipper of glass, and should one be found upon whose foot this slipper shall properly fit, such maiden shall be acclaimed the object of this search and immediately forthwith shall be looked upon as the true love of His Royal Highness, our beloved son and heir, the noble prince.

Only Ferdinand hadn't expected that *he* would have to be the one doing the questing.

King George had always been irrational when it came to matters regarding his son. It reminded Ferdinand why he was glad he'd never married or begotten any children. There were more elegant ways to leave a legacy.

He only prayed he'd find the maiden soon. Very soon.

Endeavoring to keep from falling asleep, he reached into his pocket for a handkerchief to clean his monocle, but before he had a chance to use it, the driver reined the horses to a halt.

"We've arrived, Your Grace."

Ferdinand grimaced. Reaching for his hat, he put on his most dignified expression, departed the carriage, and strode to the front door.

Inside the house, someone peeked through the curtains, hastily closing them when the Grand Duke noticed.

"It's him!" he heard a young woman squeal. "The Grand Duke. With my—"

The duke pulled his hat over his ears before he heard the dreaded words.

"—glass slipper!"

It was going to be an excruciatingly long day.

Chapter Four

The door creaked open with a soft groan, and Cinderella braced herself for her stepmother's arrival.

I'm leaving, she practiced announcing to Lady Tremaine in her head. *I won't stay here another minute.*

Only . . . where would she go? Where *could* she go? Dressed in these rags, no one would believe she'd been the girl at the ball with the dazzling gown and glass slippers.

I'll . . . I'll find the Grand Duke and show him that I have the other slipper. She inhaled, bolstered by the plan. *He'll have to believe me then.*

Her stepmother's shadow spilled through the doorway, snuffing the scant sunlight illuminating Cinderella's room. Behind her, barricading the exit, stood her stepsisters.

Cinderella couldn't remember the last time Anastasia and Drizella had come to the attic. From their wrinkled noses and contemptuous gazes, they must have been wondering the same.

"I forgot how small this place is," Drizella grumbled. "We can barely fit in here."

"It's dirty, too," added Anastasia. "All this dust is getting in my hair." She tossed a red ringlet over her shoulder and fanned herself with her hands.

Seeing Lady Tremaine's curled lip, her stepsisters' raised chins and turned cheeks, Cinderella straightened. However they mocked her now—she wouldn't let them hurt her.

"The Grand Duke has left," said Lady Tremaine evenly. "He shan't be returning."

"I know," replied Cinderella.

"Good. It has come to my attention that you have not been entirely truthful with us." Cutting off Cinderella's protest, her stepmother went on, "I have given the matter some thought, and I have a mind to report you."

"Report me?" Cinderella frowned. This wasn't what she had expected at all. "What have I done?"

"What have you done?" repeated Lady Tremaine. She turned to her daughters, laughing. "She pretends she hasn't the faintest idea."

Anastasia and Drizella didn't seem to have any idea, either, but they nervously tittered along.

"You couldn't have possibly managed to go to the ball in *that*. Whom did you steal from?"

"What?" Cinderella blustered, stunned. She bit her lip, trying to calm herself, but her voice shook. "I . . . I don't understand."

"Don't you?" Lady Tremaine sniffed. "The gown, the earrings, the carriage—the *glass slippers*."

Drizella was the first to react. "*Her?* It couldn't have been her."

"Mother!" chimed in Anastasia with crossed arms. "*She's* the girl with the glass slipper? You can't be serious."

"Indeed." Lady Tremaine's icy gaze did not leave Cinderella. "It seems we've all underestimated her. But she has made a grave error." She raised a commanding hand to her daughters. "Search the room."

"No!"

Cinderella lurched to stop her stepsisters, but they were too fast. Drizella pushed her away, nearly throwing her against the wall. In a wild frenzy, the two tore apart Cinderella's bed, pulling off the sheets and grabbing the scissors on her dresser to slash through the mattress.

Despite her determination to stay calm, Cinderella panicked. The scene was an echo of the prior night, when her stepsisters had ripped apart her dress—her *mother's* dress that she had remade—broken her green bead necklace, and cruelly tormented her until she had burst into tears. Every time she thought she was strong enough to endure their malice, they found new ways of hurting her.

She couldn't let them find the glass slipper. It was all she possessed of her time at the ball—the only reminder of a rare, treasured moment of happiness. The only thing that could actually help her obtain a new life.

"Stop, please!" cried Cinderella, trying to pry the scissors from Anastasia's hands.

"Mother!" Anastasia yelled.

Cold fingers encircled Cinderella's wrist, sharp nails digging into her skin. As her stepmother dragged her back, Cinderella's eyes widened with alarm.

Drizella had found the missing glass slipper.

"You were right!" she shrieked. "Mother, this is—"

Lady Tremaine extended her hand. "Give it here."

Before Drizella could obey, Cinderella twisted out of her stepmother's grip and scooped up the slipper.

Her stepmother's face darkened. "Cinderella, give me the slipper."

"No."

"At once, Cinderella."

Cinderella didn't budge. The royal proclamation had stated that the prince would marry the girl who fit the glass slipper he had found at the ball. If she gave hers to Lady Tremaine, Anastasia or Drizella would claim it, bring it to the palace, and lie to the king that *they* had danced with the prince. Even if he didn't recognize the women—which, surely, he wouldn't—it would be a powerful bargaining tool.

Firmly, she repeated, "No."

"Very well, then," said her stepmother, strangely calm. "Drizella, Anastasia."

Coming from both sides of the room, the sisters lunged for her, and Cinderella's mind reeled with panic. She couldn't let them have the slipper. As they tore at her, shouting, "Give it here!" Cinderella suddenly knew what she had to do.

Mustering as much strength as she could, she raised the glass slipper high above her head, watching the iridescent glass catch the light outside and sparkle like diamonds.

Then she flung it at the wall.

It shattered into a thousand pieces.

Drizella shouted, "Look what you've done!"

Breathing hard, Cinderella barely heard her stepsister. The sight of her shattered slipper stung, and a sharp ache rose to her chest. The shoe had been her key to finding the young man from the ball again, to making a new life for herself outside Lady Tremaine's domain. Now that it was no more . . .

Cinderella gritted her teeth. Now that it was no more, her stepmother couldn't use it to her advantage.

"Mother!" Anastasia cried. "How could she?"

"I don't understand how she got the glass slipper in the first place—"

"Silence!" Lady Tremaine cut in. Then her voice became lethally soft. "Girls, step outside, please."

"But, Mother!"

"I will not repeat myself."

In a huff, Drizella and Anastasia paraded out of the room and shut the door. Once they were gone, Lady Tremaine stepped over the pile of glass shards and regarded Cinderella with an icy gaze.

"So. You lied to me."

"Stepmother, you can't possibly think that I stole—"

"I don't care where you got the dress or the shoes," Lady Tremaine interrupted. "Or how you managed to go to the ball." Her pale green eyes narrowed. "You have overstepped your place for the last time. Look at yourself—you are nothing. An orphan and a servant. Who would want you? Certainly not His Royal Highness."

The words cut deep, and Cinderella struggled to keep her tone steady. "I—I'm my father's daughter. Your stepdaughter. I'm a member of this family."

Her stepmother gave a hollow laugh. "A member of this family? Your imagination is to be commended if you truly believe that."

Cinderella's lip quivered. "Why do you hate me so much?"

"Hate you?" Disbelief, then amusement glittered in Lady Tremaine's eyes. "What makes you think you're worthy of my consideration, let alone hatred?"

"But—"

"Have I ever beaten you, Cinderella? Or starved you, or publicly shamed you? That's what they do to girls at the orphanage."

Mutely, Cinderella shook her head.

"I locked you here because you were deceitful. You lied to me and my daughters."

"I never lied," Cinderella argued, gathering her courage. "At every turn, I've done what you have asked. I've cleaned, I've cooked, and I've never complained. All I wanted was for you to think of me as one of your daughters—"

"How could I think of you as a daughter of mine?" Lady Tremaine barked. Calming herself, she went on, "Until the day I met you, you'd never done a day's work. Do you remember what you said to your father?

" 'Papa! You brought me a mother.' " Her stepmother scowled. "As if I were a thing to be brought, an object to be shopped for."

Cinderella did remember. In her joy at seeing Lady Tremaine, the words had gushed out of her mouth. She hadn't meant them as an insult. "I was happy to meet you. I didn't mean—"

"I remember how you looked down on my daughters. You, with your fine dresses and music lessons. Your riding clothes and flowers and little songs for the birds and that *dog*." Lady Tremaine scoffed. "The first thing you did was mock me and embarrass my daughters in front of your father."

"I didn't—"

"Of course you didn't know. You presume ignorance is innocence. I've had to build my life from nothing. Give my daughters a place in this society. But you, you scoffed at our old clothes and Drizella's teeth, Anastasia's hair."

At the accusation, Cinderella's brow furrowed. Had she? She could remember the day her stepmother had arrived so clearly. They'd come during her music lesson, and she'd raced out of it as soon as she'd seen her father's carriage outside the window, trundling toward home. No one had told her about Lady Tremaine, so it had jolted Cinderella to see her: the heart-shaped hair piled high, making her seem even taller than her father, her long neck and unforgiving posture. She'd been wearing a wine-colored dress with a high collar. One daughter on either side, both with evenly curled ringlets, neither smiling.

"She's a lady," one of the servants had said, passing

Cinderella, who hid by the stairs. "Best not run to your papa and hug him as you always do. Keep your chin up, and curtsy when you greet his guest."

That she'd done. But maybe she'd held her chin too high or curtsied too low. Her papa had never required her to be on such stiff behavior before, and she'd so wanted to impress her new mother. She had been so nervous.

"Lady Tremaine," Cinderella had said in greeting, with her deepest curtsy. Papa chuckled, gently pulling her up.

"No need for that, Cinderella. We are family now."

"Oh, Papa!" she exclaimed, hugging him fiercely. "You've brought me a mother!"

In her excitement, her hair bow came undone, and her father retied it for her. "Why don't you show Drizella and Anastasia the music room while Lady Tremaine and I settle into the chateau?"

"I have a music lesson this afternoon," she'd said to her new sisters, careful to be polite and considerate. She'd so wanted Anastasia and Drizella to like her. "My teacher wants me to learn a new song. She's upstairs waiting now. Would you like to join me?"

"I want to sing," Drizella had said. "Anastasia plays the flute."

How could she have known that her stepsisters had no talent for music? She hadn't meant to embarrass them.

Later Cinderella had caught the servants chatting more in the kitchen. They hadn't seen her, and she hadn't meant to eavesdrop, but she had never forgotten their conversation:

"I don't like the looks of our new mistress. You see the way she eyes the finances? Just now she was telling me I've been feeding the chickens too much, and that I've a heavy hand with the butter. I fear she married the good master for his money."

"Hush, you'll get yourself in trouble talking like that! Her husband was a lord."

"Yes, but a penniless one."

"That can't be true. The master wouldn't—"

"The master's been fooled, I swear. I heard that Lord Tremaine squandered his family's fortune gambling. When he was called to serve in the war, he joined only to escape his creditors. Then he tried to desert and was hanged. It was a disgrace."

"You can't believe these sorts of rumors."

"They're not rumors! You know what a kind heart the master has. He probably met her during his travels and took pity on her and her daughters. But she isn't innocent; if only you could hear half the things people say about her! Delusions of grandeur, for one. And now that she's mistress of the house, who I truly worry about is dear Cin—"

The servants had seen her then and hadn't said any more.

At the time, Cinderella hadn't understood the importance of what she'd overheard. Even after her father had passed away, leaving Lady Tremaine as head of the household, she hadn't given her stepmother's past much thought.

Whenever her stepmother was cruel to her, she told herself she was better off staying here—in her father's home with her stepfamily—than venturing outside.

But what if she'd been wrong? Her stepmother *was* calculating, and she would stop at nothing to ensure her future as well as her daughters'. She was also ruthless. Cinderella just hadn't let herself acknowledge *how* ruthless. She'd shielded herself by burying her unhappiness in daydreams and pretending that she was fine. That they needed her.

She looked up at Lady Tremaine, a woman who'd once had everything that mattered to her: wealth, status, and the admiration of her peers. Now she lived in a dated chateau, with no servants except her daughters and so little money that she'd had to sell the draperies to pay for their gowns.

"You misunderstood me, Stepmother," said Cinderella quietly. "I wish we could have settled this years ago, if this is what's been bothering you. I didn't look down on Anastasia or Drizella. I was only wishing I had a mother, like they did. Mine died—"

"I heard enough about your dead mother from your dead father," Lady Tremaine snapped. "When he passed, I took it upon myself to reform you. I've done my best trying to raise you into a respectable girl, but I can see my efforts have been in vain." She kicked the glass shards toward Cinderella. "Clean this mess. I'll decide what to do with you later."

Her stepmother turned on her heel, and before Cinderella could lurch for the door, it slammed shut again, the key turning in the lock to keep her from leaving.

Outside, her stepsisters' voices echoed up the stairwell.

"What are you going to do, Mother?" Anastasia asked. "She can't stay here! What if the Grand Duke comes back and—"

"I am aware, Anastasia."

"W-w-well . . . we can't keep her locked up in there forever."

Lady Tremaine's tone rose a notch, as if she wanted Cinderella to hear: "I am going to send her away."

"Send her away?" Drizella repeated. "Mother, have you thought this through? If you do that, who's going to press our clothes? Who'll cook breakfast and bring us tea and—" Drizella went suddenly quiet, a sign that Lady Tremaine had cast her a deadly look.

During the heavy silence that followed, Cinderella inched toward the door, pressing her ear against the wood. Her heart roared in her ears, but she needed to hear what her stepmother was going to say.

"There's a man from the far seas who makes his trade

in troublesome girls." A deliberate pause. "It is to our good fortune that he happens to be in town again tonight."

"So . . . you're going to sell her?"

"I will certainly consider it. I *have* considered it before. The price he's willing to pay will be enough for us to hire a new maid."

Cinderella held her breath, panic rioting within her. She pressed her ear against the door to catch more, but all she could hear were Anastasia's and Drizella's laughs echoing up into the tower.

It was too cruel. Sinking to her knees, Cinderella hugged herself. For a moment, she'd let herself fantasize about a world in which she could present her glass slipper to the Grand Duke, be brought to the prince, and pick up with him where they had left off. She had thought it possible to ease away the loneliness so deeply set in her heart.

"Maybe I never should have gone to the ball," she whispered to herself. "I was happy enough before, wasn't I? Pretending that everything was all right."

She laughed sadly at how miserable that sounded. Even now she was pretending—just to get herself through what was to come.

And the worst of it was that she couldn't even fight it.

All she could do—all she had *ever* been able to do—was wait.

Chapter Five

The afternoon aged into evening, and the lengthening shadows looming over Cinderella's walls melted into the black folds of night. In the distance, the moon rose behind the king's palace.

Cinderella paced the room, her anxiety heightened by the small space. It wasn't like her to be so restless, but no matter where she looked, she couldn't avoid seeing the broken bed, the ripped sheets, and the chaos that her stepmother and stepsisters had made of her room. She couldn't avoid confronting the locked wooden door that barred her from her freedom.

She'd tried kicking the door countless times. Tried heaving her chair at it, and she'd almost had some luck picking the lock with two hairpins before one of them snapped in half between her fingers. But it would not budge. The window wasn't an option. She was too high up, and even if she could fashion some sort of rope, it wouldn't be long enough for her to climb down with.

Only when she'd run out of all ideas and collapsed onto her chair, exhausted, did she remember. Her shimmering ball gown, the mice turned into majestic stallions, the pumpkin coach, her glass slippers. None of it would have been possible if not for one person. . . .

"Fairy Godmother?" she called, tentatively at first. Quietly.

No answer.

She tried again. "Fairy Godmother? Please, help me."

Maybe her fairy godmother had been a dream. Maybe all of it—the ball, the prince, the castle—had been a hopeless fantasy. Maybe when Cinderella woke up tomorrow all would be as it had been before.

But no. The prince's kiss still tingled on her lips, and strains of the song they had danced to together still echoed in her memory. If nothing else, the shattered remains of her glass slipper, strewn across the floor, assured her it had all been real.

Cinderella looked at herself in the mirror. Her eyes were bloodshot, her cheeks stained with tears. Her hairbrush and comb still rested on her vanity, her neatly arranged hair a bitter reminder of how happy she'd been only hours before when she had been planning to meet the Grand Duke.

"What do I do?" she asked her reflection. She'd grown used to talking to herself—or the mice—all these years to keep from going mad. "How can I keep faith that things will get better when they only seem to get worse?" She buried her face in her hands. "Maybe she was right. Maybe if I *had* run off to the palace with the slipper, the prince wouldn't see the girl he'd danced with. All he'd see is . . . an orphan in rags."

She swallowed hard. "A nobody."

"Who's a nobody?" It was a familiar voice, serene and kind.

Behind her, a shimmering silhouette appeared against a backdrop of shadow. Slowly, gradually, a soft light bloomed in the middle of Cinderella's room, and an elderly woman wearing a sky blue cloak materialized.

Cinderella gasped. *"Fairy Godmother."*

"Please, dear, call me Lenore."

If the situation hadn't been so dire, Cinderella would have laughed at her matter-of-factness. "You're here," she said instead.

"I heard you call. . . ." The fairy's round eyes widened as she gestured at the ramshackle attic. "What happened?"

Cinderella opened her mouth to reply, but a lump

formed in her throat. It hurt to speak. "My stepmother . . ." She couldn't finish her sentence.

"Oh, my child." Her fairy godmother opened her arms, embracing Cinderella and gently patting her back.

When she pulled away, Cinderella noticed a frown had set on Lenore's face. She touched the ripped mattress and pillows, and her expression darkened when she noticed the constellation of glass shards on the ground. "Your step-mother discovered that it was you at the ball."

"Yes . . . she locked me here."

"Oh, that woman!" Lenore stomped her foot. "I have a mind to . . . hmph, I'd best not say. It wouldn't be appropriate."

"Can you help me?" Cinderella asked urgently. "She's going to send me away—tonight."

"Send you where?"

"I don't know." Fear edged Cinderella's voice, making it tremble no matter how she tried to keep her words even. "There's a man coming to take me away from Aurelais. I-I-I think he's going to sell me. Please . . ."

Her godmother clenched her jaw, and when she finally spoke her words were heavy with sadness. "I'm afraid I cannot, my child. I'd love nothing more than to turn your stepmother and stepsisters into toads and take you far from this place, but that is not how my magic works. I can only set you *on the path* to happiness."

How does *it work?* Cinderella wanted to ask. She had so many questions for her fairy godmother—about magic, and why she'd helped Cinderella go to the ball in the first place. Questions she hadn't thought to ask the first time her fairy godmother had appeared. But there were more pressing matters at hand now.

"Could you . . . could you unlock the door?"

"I can certainly try." Rolling up her sleeves, the fairy godmother drew up her wand and pointed it at the door.

The door shuddered, but it would not open.

With a frown, Lenore waved her wand and tried again, but this time, the spell sent her reeling back toward Cinderella's bed.

Lenore lowered her hood, her dark eyes filled with regret. "As I say, there are limits to my powers," she explained, tapping her wand on her palm. She clutched the wand tightly, looking once more at the shattered glass. "I'm sorry, dear. Perhaps I shouldn't have come to you in the first place."

"Why?"

"My magic is forbidden in Aurelais," said her fairy godmother calmly. "Oh, I bent the rules a little by putting a time constraint on the spell I used to send you to the ball— rather clever of me—but my wand won't allow me to risk a spell so large again."

"Your magic is forbidden?" repeated Cinderella, barely hearing the rest of what she'd said. "What do you mean?"

"There's a reason my magic could only last until midnight. It was borrowed magic, because magic in Aurelais has been outlawed, and all its fairies exiled. The Grand Duke—the former, that is—he made it his mission . . . oh, it happened long ago. You must not worry."

"Of course I'm worried! Are you in danger by being here?"

"I should not stay long," was all Lenore would say. Her godmother cleared her throat. "But there is one thing I can do at least. I can speak with your dog."

"Bruno?"

Confused, Cinderella glanced out the window. She couldn't see Bruno from here, but she imagined him downstairs in one of the storerooms, curled up against a rug and dreaming of chasing Lucifer, her stepmother's cat. *By now he must be starving,* she thought with a pang of guilt. Since she'd been locked up, no one would have fed him all day.

"Yes, that's what I'll do—I'll tell him you're in trouble," Lenore said, determined.

Cinderella wasn't sure how her dog would be able to help her. "How—"

"And before I forget," continued Lenore, fishing into her sleeve, "I believe these belong to you."

Out came the green beads that Cinderella had worn the previous night—before Drizella had snatched them from her—restrung.

"I wouldn't want you to leave without your mother's beads," said Lenore firmly, clasping the emerald-colored beads around Cinderella's neck.

"How did you—"

"Found them on the ground after you left last night. Your mother would have wanted you to have her beads; that horrible Drizella has had them for long enough. Keep them with you to remember where you come from."

"I will," said Cinderella softly. Carefully, she unclasped the necklace and put it in her pocket. "Thank you."

"Don't thank me. I wish I could have done more." The fairy placed a gentle hand on Cinderella's shoulder. "Be brave, my dear. The path to happiness is not always an easy one. Now I must go."

Then she vanished in a twinkle of lights—leaving Cinderella alone once more.

She blinked, fighting back a fresh wave of tears. "I can get through this," she whispered.

I won't be afraid, she told herself. *I'll find a way out, somehow.*

Then, trying to steady her racing heart, she waited for her stepmother to return.

———

The sound of footsteps returned late at night, far later than Cinderella anticipated. She'd fallen asleep on her mattress, but the harsh thumps up the tower stairs jolted her awake.

By the time she lit her candle, her stepmother stood at the door, looking calm and composed.

"I see you're awake. Good. You have a visitor." Lady Tremaine turned. "Mr. Laverre!"

A thick-necked brute of a man with a cruel leer appeared at the threshold, and Cinderella gasped.

A bundle of rope dangled from Mr. Laverre's hands, and his mouth bent into a pitiless smile. "This the girl?" he rasped.

"Yes. Will she do?"

Mr. Laverre looked her up and down. "She'll fetch a fair price. More than fair."

Setting his lamp on the ground, Mr. Laverre reached into his pocket and handed Lady Tremaine a heavy pouch of coins.

"No, please," Cinderella pleaded with her stepmother. "Don't do this!"

But Lady Tremaine ignored her and pocketed the coins. "I trust you'll take her far away."

"Oh, I've a place in mind. It's so far Aurelais isn't even on their maps."

A small smile touched Lady Tremaine's mouth. "She's a wicked child. Find her a household that works her to the bone. Better yet, have her thrown into the mines. She deserves nothing better." With a satisfied nod, she departed the room, leaving Cinderella alone with Mr. Laverre.

Cinderella cowered in a corner, her hands scrabbling behind her for something, *anything* to fend off Mr. Laverre. Her fingers closed over her hairbrush, and she swung it wildly as he advanced toward her.

Mr. Laverre batted her brush aside, grabbing her arms. Cinderella struggled, lunging for the pile of glass debris on the floor, but she'd barely managed to grab one shard when he threw the rope around her, securing her arms to her sides and her wrists together.

"Let me go!" Cinderella screamed. "Let me—"

Mr. Laverre clamped her mouth with his hand. "Don't worry, it won't be forever. A girl like you will pay off her debts, eventually."

Terror seized Cinderella, and her muscles tensed with fear.

"What's that you've got in your hand?" Mr. Laverre tried to pry her hand open. "A chip of glass isn't going to stop me, lass."

Before he could take it from her, Cinderella threw her elbow into Mr. Laverre's ribs. He staggered back, stepping into the glass slipper's remains, and let out a cry. She started to flee, spiraling down and down the stairs. But the ropes around her arms unsteadied her balance, and she didn't get very far before Mr. Laverre caught up, seized her by the waist, and hoisted her over his shoulder.

"A good effort, lass." He pitched a pillowcase over her head. "But not good enough."

Cinderella struggled, trying to use the glass in her hand as a weapon, but it was no use. The bindings restricted her movement, and her feet hit the walls instead of her captor when she tried kicking. Each thump of Mr. Laverre's boots down the tower steps, then through the corridor and down into the main hall, thundered in her ears.

When the front doors swung open and the crisp chill of the wind bit at her cheeks through the pillowcase, she heard Bruno barking.

"Bruno!"

The bloodhound was already on his way. Scrambling toward Cinderella, he leapt to attack Mr. Laverre. But the man grabbed his driving whip from his carriage and swung it at Bruno, flinging him into a puddle. As Bruno whimpered, Mr. Laverre threw Cinderella into the carriage.

"Hiyah!" he shouted. His whip cracked against the backs of his horses, and as the wheels rattled to life, Cinderella rolled violently from side to side.

The shard of glass tumbled out of her hand, and she floundered to get it back. Her fingers grazed its edge, and she bit back the pain as it nicked her palm.

It was sharp. Maybe sharp enough to cut her free. With

renewed determination, she gripped its blunt side and started picking at the ropes.

Not an easy task. Every time the carriage hit a bump, Cinderella nearly dropped the shard. Finally, when the thick twines loosened and she freed her hands, she threw the pillowcase off her head.

There was nothing around her except the carriage cushions, most of them ripped as if someone before Cinderella had tried clawing her way free. The doors were bolted shut from the outside, but the window . . .

In his haste to get away from Bruno, Mr. Laverre hadn't properly closed it. The strong winds had pummeled it open, the wooden board creaking as it swung back and forth.

Rain washed into the carriage. The storm had swelled in strength, the pitter-patter now a constant drumming against the carriage roof. Mr. Laverre's horses slowed, fighting the powerful winds, and prepared to make a sharp turn.

This is my chance, thought Cinderella, bolting toward the window.

The carriage started again, picking up speed and throwing her back. The world rumbled beneath her, every turn of the wheels throwing her from side to side in the carriage, making it hard for her to catch her balance. She gripped the underside of the seat to steady herself.

Fear made her hands shake, her knuckles bone white. Gathering her courage, she inched her way to the edge of the carriage and clutched at the open window. Rain battered her temples, and a violent gust of wind lashed at her, threatening to throw her back into the carriage.

On the count of three.

One.

Two.

Three. She meant to jump, but the horses stumbled over a broken crate on the road, and the carriage suddenly swerved right. One of the doors swung open, taking Cinderella with it and tossing her out onto the road.

She forgot not to scream. Thankfully, the rain muffled her cry as she slammed into the ground. She landed on her side, her legs scraping against the rough gravel. The carriage wheels splattered mud over her clothes, and she felt a shock of cold.

Ignoring the pain springing in her ribs, Cinderella pulled herself up and off the street, narrowly avoiding getting trampled by another coach that came barreling past. She crawled into a corner and held her breath until Mr. Laverre's carriage rounded the corner, its wheels lumbering against the pebbled roads.

Cinderella waited there, knees shaking, teeth chattering, the whole time fearing that Mr. Laverre would discover she had escaped. But when several minutes had passed and his carriage did not return, she finally stirred.

One muscle at a time, she picked herself up. Everything

hurt. Her ribs, her back, her hands. Cuts and scrapes nicked her knees, and her fingers were bleeding. But she was free.

Suddenly, she heard a familiar whimper, and a wet, furry creature brushed against her calves.

"Bruno!"

Cinderella had never been so glad to see him. "You followed me all the way from home! You brave, brave dog."

She hugged him, taking comfort in his familiar face. Together they rose and wandered the neighborhood in hopes of finding a kind soul who might take pity on them. But the streets were empty, and no wonder—no sane person would be out during a rainstorm like this. The rain had snuffed the lamps, and darkness wreathed every inch of the road ahead.

Each house was gated, every shop locked. There was no hope of finding help at this hour, not in this weather. The rain was relentless; they'd have to wait until the storm passed, or until dawn . . . whichever came first.

They found shelter under the awning of a closed storefront. Cinderella tried knocking several times, but no one came to the door. Through the glass was a marvelous display of layered cakes decorated with pink rosettes and candied fruits, chocolate-laced cookies, and buttery pastries dotted with jam.

"Come on, Bruno," she said, wincing as her stomach

growled with hunger. She leaned against the store's brick wall and gathered her dog under the awning. "Let's sleep here tonight."

She hugged him close, listening to his pulse thump steadily against her racing heart. Gradually her temples stopped throbbing, and the pain in her side dulled.

"Oh, Bruno, I'm sorry."

Her dog looked at her as if he didn't understand why she was apologizing to him.

"You could be home with a hot meal and a warm bed right now." She stroked his ear playfully. "You could be drinking a nice warm bowl of milk, or chasing Lucifer out of the kitchen." She drew him close, burying her face in his warm fur. "But I'm glad you're here, loyal as always. Thank you, Bruno."

Her terror subsided, but fear lingered. New fears. Practical ones, brought on by the unyielding rumble in her stomach, the rain sinking into her skin, and the chill moving into her bones that her threadbare shirt could not prevent.

What would tomorrow bring? Cinderella wondered as she shivered. She had no money, no family, no place to go. Without her glass slipper, she was sure the palace guards would turn her away at the front gates. In her rags, with the bruise on her head and scratches on her arms, who would believe that she had danced with the prince at the ball? That she was the maiden the whole kingdom was looking for?

One thing was for certain: if she didn't find food and shelter, she and Bruno wouldn't last long on their own.

It was what she'd always feared. Any time she'd secretly fantasized about leaving her stepmother's house, this was the reality that had chased the dream away.

"The world is a cruel, cruel place, Cinderella," her stepmother used to tell her when she was a child. "You should be grateful to me for giving you a roof over your head. How do you think you'd fare out in the world? You, without any worldly experience—an orphan, unwanted and alone?"

Those words haunted her. They were awful, but true; she *was* alone, and she had no experience being out in the world. How would she make a life for herself?

It's better than being stuck with Mr. Laverre, she reminded herself. *Anything is better than that.*

She glanced up, taking in the moon, still luminous even as the storm unfolded. Shielding her eyes from the rain, she craned her head north. There, at the edge of the city, sat the king's palace.

Her father had once told her that one could see the king's palace from any point in the city. Her view now was different from the one she'd had at home, but the palace was no less resplendent. How many hours had she spent staring at it, dreaming about how grand it would be to go inside, how wonderful it would be to dance within its marble halls?

Well, now she had.

She felt no regret about how eagerly she'd wanted to go to the ball. What she regretted was how naive she'd been, and that flicker of longing that had sprung up inside her when she realized the Grand Duke's quest was to find *her*. For an instant, she'd fooled herself into thinking reuniting with the prince was the ticket to happiness and a better life for herself.

But no longer.

So where did she go from here?

Despair gnawed at her. She could try to call for her fairy godmother again, but . . . Lenore had said her magic was forbidden. Cinderella wouldn't put her fairy godmother in danger.

I'll figure this out on my own, Cinderella thought grimly. *I cannot always depend on someone to save me.*

"Tomorrow," she whispered aloud, stroking Bruno's head. "Beginning tomorrow, I'm never going to feel this helpless again. Once the storm ends, we make a new life. You and me."

With that promise heavy in her heart, she hugged Bruno close, shifting them both deeper under the awning and away from the cold, relentless rain.

It was a long time before she finally fell asleep.

Chapter Six

The sound of Bruno barking, loudly, woke Cinderella from her dreams.

She started to rise, but the morning's bright light made her pinch her eyes tight. The sun was usually never this harsh in her room.

"Stop following me!" someone cried in the distance, sounding more distressed than irritated.

Strange, thought Cinderella blearily, *that doesn't sound like Anastasia or Drizella.*

"No, no, I can't go that way. I'm going to be late for work if I—stop chewing on my skirt. Stop that!"

Certain she was still dreaming, Cinderella covered her eyes with her arm, cherishing every minute of sleep before she had to get up and prepare breakfast for her stepsisters again. As she stifled a yawn and stretched, her knuckles brushed against hard gravel instead of the stiff cotton over her mattress.

With a jolt, Cinderella sat up and tried to make sense of her surroundings. The sun still glared at her; all she could see was the sky, bright and cloudless, an ocean of seamless blue. Everything else was blurred, freckled by dancing white sunspots.

"Bruno?" she called out. Where had he gone? She raised her tone an anxious note. "Bruno?"

Behind her, someone let out a gasp. "Oh, my! Miss! Miss, are you all right?"

Cinderella perked up, recognizing the voice of the young woman she had heard earlier.

Bruno appeared from behind the girl's skirts and scampered to Cinderella's side.

"Oh, what a relief—he's yours! I worried he was a stray, he was barking so much." The girl knelt beside her, setting down a basket brimming with neat piles of fabric, spools of thread, and a pair of scissors. A seamstress, Cinderella deduced.

"He grabbed on to my skirt and wouldn't let me go until I followed him. Now I see why, clever dog." The seamstress viewed Cinderella, her hazel eyes flaring with concern. "Are you all right? Can you stand?"

Cinderella's back ached from sleeping on the street, and

her head still throbbed from hitting the side of Mr. Laverre's carriage, but already the pain was subsiding. "Yes, I'm fine."

The young seamstress lent Cinderella her arm, yanking her to her feet. "You're lucky I was running late to work. Otherwise, who knows who might have found you!"

"Thank you," said Cinderella, staggering back.

The seamstress's eyebrows suddenly flew up, and she pulled Cinderella off the street and onto the sidewalk before a carriage rushed past, its wheels spinning alarmingly fast.

"I guess I spoke too fast," Cinderella said, catching her breath. "I didn't even know I was on the street."

"You need to be more aware of your surroundings," the seamstress chided. "You could have gotten trampled!" She furrowed her brow. "What's a girl like you doing sleeping out here anyway?"

"It's a long story," replied Cinderella, managing a smile. "Thank you again for your help. I don't want to keep you if you have somewhere to go."

The seamstress's expression softened, and she glanced at the clock over one of the shops. "Guess I'm going to be late no matter what. Besides, you look like you need my help more than some silly lords and ladies." She pushed a lock of auburn hair out of her face. She was tall, and a dimple emerged on the right corner of her mouth when she smiled.

"I get nervous when I'm running late, so I'm sorry if I was rude. Let's start again. I'm Louisa."

"Cinderella."

"Cinderella?" Louisa's eyebrow arched. "That's a name I've never heard before, and I know about most of the girls in town."

Cinderella pursed her lips and twisted the ends of her apron, unsure how to explain she'd been her stepmother's servant for years and practically a prisoner in her own home.

"I don't go out much," was all she said.

"I was beginning to wonder," said Louisa dryly. "You don't seem to even know where you are." Her hand jumped to her mouth. "That came out ruder than I meant it to. Mother always says I need to keep my thoughts to myself. Aunt Irmina does, too, but it's hard when my thoughts are so loud." Louisa made a face. "How'd you get a name like Cinderella?"

"My birth name is Ella, after my mother, Gabrielle. But no one's called me that for years."

"I like Cinderella," Louisa declared. "I don't understand the 'Cinder' in front of Ella, but it's different, I'll say."

"I used to curl up by the fire in the kitchen waiting for my papa to come home from his travels," Cinderella explained. "Sometimes I'd fall asleep and have soot all over my clothes. One time he cleaned it off, and ever since he called me Cinderella."

"Cinderella" had been her father's term of endearment

for her. Only after he died did her stepmother and step-sisters use her name as a way of mocking her.

"Is he traveling now?" Louisa asked. "He must be worried about you."

"No." Cinderella's voice faltered. "He's not traveling, he's . . . he passed away. Years ago."

Louisa smacked her mouth. "I'm sorry. There I go, saying the wrong things again."

"It was a long time ago. You couldn't have known."

"Do you at least have a place to go? Any home or family?"

Cinderella was silent. What could she say? That she'd been trapped in her father's house for the past decade, forced to wait on a cruel stepmother and two stepsisters?

Even if she wanted to go back to her father's house, she couldn't. Not after what had happened the night before.

"No," she said quietly. "Don't worry about me. You should get to work. I've kept you long enough."

Louisa eyed her face, gesturing at her forehead. "You have a bruise."

"It's nothing. Just from last night. I hit my head on a carriage."

"A carriage?" Louisa repeated, alarmed. "What were you—"

In the background, a clock chimed, cutting over Louisa's question. She shot up, picking up her basket so quickly it swung in her arms. "Heavens, it's seven o'clock already!"

They were the same bells from the palace watchtower that used to rouse Cinderella every morning. "Old Killjoy," she used to call the clock. But for the first time, she wasn't hearing it ring in bed; she wasn't in her tiny room in the attic, watching the city come alive. She was in the heart of Valors.

Something about that realization made a lump rise in her throat; she'd missed being in the city. She just hadn't expected this—being forced out of her home and sold by Lady Tremaine—to be the way she found herself there.

"Go on," Cinderella said over the clock's chimes. She inhaled a shaky breath. "I'll be fine. I have Bruno with me."

"I hate to leave you, but I really—oh, no!" Louisa suddenly exclaimed. Bruno was gnawing on a scrap of fabric from her dress. "My uniform!"

"Bruno," Cinderella scolded. She tsked at him, then turned to Louisa. "It's torn in the back. I'm so sorry. But I can help you mend it if you have a needle and thread handy."

"It's all right," said Louisa, already trying to assess the damage. "He was trying to get my attention so I could find you. I can manage. I wasn't raised a dressmaker's daughter for nothing!"

"Even a dressmaker's daughter would have to have eyes in the back of her head to mend that rip," Cinderella pointed out, laughing. "Can you even see it, behind you?"

Louisa craned her neck to look. "You're right." The seamstress made a worried face. "I'll be sent home if I show up at the palace with a tear in my skirt."

The comment startled Cinderella. "The palace?"

"I work there."

Cinderella's heart skipped a beat. Quickly looking down at Louisa's skirt to hide her emotions, she took the needle and thread her new friend offered. "You must be very skilled."

"Hah." Louisa held up her skirt so Cinderella could begin working. "My mother owns a small dress shop in the Garment District. I've been sewing for her since I was little, but I'm still the slowest in the palace."

Cinderella didn't speak until she was nearly done mending Louisa's skirt. "Is this good enough?"

"Oh, that's wonderful. You're a fine seamstress yourself."

I used to sew for my stepsisters, Cinderella almost said, but she stopped herself. The memory of Mr. Laverre and her stepmother trying to indenture her as a servant were too fresh. Best not to speak of them, not only because she was worried they might find her, but also because her stepmother's cruelty still stung.

"Very neat," Louisa said admiringly. Then she hesitated before observing, "Your hands are shaking."

"Are they?" Cinderella stuffed them into her pockets. "Just a little chilly, I guess."

"Goodness, you don't even have a coat?" Louisa frowned, then took one of the sheaths of cloth from her basket and wrapped it around Cinderella's shoulders. "You don't have to tell me how you ended up on the street, but . . . tell me the truth. You don't have anywhere to go, do you?"

Slowly, Cinderella shook her head. Hunger sharpened in her gut, and her stomach growled before she could stop it.

"I knew it! Why don't you come with me? I'll make sure the cooks get you a nice bowl of soup. I think it's onion soup today, and that's one of my favorites." Louisa paused, glancing at Cinderella's dirty dress and the apron over it. "Maybe we can even find a job for you."

"In the palace?"

"No, the tanneries. Of course, the palace!" Louisa giggled at Cinderella's wide eyes, misreading her startled expression for one of awe. "It's less grand when you're the one cleaning it. But given the urgent search for the missing princess, no one in the palace is paying close attention to us servants. I'm sure I could convince Aunt Irmina to give you a few days' work at the very least."

Cinderella swallowed. The palace was where Prince Charles lived, but she wasn't a fool. She knew that the chances of running into him would be slim. And yet . . . maybe—just maybe, if he saw her again, even dressed as a member of the palace staff, he might recognize her.

She shook the possibility away. *What am I thinking,*

clinging to some silly fantasy about a silly prince I've only met once? She inhaled, trying to reason away her feelings for the prince. *A job in the palace is more than I could have hoped for. It's work that will pay, and it's a life away from my stepmother. It's the new start I've been waiting for.*

"Well?" Louisa asked. "What do you say?"

Cinderella almost agreed, but then she remembered Bruno, who was staring morosely at the two girls. "What about Bruno?"

Louisa eyed the bloodhound nervously. "I can try to sneak him into the servants' quarters, but we'll have to keep him hidden. Aunt Irmina is not fond of animals."

So it was settled, and Cinderella followed her new friend, Louisa, to the last place she'd thought she would see again.

The palace.

Chapter Seven

"Announcing the Crown Prince Charles Maximilian Alexander, son of King George-Louis Philippe III, noble prince and beloved heir to the throne of Aurelais—"

Charles usually would have waited for the royal crier to finish declaring his entrance, but this morning he barely even heard the man.

He stormed into the royal dining chamber. Inside, he found his father calmly breaking his fast with a plate of almond cakes, freshly baked pastries, and raspberry jam, and the Grand Duke reading aloud from a scroll.

"That is one hundred and twenty-three households, sire," declared Ferdinand. "None of the maidens came close to fitting the slipper. At this rate, I suspect the search is futile and that the missing young lady will not be foun—"

The duke lowered his scroll, noticing Charles. "Why, good morning, Your Highness."

A flurry of servants trailed Charles. Any other day, he might have felt horrible about causing a ruckus with his unexpected appearance at breakfast. But not today.

King George brightened at the sight of his son. "Good morning, my boy. Sit down, sit down."

"Good morning, Father," replied the prince, managing an awkward bow. A servant hastily pulled out a chair for him, but he did not sit. Instead, he directed his gaze to the Grand Duke. "I thought I made it clear that I wished to be present for every report regarding the glass slipper."

"It is half past seven, Your Highness," replied the duke smoothly. "We waited as long as we could."

As always, Ferdinand had an excuse for everything, but Charles detected an undertone of fatigue behind his usual unflappable charm. Dark circles hooded the Grand Duke's eyes, and his uniform, typically pressed to perfection, was wrinkled at the hems. Evidently, he had not slept well.

Charles had not, either. In truth, he hadn't slept at all.

How could he? The last thing he had wanted was for Ferdinand to find his intended bride. Charles had wanted to search for her himself. Unfortunately, his father had insisted on appointing the Grand Duke for the job.

Ferdinand is the most capable man in the kingdom. He will find her, he'd said.

Her.

Charles hated that he didn't even know her name. Everyone was calling her "the mysterious maiden" or "the runaway princess" or simply "the girl with the glass slippers."

To him, she'd been more. The girl who had captured his heart. His true love, perhaps. Until he saw her again, he couldn't be sure.

"Did you find her?" he asked.

"I regret not, Your Highness." Ferdinand blew his nose into his handkerchief and waved a hand at the servants to disperse.

Charles knew the gesture. *These are matters of state, meant only for the sovereign's ears.*

Which meant there was bad news to come.

The duke straightened as the staff retreated outside. "I've searched everywhere. The maiden has vanished."

It was as Charles had feared. "Continue your report, please."

"As you wish, Your Highness." Ferdinand returned to reading his scroll. "From dawn to dusk, one hundred and twenty-three households were searched yesterday in the first and second precincts of Valors. None were residence to the maiden with the glass slipper. I regret I must conclude my search—"

"After only one day?" interrupted Charles.

"Yes. I made a thorough inquiry of the first and second precincts—"

"There are *nine* precincts in Valors, and more than a hundred and twenty-three households."

"There are only one hundred and twenty-three *noble* households."

"I thought I'd made myself clear," Charles said through his teeth. "*Every* house. Noble *and* common."

The duke frowned. "B-b-but, Your Highness—if the girl's a commoner—"

"*Every* eligible maiden was invited to attend, wasn't she?" Charles said, quoting the invitation. "Then the girl could be anyone. A countess, a farmer, a scullery maid. Search *everyone.*"

"I am afraid that will be impossible," said the duke. "There is a council meeting this morning regarding urgent matters of state. My presence is not to be missed. Sire, don't you agree?"

"Hmm?" said the king, who was more focused on his plate of eggs than on the conversation at hand. "Ah. Yes. Urgent matters of state. Everyone's been searched."

He seems distracted this morning, Charles thought, observing his father. "No, I said to search *everyone.* If I could go myself to look for her—"

"That's out of the question," interrupted Ferdinand.

"Your Highness, it would be neither appropriate, nor safe, for you to venture into Valors on such a quest—"

"I was addressing my father, not you."

"Ferdinand's right," said the king, finally snapping to attention. "A prince does not go out on a manhunt, knocking on doors in search of runaway princesses!"

"It's not a—"

"Besides, your aunt Genevieve arrived this morning and expects you to accompany her to lunch."

The prince started. The name was one he hadn't heard in years. "Aunt Genevieve is here?"

"That's what I said, isn't it?"

A muscle twitched in Charles's jaw. Now he understood why his father looked so preoccupied. His aunt, the Duchess of Orlanne, hadn't visited in nearly a decade; in fact, the last time she'd been there, she'd sworn never to return to the palace. She and his father famously did not get along—and Charles didn't understand why, given he thought the world of her.

"Where is she now?" Charles asked.

"Still sleeping, I should hope." King George shoveled the rest of his pastry into his mouth. He began to cough violently as he chewed, the color draining from his face.

"Oh, dear!" exclaimed the Grand Duke, springing to action. He tapped the king's back with his scroll, but it only made the coughing worse. By now, the king's face had turned an alarming shade of purple.

Charles rounded on his father, hoisting him out of his chair and pumping his chest as the duke rang the nearest bell.

"Come help His Majesty! He's choking!"

Just as the servants began clamoring inside, the pastry shot out of his mouth onto the table.

"Breathe, Father, breathe."

The king tugged at his collar, recovering his breath.

"Sire," said the duke, "that's the third time this week. Are you—"

King George grunted, a signal for the duke to be quiet. "Nothing's the matter with me. Drank my tea too fast, that's all. Pass me the sugar, will you?"

"Father, are you sure that's a good idea? You just choked."

The duke complied before Charles could argue further, scooping a heaping spoonful for the king. George leaned back in his chair, a contented smile cheering his expression.

"Perhaps you ought to sit out on meeting with the council this morning, Your Majesty," Ferdinand said, once Charles's father took another long sip. The duke had taken the tone Charles detested most; it was far too nice, far too suggestive that he was angling for something. But what?

"Sit out the meeting?"

"Yes. The physician said—"

The king shot the Grand Duke a deadly look. "I can handle a council meeting, thank you very much."

"But sire—"

Charles frowned at both of them. "What did the physician say, Father?"

"Only that all this party-throwing business is too much for a young man like me." King George leaned back in his chair, exhaling then letting out a chortle. "What does he know?"

The Grand Duke was watching them, a corner of his mouth lifted. Charles didn't like the look.

"Shouldn't you be resuming your search in Valors?" he asked Ferdinand.

"If Your Highness insists, I will certainly continue my search. But only *after* the council meeting. There are important laws being discussed this morning, and His Majesty greatly values my opinion."

Charles frowned. "Important laws? Father, I could help you—"

"No, no, you must not be late for your luncheon with the duchess," interrupted Ferdinand smoothly. "Now, if you'll excuse me, I must prepare my statement for today's council." He rolled up his scroll, tucking it under his arm, saluted the king, and bowed.

Then the door closed, leaving the prince alone with his father.

Charles opened his mouth to express his doubts about the Grand Duke, but his father spoke first: "Why the frown, my boy? Don't be so hard on Ferdinand. He's doing the best job he can."

"I don't trust him."

"Why not? He's doing you a great favor, searching the kingdom for the girl with the glass slipper."

Charles tried not to cringe. The last person he wanted to be indebted to was the duke.

"Curious maiden, this young lady of yours." The king laughed heartily. "I've heard of many things in my time, but not glass slippers. Cheer up, my boy. We'll find her. How far could she have gotten on glass? And only one shoe!"

Slowly, Charles relaxed, and he couldn't help smiling. Hearing his father laugh reminded him of the man he'd missed while he was away at the Royal University: the vibrant and energetic father who'd bounced him on his knee when he was a boy and spent every precious free moment he had with his son. Then the king's shoulders sagged, and his laugh became a dry, hacking cough.

Panic seized Charles. "Father!"

King George clutched at his chest, pounding on it with his fists. His cough spluttered into a coarse wheeze. Then he forced a laugh.

"It's nothing, my boy." He waved a croissant at Charles, then picked up his teacup again. "Just choked on my good humor."

"That didn't sound like you were choking—"

"Lord knows I won't have anything to laugh about when Genevieve's around," interjected the king dryly. "The last time your aunt smiled, I still had all my hair!" He patted his bald scalp. "Why else do you think I sent her away? She's no good for my blood pressure. No good for my sleep, either!"

But his father hadn't sent her away. From what Charles remembered, Aunt Genevieve had chosen to leave. He didn't know much more than that; it was always a sore subject with his father, one he had never dared to broach himself.

"Now, are you going to keep standing there or are you going to join me for breakfast?"

"Some other time," said Charles. He had a feeling his father was simply trying to change the subject.

The king harrumphed. "Very well, then. Be sure you arrive on time for lunch. The last thing I need is Genevieve haranguing me for not teaching you proper manners."

"I'll be there." Charles started to leave, then paused in his step, tensing.

"What is it, my boy?"

"It's a matter of the council," said Charles. "I'd like to join. Your daily meetings with Ferdinand, too."

"Ah . . ." The king's voice drifted. He coughed into his

sleeve. "Naturally, you will, Charles. In due time. Let us focus on getting you settled back in the palace—"

"I *am* settled."

"Then let's wait until Ferdinand finds your girl, and then we'll talk. All right? Best for you to have a proper introduction to the council once that is sorted." The king leaned back against his chair's cushioned headboard. "You'll be happier, too."

"Very well, Father." The prince bowed. "Enjoy your breakfast."

On his way out, Charles noticed his father's chamberlain lingering outside the door.

Keeping his voice low, the prince said, "Sir Chamberlain, would you have the royal physician visit my father again today?"

The older man blinked, as if surprised by the question. But, befitting the truly trained and skilled servant he was, he quickly hid his confusion and bent his head. "Yes, Your Highness."

"Thank you, Sir Chamberlain." Feeling slightly better about his father's health, Charles strode on, but he didn't know where he was going.

The gardens, perhaps. He had spent almost all of the day before there, trying to retrace the steps he'd taken with *her*, to see if he could remember anything that might help him find her. He hadn't, but maybe today would be different.

It was better than waiting for Ferdinand to come back with news.

Three corridors down, Charles passed the physician hurrying to the king's chamber.

"That was quick," he murmured. "Dr. Coste! Are you on your way to see my father?"

"Why yes, Your Highness." The physician shuffled backward, and a flash of parchment peeked out from under his arm, stamped with Ferdinand's seal.

Curious. What did Ferdinand want with the royal physician?

"I am concerned about his health. Was he ill much while I was away?"

"His Majesty the king is in excellent health!" Dr. Coste replied, a little too brightly. "His appetite is vigorous, and his energy boundless. I *have* recommended that he exercise more, perhaps a daily morning walk about the gardens, but His Majesty has been so excited for Your Highness's return from the Royal University this month that he has not yet implemented my suggestion. Even still, there is nothing to be concerned about."

"You are certain? His cough sounded worrisome."

"It's happened before," the physician assured him. "Likely, His Majesty is simply growing more sensitive to things like dust—not unusual for a man of his age. That, and his blood pressure is slightly elevated . . . but it's nothing a good week of rest can't fix. Think nothing of it."

"I see," Charles replied. That was what his father had said. "Well, if there's anything you can do . . ."

Dr. Coste stroked his beard. "I know the Grand Duke enjoys visiting His Majesty after the evening council meetings, but I would suggest that your father not take any tea after dinner. A better night's rest should relieve his coughing fits. I'll propose a sleeping draught instead."

That eased some of Charles's concern. "Thank you, Dr. Coste. Carry on."

Unclenching his fists, the prince headed to the stables. He might not be allowed to leave the palace to help search for the girl of his dreams, but a brisk ride through the royal grounds would help clear his mind.

Even if just for a few hours.

Chapter Eight

At precisely seven thirty in the morning, the city of Valors came alive. One by one, the shopkeepers opened their doors, sweeping the floors and throwing buckets of water onto the streets to clean their storefronts. Bright yellow and purple awnings hovered over the tiled roofs, and aromas of bread, oranges, and fish wafted into the crisp air. Carriages darted out of narrow side streets and rumbled onto the roads, and the fountains in the town squares gurgled to life.

As Cinderella followed Louisa deeper into the city, she marveled at the scene. Everywhere she looked there were people. Children clinging to their mothers' hands, young couples on a morning stroll, and elderly women lining up at the market for the day's first pick of fruits and vegetables.

Years of loneliness, so deeply carved into Cinderella's heart, were slowly whittled away.

This was what she had missed during her years with Lady Tremaine. Going out to the market with the servants, meeting strangers and chatting with other girls her age, wandering the streets of the city with her papa until she got lost. Having dreams of what she could do . . . She allowed herself a moment of hopeful thinking. Maybe she could open a flower shop one day, like the one she'd just passed, and have her own garden of roses like the ones her mother had grown.

"Come on," said Louisa, helping her navigate the growing crowds. "Once we're out of the square there's a shortcut we can take to the palace."

Cinderella's nerves fluttered as she glanced up at the king's residence. It crowned the top of a nearby hill, and was so close she could make out the lions embroidered on the tower flags and the pink roses lining the roads up to the main gates.

Soon she'd be there again.

"Isn't it marvelous?" Louisa asked, catching her staring. "It's even grander inside. You'll see."

Cinderella *had* seen, but she simply nodded. After all, what could she say? That she'd ridden an enchanted pumpkin-turned-coach up the winding starlit path just two nights ago?

From her window, it'd been like a painting out of a fairy tale, not an actual place people lived in. She still remembered how intensely her heart had raced, how she'd listened to the horses' hooves beating against the pavement, steadily bringing her closer to the castle.

Even the air there had been sweet, with the scent of lilies and roses and flowers she could not name. Of freshly watered bushes, of pebbled stones, of horsehair and gaslight. It had smelled heavenly.

The streets of Valors did not smell heavenly. Smashed oranges, rotten vegetables, and broken carriage wheels splattered with mud littered the roads. While Louisa chattered away, her conversation vacillating between worrying about being late for work and instructing Cinderella on how to behave in the palace, Cinderella focused on avoiding a series of suspiciously colored puddles, piles of horse manure, and broken wine bottles.

Before she knew it, she'd followed Louisa up the hill toward the castle.

"If you ever get lost," said Louisa, pointing at the clock tower, the same one that had struck midnight during the ball, "head to the clock tower. The palace is a bona fide maze, and it's the tallest building you'll see from any point. Turn left at the purple tulips and follow the hedges. The servants' quarters are right past the iron gate."

"Purple tulips," repeated Cinderella, brushing her

fingers across the leafy walls, "down to the iron gate. That's easy enough."

At her side, Bruno let out a growl; he'd spotted a stray cat scampering out of a bush.

"That reminds me," added Louisa. "We'll have to keep your dog here for now." She gestured at the hedges, whose branches were loose enough that Bruno could easily crawl inside to hide. "I'll sneak him inside during lunch."

As Cinderella nodded, Louisa tilted her head to the side, studying her. "Just a minute. Aunt Irmina's a stickler for appearances." Removing a few pins from her own hair, she wrapped Cinderella's ponytail into a neat bun. "There. That'll help a little."

She motioned at the gate ahead, guarded by four sentries. Hooking her arm under Cinderella's, Louisa whispered, "Don't say anything. Stay a step behind me, smile, and follow my lead."

Cinderella's new friend strode up to the guards, greeting them with a winsome smile. "Francis, Theodore, Jules, Jean, good morning."

One by one, they returned Louisa's infectious smile. "Morning, Louisa. Late again?"

Louisa raised a finger to her mouth, pretending to shush them. "Hoping Aunt Irmina is too busy to notice I'm a few minutes behind."

"You're in luck, as always."

"The palace still in an uproar?" Louisa exhaled with relief. "I thought so."

"You better hurry before those few minutes become half an hour. It's nearly eight."

They parted to let Louisa through, but at the last minute, the fourth guard intercepted Cinderella.

"Papers, miss?"

"She's a new maid," cut in Louisa. "No papers yet."

"New maid?"

"Yes, for . . . for the new princess."

At the words, Cinderella flinched, the blood rushing to her head. Luckily, no one was paying attention to her.

"Weren't you paying attention to the morning announcement?" Louisa was saying. "About His Royal Highness searching for the love of his life?"

The guard narrowed his eyes. "You know we don't listen to the servants' morning announcement, and I don't recall anything about His Grace hiring a new maid."

"We're about to have a new princess, aren't we?" Louisa huffed. "Then obviously the palace needs a new maid. Come on, let her in. I'm already late as it is, and you know how Aunt Irmina is. . . ." She clasped her hands together in entreaty.

"Go on, hurry before we change our minds."

Once they were out of the guards' earshot, Louisa squeezed Cinderella's hand and let out a little squeal. "See? That wasn't so hard. Now for the tricky part . . . Aunt Irmina. *Madame* Irmina to you."

"Is she in charge?"

"Yes, of the Blooms and Looms," Louisa explained breezily.

"Blooms and Looms?"

"That's what we call the quarters for all the maids and the seamstresses. We change into our uniforms, report to duty, and eat there. Some of the girls even live there, depending on their posts." She gestured left at the fork in the hallway. "That way leads to the Cooks and Looks wing. Quarters for all the butlers, valets, chefs, and so on."

Cinderella chuckled. "Who came up with these names?"

"I don't know. They were around long before I even got here." Louisa guided her down a long corridor wallpapered in cream-colored brocade. She was talking so fast now that Cinderella could barely understand her. "But they're not official, mind you, not like all the names for the rooms *upstairs*. The Amber State Room, the Hall of Westerly Mirrors, the Emerald Lounging Room. The Royal Apartments. Only the servants use Blooms and Looms, and Cooks and Looks. When you're stationed up there, and the nobles start talking about downstairs—*this* is where they mean."

Upstairs. Downstairs. It all made sense to Cinderella. Upstairs was where the masters and mistresses lived—like her stepmother's and stepsisters' quarters. Downstairs was the kitchen, the pantry, the chicken coop, the stables—all the places where Cinderella had spent her days working.

She may have returned to the palace, but being downstairs here felt just as far away from the prince as her old attic.

The main chamber came into view. This part of the palace didn't look anything like what Cinderella had seen at the ball. In fact, it reminded her of home: checkered floors, wooden walls coated with burgundy wallpaper, and silver tables with slim vases of tulips. There was even an impressive line of bronze call bells lining one side of the wall.

"Records," Louisa said hurriedly, gesturing at a long piece of paper tacked against the wall, "for keeping track of our chores and hours. Write your name every morning when you come in for breakfast. That is, unless you end up as a personal attendant. I wouldn't wish that on anyone, though."

"What do you mean?"

"All the royals have regular attendants—those positions aren't open. But visitors are a different story. They usually bring their own retinue: ladies-in-waiting and butlers and maids—even though it is hospitality for the king to offer his own staff. Father says the tradition was meant to prevent conspiracies back in the old days." She shrugged. "The point is, personal attendants are at their master's beck and call."

"I wouldn't mind," said Cinderella.

"You have no idea what you're in for." Louisa shuddered. "They say the last time the Duchess was here, she wouldn't drink the palace water—only water brought to her from the streams of Mount Bonclare. Her attendant had to write letters to every lord in Valors to get her some. She likes her tea scalding hot and throws it back at you if the temperature is wrong, and once she made her attendant bring a caged lark to wake her in the morning, because she said that the girl's voice was too shrill! Lucky for you, we had to draw straws yesterday to see who'd have to serve her . . . but—"

Before Louisa got a chance to finish, a low voice interrupted them.

"Late again, I see."

From the way Louisa instantly straightened, Cinderella deduced the woman who'd spoken had to be Madame Irmina.

"Stay here," Louisa whispered, waving Cinderella back into the hallway.

Dipping into the shadows, Cinderella pressed her back against the wall and peeked out. Madame Irmina was shorter than she'd imagined, given how tall her niece was, but she stood as though she towered over Louisa, her back stiff as an ironing board. Everything about her was precise: her hair was meticulously arranged into a neat, round bun with not a gray tendril out of place, and her apron was the whitest, most spotless swath of fabric Cinderella had ever seen.

Not a woman to be crossed.

"That's the third time this month, Louisa."

"Yes, I know. I was up late last night helping my mother, and—"

"No excuses. You know the rules."

Louisa quieted. "I'm sorry. It won't happen again."

"Don't think because you're my niece you have the privilege of flouting the rules. I warned you last time that—"

"Have a heart, Aunt Irmina," Louisa interrupted. "Papa's—"

"Save the speech. I've heard it all before. Your papa's been here ever since you were born—and it's always been your dream to work here with him." Irmina huffed. "If it really is your dream, try being on time."

"My ma's shop needed extra help last night. I'll do double my tasks—"

"How can you? You're the slowest seamstress in the entire palace—"

"Yes, but that's because my stitches are the neatest."

"And your mouth is certainly the rudest." Irmina glared at her. "Rules are rules. All I ask is that you be on time, and I will not make an exception for you because we're family."

"I'm the reason she's late," Cinderella spoke up. "Please don't punish her on my behalf."

No, Louisa mouthed, trying to wave her away. "Get back in the hall," she whispered.

But it was too late.

Madame Irmina spun to face her. "And who are you?"

"Cinderella, ma'am."

A deep frown set Irmina's tight features. "There is no Cinderella among my girls."

"I brought her," Louisa said. "We'll be in need of more staff if there's to be a new princess, and she's a decent seamstress—"

"And who are you to judge whether someone is a decent seamstress?" Madame Irmina said testily. "I make the decisions regarding the household, and we do not need another seamstress."

"She has no other place to go. I found her on the street."

"The street!" Irmina repeated with horror. "You cannot simply bring runaways into the palace. There is a long interview process. Not just anyone is fit to serve His Royal Majesty's household. References must be made and inquired after."

"Please," begged Cinderella. "I have nowhere else to go. I can cook and clean and sew—"

"This is the palace." Madame Irmina sniffed. "If we wanted just anyone who could cook and clean and sew, we would have asked for a wench from the local tavern."

"Have a heart, Aunt Irmina," repeated Louisa.

"That's *Madame* to you," Irmina snapped. "Rules are rules. She will have to go. There's absolutely no room. And as for you, Louisa, it's high time I had a word with you. If it weren't for your mother—"

Before she could finish, a bell clanged behind Madame Irmina and she stiffened. Cinderella glanced behind her, noticing once again the wall mounted with dozens of bells, all coded with different stripes of color. The one ringing was in the top row, labeled with a stripe of blue paint.

All the servants immediately scrambled to form a long straight line in the reception room. Booted footsteps echoed down the hall, and a tall figure approached.

"What is this din?" entered a new voice. Aristocratic and exasperated.

Louisa nudged Cinderella to take a place beside her at the end of the line. Cinderella straightened and bent her head, copying everyone's posture. But she peeked up at the last moment, curious what was going on and who this visitor might be.

As soon as the door into the servants' quarters opened, she let out a quiet gasp.

It was the Grand Duke.

She had only caught a glimpse of him during the ball, and again when he'd visited the chateau. His black hair was smoothly combed, a monocle hung on a golden chain from his coat pocket, and his blue epaulets bounced slightly as he walked.

He looked tired. His eyes were bloodshot, mustache flat and uncombed.

"That's the Grand Duke," Louisa whispered, assuming Cinderella didn't know. "He's the king's closest confidant and adviser. Some say he's become the most powerful man in Aurelais."

"Besides the king, of course?" Cinderella whispered back, but Louisa didn't get a chance to reply.

"Your Grace," blustered Madame Irmina, "I was not expecting you."

The Grand Duke surveyed the line of female servants with a curled lip. "Disorder is the precursor of disgrace," he said. "I expected more of you, Madame Irmina. Your girls seem to have forgotten their manners."

At once, all the young women in the room curtsied. The move did not seem to mollify the Grand Duke, however, for he simply sniffed in disdain.

"He's been in a foul mood ever since that mysterious princess vanished from the ball," Louisa whispered.

At the mention of the mysterious "princess," Cinderella's knees stiffened. "Why?"

"The princess left a shoe at the ball. A glass slipper, so I hear. It's all the prince has of her, so he sent the Grand Duke all over Aurelais to find her." Louisa let out a quiet sigh. "It's so terribly romantic. They say the prince will go to the ends of the earth to find her. All day and night the duke's been searching, but no luck so far. Can't be long now, though it *is* odd she hasn't come forth herself. I know *I* would if I had a chance to marry the prince. I'll bet the duke's going to start the search again today."

"What happens if he doesn't find her?" murmured Cinderella.

"The king's fickle." Louisa leaned closer, lowering her voice. "On a good day, the duke might get away with a rap on his knuckles. But His Majesty's been extra irritable lately, and he's very keen on the prince finding a bride right away—says it's a matter of national importance. So who knows?"

That was news to Cinderella, though she supposed she shouldn't have been surprised. A ball that invited every eligible maiden to attend could only be intended for one purpose: to find the prince a wife. Was that the only reason he had danced with her—to please his father? She wondered what he had thought of it all.

"Ahem," said the Grand Duke loudly, the rebuke aimed at Louisa and Cinderella.

Louisa's cheeks burned, and she curtsied lower. Cinderella did the same.

"I don't recognize you," said the duke, pausing in front of Cinderella.

"She's a trainee, Your Grace," offered Louisa.

"A trainee?" He inclined his chin at Madame Irmina. "Is this the new attendant you hired for the duchess?"

"Oh," Madame Irmina said, startled. "She dismissed the one I sent this morning already?"

"Never try to comprehend Genevieve's actions," replied the Grand Duke. "The woman is all madness and no reason, just like her husband. A pity she, too, wasn't banished from court." He turned to Cinderella. "Come along now, you should already be upstairs."

"But I haven't even—"

"Ah!" The Grand Duke's eyes widened, as if he were seeing her for the first time. He wrinkled his nose at her appearance. "Have we run out of gold? Someone see to it that she gets some proper clothes. I'll never hear the end of it if I send a servant in rags to Genevieve."

"Louisa, come with me," shouted Madame Irmina,

pulling Cinderella into a private room. Inside was a wall of identical dressers. "It must be your lucky day, girl."

She pulled open one of the drawers and thrust a lavender sash and an apron into Cinderella's arms. "Put this on after you've changed. I hope you've bathed recently. I suppose it doesn't matter, since you won't last long anyhow. Louisa! Get this girl an attendant's dress. And don't forget the wig."

Cinderella raised an eyebrow. *Wig?*

"Come on," Louisa whispered, guiding her to the staff's changing room as Madame Irmina returned to the Grand Duke.

"I told you not to say anything," Louisa said softly. "Now you're going to be the duchess's attendant."

"Madame Irmina was going to fire you."

"Aunt Irmina's family," Louisa explained. "She loves making threats, but she's not as mean-hearted as she sounds. So long as you pretend to be afraid of her."

"I've had some practice with that," muttered Cinderella, stifling unpleasant memories of Lady Tremaine. Madame Irmina didn't seem half as bad as her stepmother.

"Here," said Louisa, after rummaging through the closet for a rose-colored dress with frills along the cuffs and collar. She scrunched up her face. "I know it's hideous. I didn't design it."

Cinderella slipped the new uniform over her head.

"What's this for?" she asked, touching the lavender sash.

"The color tells us who you're serving. In your case, the duchess. It'll match her call bell on the wall." Louisa pinned the sash at her side, then spun Cinderella toward the mirror. "One last thing."

Louisa rifled through the drawers again until she found a wig with white ringlets that looked like they'd seen better days.

While Cinderella pinned the wig to her hair, Louisa hastily brushed its ivory curls. "It's a little big for your head, but it'll have to do for now. All attendants wear one. Come on, the duke is waiting."

"Ah, that's much more tolerable," he said, throwing a cursory glance over Cinderella when she returned. "Madame Irmina, this is not to happen again. My time is far too valuable to check on every girl we send to Genevieve."

"My deepest apologies, Your Grace."

"See to it that she's promptly directed to the duchess's chambers. I must be off."

"Eyes down, girl," muttered Irmina, pushing Cinderella's neck toward the ground. "When you're with any person of importance, stay three paces behind at all times. Don't speak unless spoken to, got it?"

"Yes," Cinderella murmured.

From behind, the Grand Duke cleared his throat. "On

second thought, you"—he pointed carelessly at Cinderella—"follow me. I'll direct you to the duchess myself."

Keeping her head low, Cinderella tried to focus her gaze on the ground, but her eyes kept drifting up.

This was the man who'd visited the chateau looking for her. All she had to do was ask him to let her try the glass slipper.

Under his arm, the duke carried a thick scroll loosely bound by a satin ribbon. It looked like a list of addresses—presumably, residences that he had to visit today in search of the missing princess.

In search of *her*.

"Have you found her yet?" Cinderella asked, filling the heavy silence between them.

Startled from his distraction, the duke scowled at her. Who knew whether it was because she had dared speak to him without first being given permission, or because she'd brought up an unpleasant topic, but she simply couldn't help asking.

"Who?"

Cinderella inhaled, summoning her courage. "The girl with the glass slipper."

"Heavens, no. If I had, the council wouldn't have canceled the meeting this morning, and I—" He stopped, his expression stony as he plodded ahead.

Tell him, her heart urged her. *Tell him you're the girl who danced with the prince at the ball.*

Cinderella opened her mouth to try again, but the words came out as a question:

"Can any girl try on the glass slipper?"

"Every eligible maiden," he said wearily, as if the phrase had been beaten into him.

"So someone . . . someone like me?"

The duke eyed her sharply. "No. You are a servant of the royal household. It would be impossible. Impossible. What will we have next, commoners serving on the Royal Council?"

Stung, Cinderella drew back. More than anything, she wanted to tell him: *I am* the girl you're looking for. You can call the search off.

But she couldn't bring herself to do it. After all, she no longer had her glass slipper to prove it. She could practically hear him laughing at her. *A pretty picture, young lady—imagine, a maid becoming a princess.* Then he would dismiss her, and she'd never be able to enter the palace again.

What was more—she couldn't forget her fairy godmother's uneasiness when she'd said, *My magic is forbidden in Aurelais.*

Even if the Grand Duke *did* let her try the slipper,

a man like him was bound to question how she had gotten her beautiful ball gown, her glass shoes, her fine coach and horses. What if the answer—magic—led to trouble for Lenore? That wouldn't do. She couldn't risk it.

She'd have to wait and try to find the prince. Prince Charles would remember her, and then everything would fall into place.

Or you could focus on creating a new life for yourself and Bruno, she reminded herself. *Not some fantasy you've made up for yourself after one night dancing with a man you just met.*

She curtsied stiffly. "I apologize, Your Grace."

"Quite so. Quite so." The duke removed his hat, fanning himself with it. When he spoke next, he sounded almost apologetic. "I have had a long day, young lady. Do not pester me further with such bizarre inquiries."

He waited for her to nod before going on. "Normally, such undignified questions posed to your superior would be most unwelcome. But curiosity happens to be a trait I need in you."

Cinderella must have looked confused, for he replied, "All will be explained as necessary."

He stopped in front of a gilded door so tall it touched the ceiling. Cinderella only now realized they had left the servants' quarters: the carpets had turned a rich, deep burgundy embellished with silver tassels, the vaulted ceilings were painted with historic scenes of Aurelais's first kings and queens, and the doors were furnished with gold-plated knobs.

"Welcome back, Your Grace." The guard on the right opened the door, and the duke strode inside his office.

"Quickly, child," said the duke. "I'm a busy man, and I have many matters of state to attend to this morning."

Cinderella hurried inside, standing awkwardly in front of the duke's desk. Imposing portraits of him stared from every direction, with the odd effect of making his real self seem small.

"Now, Duchess Genevieve is the king's sister, and you have been tasked with the very important role of serving her." The duke looked off to the side, making sure the door was closed. He lowered his voice. "I'd like you to keep an eye on her. Report to me everything about the duchess— what she eats for breakfast, what she says and does with her day. Everything."

Cinderella fought to keep her features expressionless. *Why?* she wanted to ask.

"I will be away today in search of the missing maiden with the glass slipper, but I shall anticipate your report when I return. Do I make myself clear?"

"Yes, Your Grace."

"Splendid. Now, off you go." He rang one of the bells on his desk, and within seconds, an attendant attired in a sleek velvet coat and a wig of white curls sprang into the room.

"Have my carriage readied," commanded the duke, "and see to it that this young lady is dispatched to Her Highness's quarters."

The duke's attendant cast Cinderella a sidelong glance, one that plainly showed he did not envy her position. After a quick look up and down at her appearance, he sniffed just as Madame Irmina had; even he didn't think she would last long here.

Cinderella's stomach sank. Somehow, she'd have to prove them all wrong.

Chapter Nine

The palace was a labyrinth of hallways, but the duke's attendant did not deign to give Cinderella a tour. For her part, she
was so focused on trying to keep up that she almost didn't
notice when they arrived in front of the duchess's chambers.

"She'll be expecting you," was all her guide said before
he swiftly deserted her.

"Wait, do I—"

The duke's attendant had already turned the corner.

"—knock?" Cinderella whirled to face the duchess's
massive doors, both sides flanked by unsmiling guards.

"Do you suppose I go inside?" she asked them.

No response.

Report to me everything about the duchess, the Grand
Duke had instructed.

Cinderella bit her lip. That didn't strike her as a typical task given to royal attendants.

Gathering her courage, she took the gilded knocker and tapped softly. Then she clasped the knob and turned, entering the duchess's apartments as quietly as she could.

"That was fast," rasped a voice, startling Cinderella. "I take it you're my next victim?"

Before her, the Duchess of Orlanne sat at her writing desk. A coil of salt-and-pepper hair gathered at her nape, punctuated by emerald and amethyst hairpins that matched her violet gown and its green trimming. Her face didn't seem to match the refinery of her garments; it was like a quill, long and narrow, with gray eyes as sharp as polished nibs.

"I'm sorry, Your Grace," said Cinderella, bowing. "I did—"

"I *am* sorry, *Your Highness*," corrected the duchess. "I'm a member of the royal family, unlike Ferdinand." She snapped her book closed and harrumphed. "They send me a girl who doesn't even know how to address me properly. How like George. How absent-minded!"

Venturing deeper into the sitting room, Cinderella was about to repeat her apology when the duchess grabbed the walking stick beside her desk and rose.

"Stay off the rug," the king's sister barked. She wrinkled her nose at Cinderella, her sharp eyes taking in the cuts on her hands, the bruises on her temples hidden under her ill-fitting wig. "You smell dirty. Have you been out in the rain?"

Heat rushed to Cinderella's cheeks. "There was a storm last night, Your Highness, and I only—"

"Stop." The duchess raised a gloved hand. "I don't want to hear any more. You are dismissed."

Cinderella bit her lip to keep it from trembling. Madame Irmina had warned her that she wouldn't last in the palace. But even she must have expected her to last more than five minutes.

"On your way out, you may tell whoever thought you fit to attend me to turn in their resignation as well."

"But, Your Highness—"

"Out, I said. Can you not hear?" The duchess reached toward the nearest table, picking up a silver call bell and muttering, "Wait until I get my hands on George. Does he think this is some sort of practical joke? How dare his staff send me a servant who—"

"Oh, you mustn't blame Madame Irmina!" Cinderella cried.

"What was that?"

She drew a breath. "It wasn't her fault. Or the king's."

The duchess clamped the bell in her palm, suffocating its clang. "Of course it wasn't my brother's fault. Do you think he has time to oversee the hiring of servants? Ferdinand manages the royal retainers."

"Please don't dismiss anyone because of me," Cinderella said quietly. "I'll leave now, so Madame Irmina can send you a new girl right away." She gave a despondent curtsy, then turned for the door.

"Wait. I've changed my mind." The duchess pounded her walking stick on the ground, a cue Cinderella did not understand. "Well, don't be a mouse. Come here and let me take a look at you."

Trying to hide her confusion and careful to avoid stepping on the carpets, Cinderella traced back toward the duchess.

"Hmm," said the king's sister, considering. "Your dress is a size too large, and your wig—impossible! It's practically slipping off your head." The duchess let out a sigh. "I suppose your smell isn't *that* offensive. See to it that you bathe tonight. Thoroughly, is that clear?"

"Oh, yes, ma'am—"

"Shush. I am not finished. I should be insulted that my attendant has little experience in the palace, but I supposed it would be Ferdinand's way to find yet more petty ways to slight me." Duchess Genevieve glowered at her. "He sent you specifically to insult me, didn't he? Well, I will not give him the satisfaction of sending you back."

The duchess circled Cinderella, studying her with a frown. "You're a rather pretty girl, aren't you? Bright-eyed, cheery, and earnest-looking. Clearly an inexperienced member of the royal household. Don't expect that to make me like you more. Don't expect that to make me *trust* you, either. But it appears I don't have a choice but to keep you, do I? Lunch is in an hour, and I need assistance dressing for the occasion."

Her thin brows knit together skeptically. "You do know how to dress a lady, don't you? Heavens, judging by your own outfit I am not sure I want to know the answer to that question."

Cinderella hesitated. She had fitted her stepsisters into their fine clothes plenty of times, but a duchess's gowns would be far more elegant and elaborate than anything Drizella or Anastasia ever wore.

"I don't know, ma'am," she replied truthfully.

"Don't know?"

"I have never served a duchess before."

"You don't say," said the king's sister with a scoff. "You had better learn quickly. Otherwise, you will not be staying past lunch."

"Yes, ma'am."

"Unless I address you, you are a statue," continued the duchess, taking on an instructional tone. "All servants of the palace are to be invisible. Not to be seen, heard, or even noticed. Hear me—I do not intend on being made an embarrassment of in my brother's court."

"I understand."

"Good." The duchess harrumphed again, then strode into her bedchamber to retrieve the fur stole draped over the chair. "What do you think of this?"

"That?" Cinderella stared at the stole and tried not to wrinkle her nose. She might not be knowledgeable about the latest fashions at court, but it didn't take much of an eye to tell it was the most hideous thing she'd ever seen.

"Out with it, girl."

"If I may be honest, Your Highness . . . it is not very flattering on you. I would suggest a simple cape— perhaps an emerald green to match the trimming on your gown—instead."

Duchess Genevieve's thin lips curved in surprise. "It isn't, is it? Funny that Lady Alarna should say it suits me perfectly. Yet that's the thing with my brother's court. Everyone says what you want to hear."

She tossed the stole onto her bed and cast a glance at the clock. "We'll need an entirely new ensemble, then. If that makes me late for lunch, so be it. My brother can wait. Women are always waiting on men—let it be the other way around for a change."

Cinderella tilted her head, surprised that the duchess should act so impertinent toward the king. But she didn't question it. "Yes, ma'am."

"I should have at least three girls waiting on me," the duchess said testily as Cinderella helped her select a new outfit. "Short on staff, indeed." She fluttered her handkerchief at the swarms of maids outside the window skittering across the royal lawn. "What do you think *they're* all doing?"

Cinderella wasn't sure whether she was supposed to answer. "They're on their way inside, ma'am. To do the dusting, and polishing, and sweeping, and—"

"Heaven knows what else," the duchess interrupted. "The chandeliers don't need to be cleaned twice a day, and the windows certainly don't need to be wiped every hour." Her gaze swept across her chambers and she crossed her arms. "My desk *could* use a better dusting, though. You missed a button, girl."

Cinderella bit her lower lip. It wasn't like her to be so careless. After years of working under her stepmother's careful scrutiny, she had learned to be quick yet efficient. Her nerves were failing her.

"Enough," the duchess said. "I can finish the rest myself. Go away."

Cinderella blinked. "Pardon?"

"What don't you understand, girl?" the king's sister huffed. "I'm off to lunch and I do not want some grubby young girl I've barely met scrounging around my chambers, so be off. And I don't mean wandering off for the rest of the day. I can barely stand longer than an hour's lunch with George, and I have a perfect internal clock. If you are not back before I'm finished, I will have no choice but to send you back for good."

Relief flooded Cinderella's chest. "I see. Yes, ma'am."

"And if anyone asks whose attendant you are, you are not mine."

"Understood, ma'am."

Cinderella had no idea where to go. An hour wasn't long enough to explore the castle with its maze of hallways, anterooms, and courts.

Deciding it was best not to wander too far, she made her way around the duchess's wing and stopped before a long hall that housed a gallery of portraits.

To her immediate left was a portrait of the king and duchess as children. Genevieve carried her baby brother in her arms, a half smile perched on her lips as George tugged on her sleeve. In another painting, the two were slightly older, riding the same pony in front of a fountain in the royal gardens. The duchess had a mischievous glint in her eye, and a wide grin Cinderella couldn't imagine the stern lady wearing now.

Seeing the duchess as a girl of five or six made Cinderella smile.

They looked close, the king and his sister. I wonder what changed.

With a sigh, she progressed down the hall, observing

the king growing older with each painting she passed. In the middle of the gallery, a regal young woman appeared by King George's side.

The queen.

Whoever had painted her had captured the intensity of her gaze, for it was so arresting that when Cinderella stopped to get a closer look, she almost curtsied before the portrait.

She leaned toward the painting, studying the queen. Her hair was raven black like her son, the prince's, her eyes dark yet luminous.

"Back from your morning ride, Your Highness?"

Cinderella threw a glance behind her, and her heart nearly stopped. At the other end of the hall—was the prince!

A deep frown beset his face as he strode down the hall, looking harried. His attendant practically had to run to keep up with him.

Do I bow? she wondered frantically. She needed to make a decision before he passed her.

Hastily, she bent into a curtsy. She knew she was not to peek up and glance at him, not to say a single word unless addressed or spoken to. But she couldn't help it.

She looked up.

Seeing him again, a wash of memories overwhelmed her. How wonderful it had been to dance—for the first time in years! When she closed her eyes she could still remember the smell of the ballroom: a potpourri of perfumes from the hundreds of guests, with the faintest hint of lemon from the shining floors. She could feel the soft ruby carpet under her heels, and hear the lush waltz music echoing up to the high ceilings of the ballroom.

And how kind he had been to her. Not a trace of the arrogance she would've expected from the royal heir to the kingdom—she supposed that was why she hadn't even known he was the prince.

And their kiss.

Simply remembering it made Cinderella's face warm.

Your Highness— she almost said, but she stopped herself. *Your Highness, what? Your Highness, I'm the runaway princess. Only, I'm not really a princess. I'm just Cinderella.*

She bit her tongue. She couldn't do it.

Why not?

She stared after him as he passed her, not sure if she knew the answer.

The prince wasn't dressed in formal attire, but in a navy suit with a thin cord of silver trimming the sleeves and collar. No medals adorned his jacket, and no epaulets sat on his shoulders. Yet Cinderella found she liked him even more like this, with a smudge of dirt on the cuff of his sleeve and a stray piece of hay clinging to the side of his pants.

How much he looked simply like a young man she might have met in town. She could almost have forgotten he was a prince.

Almost.

Prince Charles was nearly at the end of the corridor when he suddenly stopped. He turned and retraced his steps until he stood in front of her, and Cinderella held her breath, her pulse hammering in her ears.

He smiled at her, and something flickered across his dark eyes—a spark of recognition.

Cinderella's heart lifted.

"You," he said quietly. He gestured at her lavender sash. "You must be Aunt Genevieve's new attendant."

Cinderella blinked, sure she had misheard, but the prince kept speaking.

"Welcome. My aunt is very dear to me, and I would be most grateful if you saw to it that she is comfortable here."

Cinderella's lips parted with disappointment. Struggling to find the words, she curtsied again. Before she could utter anything at all, Prince Charles wished her well and was gone.

"Yes, Your Highness," she whispered, watching him disappear down the hall.

Slowly, as her heart sank, a terrible ache rose in her throat. She had been sure he would recognize her. Was it the wig?

Why didn't I take it off? Why didn't I say anything?

She inhaled, trying to ease away the sadness swelling inside her. Even with the wig, she thought he would have known her. Maybe . . . maybe it hadn't been love, after all. Maybe he was only searching for her because his father wanted him to get married.

What does it matter? she admonished herself. *This is the chance at happiness I've always wanted. I'm free of my stepmother, and I have a new life in the palace. It'd be silly to risk losing that new life and throw my heart away on a boy—prince or not—that I don't even know.*

I'm not going to look for him again, she decided, pushing all thoughts of Prince Charles aside. She needed her work as the duchess's attendant more than she needed a prince. She'd pour all her energy toward her position in the palace. Then she'd make new dreams for herself—dreams like seeing more of the world, and helping others.

Like her fairy godmother.

She frowned, murmuring to herself. "The next time I see her, I'll have to ask what she meant by her magic being forbidden here."

But she had no idea when she'd see Lenore again; she couldn't summon her fairy godmother while she was working in the palace . . . not after what she had said—or *hadn't* said—about the ban on magic. Certainly not with the Grand Duke constantly lurking about, waiting on her for reports.

His portrait stared at Cinderella from the wall, and a wave of dread rushed over her. In her first hour serving Duchess Genevieve, she'd done nothing but help the king's sister dress for lunch. What exactly was the duke expecting her to report to him? What her fashion tastes were? What flavor tea she liked to drink?

Cinderella hoped she wouldn't have to find out.

Chapter Ten

Prince Charles wished he had something—or *someone*—to blame for being late to lunch. Under his breath, he ran through a list of excuses, each more pitiful than the last.

"Apologies, Aunt Genevieve. My horse stumbled over a fence during my morning ride. It's my fault . . . I was distracted.

"Apologies, Aunt Genevieve. I was so engrossed in the book I'm reading, and I didn't hear the clock strike noon. What book is it? I . . . I can't recall the title."

He shook his head, trying again, "Apologies, Aunt Genevieve. I wandered too far from the palace and got lost. Where was I, you say? In the gardens . . . I wanted to see whether the roses have bloomed."

He shook his head at himself. *Got lost? On the palace grounds, where you spent every free moment of your childhood exploring? Where there are at least five guards watching you at all times?*

None of his excuses were true, but worse, they weren't even good lies, and he knew it. Passing his horse's reins to the stable hand, he returned to the palace and made for the royal dining hall, where his aunt and father awaited.

In all honesty, he'd been well aware of the time. He'd ridden out to the edge of the palace grounds, to a quiet part of the hill overlooking the city. Instead of heading back early so his valet could help him change out of his riding habit, he'd stayed out until the last minute, breathing in the fresh spring air and gazing down at the vast expanse of Valors.

Even after four years away, he still knew the bend of every path and the shape of each grove across the royal grounds. How good it had felt to be out of the palace, away from the perfumed halls and the watchful eyes of his ancestors' towering portraits—and from the responsibility that weighed on his shoulders.

How good it felt to try to forget, even if only for a moment, that the lofty trees and clipped hedges surrounding the palace perimeter were walls designed to keep him in—and everyone else out.

Only half mindful of his whereabouts, he soon found himself a mere turn away from the royal dining room. Its cream-painted doors, adorned with gilded angels and olive branches, were slightly parted; Charles could just make out his father's throaty voice inside. And his aunt's . . .

He'd better hurry if he didn't want to disappoint Aunt Genevieve.

As he quickened his pace, a young woman to his left curtsied, a servant he'd never seen. She wore a lavender sash, with a wig slightly too large for her head. Her eyes were the clearest shade of blue he'd ever seen.

He stopped to greet her—he always made an effort to welcome the newer staff, but his words were hasty and rushed; he didn't want to keep Aunt Genevieve waiting.

Yet as soon as he continued on his way, he regretted not having spoken longer to the new girl.

There was something about her . . . the blueness of her eyes had arrested him in his place. A hint of sadness had touched them when he'd spoken, and he wondered why. Part of him wished he could go back to her and make her smile.

A mad possibility entered his mind. It made no sense at all, yet he couldn't get it out of his head. She'd looked so familiar. . . .

No, it couldn't be her.

It had to be the sash, he reasoned. He hadn't seen any of the servants wear lavender, his aunt's color, in a long time. Yes, that was it.

His mind made up, he made for the hidden panel in the wall where the servants entered and exited the royal dining room. The first person he encountered was just the one he was looking for.

"Madame Irmina, I was hoping you could help me with something."

"But of course, Your Highness." She beamed.

"Thank you." Charles cleared his throat. "The new girl serving my aunt," he began, not at all sure what he was trying to get out of the conversation but unable to stop himself from asking. "What's her name?"

"The new girl?" Madame Irmina tilted her head. "I do not know who you mean, Your Highness."

"She . . . she reminds me of someone." The prince shook his head. "Never mind, it's—"

"Oh, you must mean Louisa's street urchin. Yes, she was assigned to your aunt this morning."

"Ah." Hearing his voice brighten, he cleared his throat self-consciously. "I believe so. But what do you mean, street urchin?"

Madame Irmina's composure wavered, and she tucked a stray strand of hair behind her ear. "A slip of the tongue,

Your Highness. My niece brought the girl in this morning. She had nowhere else to go."

"This morning," Charles repeated. "So she only just arrived."

"Yes. Just. Sounds like she's an orphan, poor thing."

He sighed. An orphan with nowhere else to go. His father and the duke were convinced his mystery maiden was of noble birth, but her guilelessness and the earnest way she'd spoken to him weren't anything like the ladies at court he'd met. Still, common sense dictated that no penniless orphan could be the young lady he'd danced with, a girl with glass slippers and a pale blue gown that shone like moonlight.

But those eyes . . . he couldn't shake the feeling that he'd seen them somewhere before.

"Thank you for your help."

Madame Irmina curtsied. "It is my pleasure, Your Highness. I haven't had a chance to tell you this personally until now, but everyone in the household is so happy to have you home from your studies."

"And I have looked forward to returning," replied Charles. He gave a slight, grateful bow of his head. "Now, if you'll excuse me."

It wasn't a lie, not entirely. He *had* been looking forward to returning to the palace and seeing his father. But was he happy to be back? Of that, he wasn't quite so sure.

Four years at the Royal University of Aurelais had changed him. He'd lived in a dormitory instead of a palace, and his professors had called him by his name instead of his title. His classmates whispered behind his back, turning up their noses at him for sending away his valet and for staying in the university dormitory instead of at one of his father's nearby estates, but he'd never minded. He relished not being reminded of his royal status at every turn.

The girl at the ball was the first person he had ever met who seemed to want to get to know him for *him*, not because he was the crown prince of Aurelais. She'd had no idea he was the prince, and Charles could not forget how refreshing that was, how wonderful it'd been to simply talk to her.

She hadn't cared about his title, and he wouldn't care about hers. Whatever—*whoever* she was, he was utterly smitten all the same.

But she had vanished, and with each passing day, Charles despaired that he would never see her again.

"The young lady has left without a trace," the Grand Duke had reported on the night of the ball, after sending his men to chase after her coach. Then, after a snide pause—in which he had taken undisguised pleasure—he had added, "Don't you suppose that if she had wanted to marry His Royal Highness, she would have stayed?"

Charles couldn't get Ferdinand's words out of his head. What if they were true? He wanted to believe she had fled the ball because it had been midnight, as she'd said—but what if she had left because of *him*?

The doors to the royal dining room opened, and a familiar voice from inside called to him, "Charles!"

Lifting his head, Prince Charles smiled, filled with a new sense of hope and determination.

If anyone would help him find the girl of his dreams, it was Aunt Genevieve.

Chapter Eleven

Try as she might, Cinderella could not forget her second encounter with Prince Charles.

Every free moment she had, she ran through their brief conversation in her head. She couldn't forget how her heart had swelled when he'd stopped to speak with her. And how it sank once she realized he hadn't recognized her at all. It still stung whenever she thought of it.

"You have your answer," she told herself. "He doesn't remember you. So you should stop thinking about him."

Easier said than done. The only way that would happen was if she didn't have any free moments to think about him.

She threw herself into her new routine as the duchess's attendant, working from dawn until long past dusk over the next week. Being a royal attendant was taxing; Cinderella had thought that serving only one mistress instead of three would be easier, but the palace was far bigger than her stepmother's house. The walk alone from the kitchen to the duchess's chambers with her tea took a quarter of an hour.

Not to mention, Genevieve was a demanding mistress with a keen eye, and few things pleased her.

"My collar is crooked," she would say. Then, a minute later: "My hair is uneven. You'll have to do it again."

Or: "The rouge on my left cheek is darker than on the right. Can't you do anything properly?"

And before breakfast: "I specifically asked for my tea to be steeped for four minutes. Not three, not five. *Four*. Any more makes it much too strong."

On top of that, Cinderella was tasked with helping the duchess prepare her bath, taking her clothes to be laundered, steaming the curtains, beating dust out of the rugs, and polishing the duchess's jewels until they sparkled. Duchess Genevieve was used to having at least three girls to wait on her, but no other servants arrived to Cinderella's aid.

All the same, Cinderella didn't mind. Duchess Genevieve was stern and eccentric, and as often as she berated Cinderella for her incompetence, she wasn't mean-spirited, as Lady Tremaine had been. Maybe it was the portraits Cinderella had seen in the royal gallery of the duchess grinning, or the way she pored over her novels, chuckling to herself when she thought Cinderella couldn't hear, that made Cinderella like the woman.

Her stepmother had never read; in fact, every time she caught Cinderella in the act, she tore the book away and burned it. In the palace, Cinderella had already stolen a few peeks at Duchess Genevieve's novels, luxuriating for a few moments in a far-off adventure. Cinderella was certain that no one who read such thrilling tales could be *that* bad.

Besides, the extra work made the days pass faster. Every day she survived in the palace meant another night with a roof over her head and three hot meals, the leftovers of which she and Louisa always sneaked over to Bruno late at night.

But it didn't help that she was living under the same roof as the prince.

The prince, Cinderella thought with a sigh, as she slid a pearl-studded pin into the duchess's chignon to hold it firm. *I don't even know why I'm still thinking about him. Maybe I'm in love with the idea of him, just as he's in love with the idea of me. So much that he didn't even recognize the* real *me.*

"You're looking rather dour today," the duchess remarked while Cinderella finished buttoning the back of her dress. "What's the matter?"

"Nothing, ma'am," Cinderella mumbled.

"Then? For heaven's sake, girl, can't you say anything entertaining? The lot of you all are so dull."

Genevieve sighed and reached for a book on her dresser. "I am beginning to remember why I stayed away from this place for so many years. This is the capital of ennui."

"Would Your Highness like me to fetch you some embroidery? I have a friend who works in the sewing room, and she could bring something—"

"Embroidery?" Genevieve looked up from her book. "Goodness no, what do you take me for, my mother?" Scowling, she fluttered her hands westward. "Fetch me something new from the library. No, make it two. Make sure they're adventures—with pirates and beheadings and the lot."

Cinderella resisted the urge to raise an eyebrow. "Yes, Your Highness."

"If that old prig Martin is there, let him know it's for Grinning Ginny." In spite of her efforts to remain deadpan, the duchess disclosed the barest of smiles. She quickly repositioned her lips into a thin, stern line. "He should know what I'm looking for."

Grinning Ginny? "Yes, Your Highness."

"What are you standing there for? Don't make me regret keeping you on."

Cinderella hurried out of the duchess's apartments.

On her way to the library, she took a few wrong turns and ended up in the middle of Blooms and Looms. She decided there was no harm in quickly checking on Bruno while she was there. She and Louisa had found a hiding spot for him behind the henhouse, and they been taking turns sneaking him snacks from the kitchen. Cinderella only hoped Bruno had behaved himself and hadn't become tempted to chase the—

"I found this mutt hunting the chickens!" Irmina said, dragging a regretful-looking brown bloodhound into the servants' quarters.

Bruno whimpered, a thick leather leash knotted around his neck.

"He's mine!" Cinderella exclaimed, racing to him.

"Yours?" blustered Madame Irmina, tightening her grip on Bruno's leash. "Why am I not surprised?"

Fear spiked in Cinderella's heart. "Please," she pleaded. "He's a good dog. He has no place to go."

"There are no pets allowed in the palace. Either he goes or you both go."

"Oh, please," said Cinderella. "Bruno's been with me since I was a little girl, and he—"

Irmina's jaw tensed. "Need I repeat myself?"

Cinderella was about to plead her case again when a sharp voice from behind interrupted, "What is going on here?"

Instantly recognizing the speaker, Cinderella fell into a curtsy.

"Your Highness," Irmina spluttered, startled by the duchess's unexpected appearance. Behind her, Bruno growled and nipped at the hem of her dress. Irmina kicked him back, locking him into one of the pantries behind her.

She cleared her throat, her tone becoming honeyed and warm. "What an honor it is to welcome you here. My deepest apologies—I was not expecting you."

Genevieve harrumphed. "And why should you? I do not make a habit of having my comings and goings announced."

"To what do we owe the pleasure of your visit, Duchess?" asked Irmina, wisely changing the subject.

"I was wondering what was taking so long with my book. Imagine my displeasure when the guards informed me they spotted my attendant here instead of in the Royal Library."

A smug sniffle escaped from Madame Irmina's direction, and Cinderella tried not to panic.

"I apologize, Your Highness—"

"I'll see to it that the girl's dismissed," cut in Madame Irmina, starting to shoo Cinderella away. "Come with me, you *and* your mutt, before you embarrass us—"

"No, please!" Cinderella twisted away, untangling her arm from Madame Irmina's grip. She freed Bruno from the pantry, and as he spun toward the door, the duchess stepped on his leash.

"Halt!" she commanded, and to Cinderella's surprise, Bruno stopped. "Now, explain yourself."

Flustered, Cinderella saw she had no choice but to tell the truth. "I wanted to check on Bruno, my dog. You see, we're both new here, and he had nowhere to go, so—"

"Animals are not permitted in the palace," Madame Irmina interrupted, reaching for Cinderella's arm again. "I must apologize for disturbing you, Your Highness. I'll see to it that she leaves the palace straighta—"

"I'll take him," interrupted the duchess.

Stunned, Madame Irmina blinked. "Pardon, Duchess?"

"I said, I will take him. The mutt, the dog—Boris, whatever it is his name is." Genevieve glared at the maids eavesdropping on the scene, and everyone hastily returned to work. "Untie that ridiculous cord from his neck."

"Y-y-yes, Your Highness."

"Thank you for reminding me why I prefer the company of animals to the lot of you. Servants, lords, kings—you're all the same. Squabbling ninnies. Come, Bruno." Genevieve gestured at the bloodhound, then fluttered a beringed hand at Cinderella. "And you, girl, get to the library and bring me my book. Chop-chop."

"Yes, Your Highness," Cinderella breathed. "Thank you."

"Don't thank me yet. It's only out of boredom that I decided to save your mutt. My brother and nephew are hardly good company when all they've been doing is moping about."

Cinderella hoped the duchess didn't see her flinch. *Moping about?*

"Now why are you still standing there? While you're at it, I want a fresh cup of tea. Remember, two lumps of sugar and a splash of milk." Genevieve turned to Bruno. "And you—you're the skinniest dog I've ever seen." She clapped her hands and next directed her severe tone at Madame Irmina. "You, see to it that Bruno has a bountiful meal. I want to see some meat on his bones."

Madame Irmina hurried to fulfill the request.

"I'll fatten you up, you scraggly beast," the duchess murmured to Bruno. She wrinkled her nose, picking a chicken feather out of his coat. "And I'll see to it you're bathed, too."

Hiding a smile, Cinderella turned for the library to procure a book as the duchess had requested. If Genevieve had a soft spot for dogs, she couldn't be as irredeemable as everyone said.

A half hour later, Cinderella returned to Duchess Genevieve's chambers, out of breath but with an armful of novels that the librarian had eagerly recommended.

Her mind was reeling. While walking back, she'd secretly

flipped through the top book, unable to help herself. It was titled *The Pirates of Ild-Widy and the Enchanted Forest*.

The word *enchanted* had caught her eye. Before she'd met her fairy godmother, she'd thought magic and spells and curses were long gone, now only existent in tales meant for small children—or novels such as these. But it seemed there was more to it than that. As she absently glanced through the pages, she noticed one that was dog-eared.

It wouldn't do for the duchess to read a book with bent pages. Cinderella turned to it, only to be confronted with a handwritten message:

We must bring magic back. Maybe 36 ships and 47 pirates can help. —Art

The rest of the message had been smudged. It made no sense at all.

Cinderella stopped. What could it mean, and who had written it there? There was no other message in the book, nor in any of the others Cinderella had borrowed.

Before she had a chance to investigate further, Genevieve appeared.

"Hand those here," she said, taking the books. The duchess barely glanced at them. She pushed them to the side of her desk and collapsed onto the brocade daybed in her parlor.

"What is wrong with this dog?" she demanded.

Hastily setting aside the book, Cinderella asked, "What do you mean, Your Highness?"

"I bring him here, out of the gutters into one of the grandest apartments in the palace, but all he does is stare mournfully at the door. I do not understand him at all."

"Where is he now?" As soon as Cinderella asked, Bruno started scratching against the bedroom door.

Genevieve opened it, and he practically leapt into Cinderella's arms.

Forgetting her present company, Cinderella embraced him, stroking his fur and tickling his ears.

"Ahem."

The duchess was watching them with a stern expression. Quickly rising again, Cinderella nudged Bruno toward the duchess.

Genevieve rubbed one of his floppy ears, and after his hesitation eased, Bruno luxuriated in the attention. She drew back her hand. "When was the last time he had a bath?"

Before Cinderella could reply, the duchess fluttered her fingers at her. "No, don't tell me. I'd rather not know. I don't see any fleas, thankfully. See to it that he is washed tonight."

"Yes, ma'am."

Duchess Genevieve sighed, petting Bruno again. "You know, it's been a long time since I've had a dog. I didn't expect to find this mongrel so delightful, and yet he grows on you quite unexpectedly."

It wasn't the first time a smile had graced the duchess's lips, but as before, her expression quickly became stern once again. "How did this creature come to you?"

"My father and I found him on the street outside our home," Cinderella said. "I was nine, and my mother had just passed away." Her throat tightened. "He looked lonely, like my papa and me, so we took him in."

"Sometimes I wish George would get a dog," Genevieve said with a harrumph. "Though I guess he's got a pack of other animals nipping at his feet."

"Excuse me, ma'am?"

"Oh, all the gentry and the lords on the council. The Grand Duke, especially. But a real dog would do him good. It would do Charles good, too."

Cinderella inhaled at the mention of the prince. "Why is that?"

"His mother died when he was a young boy, too, of course," mused the duchess. She cleared her throat, as if suddenly aware she was sharing too much. "And why the name Bruno?"

"My papa picked it. He said it meant 'brown,' like his coat. But also 'protector.' We didn't mean to keep him at first. But he came to us looking so starved and sad that we took him in, and once he'd been fed, Papa and I couldn't part with him." Cinderella smiled at Bruno. "He's been my sweetest companion ever since. And my most loyal protector."

"I like dogs much more than people," said the duchess. "For that very reason—they don't let you down as much." She sniffed. "I have six children, you know, but my husband died three years ago. He was a good, practical man, one who never grew up with a golden spoon in his mouth or with a crown dangling over his head. My children, on the other hand . . ." She shuddered.

"When Arthur died, he left the estate to me instead of our eldest son. Unheard of! My children love me, but they rarely visit anymore. They say I embarrass them by throwing away our wealth to charity and hobnobbing with poor intellectuals. So you see, even though I'm always surrounded by people, it is rather lonely sometimes."

Cinderella understood, more than she could express. Her heart opened to the duchess, and she began to wonder why the duke disliked her so much. "Then why don't you visit more?"

"Visit George?" Genevieve's shoulders shook with mirth, but her expression grew quickly somber. "Perhaps I should have. Charles has been away at school, and I suppose I never forgave George for casting Arthur away from court. I can hold grudges for years, you see, and I left with a promise never to return."

A promise never to return? Cinderella bit her lip to contain her curiosity. What did that mean?

"But now here I am, back again in the palace." Genevieve cleared her throat. "Tell me, what does your father do?"

"My father passed away a long time ago," Cinderella said softly.

"I see. You must miss your parents terribly."

"Every day," confessed Cinderella, swallowing the lump in her throat. It had been so long since she'd permitted herself to mourn her parents. While she had lived with her stepmother, Lady Tremaine kept her so busy that she hadn't had much time to think about her father or her mother. But now she missed them more than ever.

"I don't remember my mother well," Cinderella began, "but she used to sing a lullaby about a nightingale every night."

"Did your father remarry?"

"Yes," said Cinderella carefully. "My stepmother has two daughters."

"Ah, therein lies the problem. You fell into their shadows, didn't you?"

Cinderella barely nodded.

"Poor Charles," Genevieve murmured. "He's been alone a long time, too."

"Alone?"

"My brother didn't spend much time with him. He hopes to rectify that, I think."

"How?"

The softness in Genevieve's expression immediately hardened as she realized she'd revealed something she should not have.

"I'm sorry, Your Highness. I shouldn't have—"

"Can you keep a secret?" Genevieve interrupted softly.

Cinderella blinked back her surprise. "Yes."

"He's not a young man, my brother. He is tired of ruling, and plans to pass on the throne."

"To . . . to the prince?"

"Charles doesn't know it yet, but that's why George is so adamant that he find a wife and start a family—so that the succession will be secure, and none of our neighboring kingdoms will sense any weakness."

Cinderella remained quiet. She didn't know what to say.

"That's why George asked me to come. Oh, he says it's to help Charles and his future bride settle into their new roles as king and queen, but I think he's finally feeling guilty about what he did to my husband. He'll never apologize for it, though. He's proud, just like me."

Again, Cinderella's interest was piqued. *What happened between the Duke of Orlanne and the king?* she wondered.

"No one knows this yet—not Charles or the Grand

Duke. It is of the utmost importance that it remains this way, until my brother is ready. Though I have a feeling Ferdinand suspects something, given my return to the palace."

Cinderella winced, remembering the duke had asked her to collect information on the duchess. Now she wished Genevieve hadn't told her anything. "What makes you think he suspects something?"

"Ferdinand's a sly old fox. Always has been. Why else do you think he's plastered himself next to the king as his most trusted adviser for all these years? George's always been a child at heart, and Ferdinand's taken advantage of him to increase his influence. I can't stand the man."

"Why are you telling me this?"

The duchess picked up her fan and batted it carelessly. "I'm good at reading people. I only wish my brother were, too. Let's just say you've got an honest way about you—and a sharper eye than I initially thought." She brushed her fingers over the nearest table. "Not a speck of dust."

"Oh." Cinderella felt little pride from the compliment. "It is my job," was all she said.

"I'm glad you understand that, girl. Though no one told you to reorganize my books."

There was a note of accusation in the duchess's voice, and Cinderella didn't know how to respond. "I apologize, ma'am. I—"

"Most of my attendants arrange them like flowers, by

color and size, but you did it by substance and author. You couldn't have done that without reading them."

She swallowed. "I didn't have time to read any, ma'am . . . but I couldn't resist skimming a few."

"Which ones? The pirate adventures? Never mind, don't tell me. There's a library in the palace for good reason, you know."

"I'm so sorry—"

"They're books, not diaries, girl. I'll *tell* you when you've committed a crime. The girl before you I caught reading my letters. I fired her on the spot. So far you've passed the test." Duchess Genevieve paused. "Speaking of which, what is your name?"

The past few days, the duchess had only called her "girl." Now that she'd finally asked her name, Cinderella became tongue-tied. "It's . . . it's Cinderella."

"Cinderella," repeated Genevieve. "An odd name, but you must be aware of that." She sniffed, stifling a yawn. "Heavens, it's four o'clock already? I've been dawdling so long with you and your mutt I've forgotten my afternoon nap. All this traveling has made it impossible for me to sleep. Over there, on my writing desk—bring me my sleeping draught."

Obediently, Cinderella grasped the glass bottle and followed the duchess's instructions:

"Three drops into my tea. And a squeeze of lemon, for good measure. No, child! That's four drops, can't you count?"

"I'm terribly sorry, Your Highness."

"I suppose one extra drop won't kill me," said Genevieve, bringing the teacup to her lips. She sipped, and almost instantly, her hooded eyelids drooped with drowsiness. "I don't know how George drinks this stuff every night."

She finished the tea, then passed the cup to Cinderella.

"Now off with you. It's time for my afternoon nap. Be back precisely in an hour, you hear? I'll expect a fresh pot of tea, and some biscuits would do nicely, as well. And Cindergirl—if you ever do go to the library, tell those over-stuffed scholars there that the books you're looking for are for me. Fewer questions that way."

"Yes, Your Highness. Thank you."

Cinderella took one of the silver trays from the duchess's table, set the empty teapot on it, and slipped out of the apartments. No sooner did she step outside, though, than the duke's attendant bumped into her.

"Oh, I'm sorry!" she said, but the man had whirled away from view.

When she looked down at her tray, there was a sealed letter that hadn't been there before.

Heart hammering, she waited until she was down the corridor, away from the guards' inquisitive eyes, before opening and reading the note.

I await your report. Come see me at once.

Chapter Twelve

Cinderella dreaded meeting the Grand Duke again, and her apprehension only intensified when she arrived at his apartments.

She'd simply evade his questions as best she could. That was all there was to it.

He hadn't been in his office by the servants' quarters, so the palace staff had directed her to his apartments. They were even larger than the duchess's, and room after room smelled of burnt wax and worn leather. She followed the smell past the sitting room into a short hallway whose walls were mounted with portraits of the duke's forebears. At the end, a door had been left slightly ajar, the frantic scraping of pen to paper growing louder as Cinderella approached.

Buried behind a stack of papers and a cup of tea that

looked barely touched, the Grand Duke scribbled away at the sheet of paper, his back hunched and his neck bent toward the sunlight that pooled on his desk. His black hair, which had been neatly slicked back the last time she saw him, spilled across his forehead, and his mustache curled at its ends.

Quietly, Cinderella slid into the office, her steps muffled by the wool carpet. She shuffled off onto the parquet.

The duke didn't look up.

The minutes stretched, and finally, she cleared her throat. "Your Grace, you summoned me."

His fountain pen rattled against the inkpot. "Ah, it's you." He held a red stick of wax against the lone candle burning on his desk, then affixed a seal to his document before putting it aside.

"At last. You must be brimming with news, my child. Come, what is your report?"

Two key pieces of information clung to Cinderella's mind. But she remembered what the duchess had told her about Grand Duke Ferdinand: that behind his sterling reputation was a sly old fox—a man not to be trusted.

She pursed her lips. "I'm not sure what to report, Your Grace."

"Not sure?" The Grand Duke eyed her skeptically. "You've had days to observe the duchess. I told you I wanted to hear everything."

"She takes her tea three times a day, steeped for four minutes—"

"I don't care about her tea-drinking habits!"

"Forgive me, Your Grace. You never told me exactly what you *do* care about."

He seethed at her. "Need I remind you that I gave you this position? I could easily take it away."

"I apologize, Your Grace," she said quickly, fervently hoping to be released from this meeting as soon as possible.

"There is nothing unusual about the duchess?" he asked impatiently. "What does she do during all her time? Write letters, go on long walks?"

"She reads, Your Grace."

"Reads what?"

"Novels. Mostly pirate adventures."

The duke let out a snort. "A front. Come now, there's more. You're twisting your hands."

Cinderella's hands flew apart. She hadn't even noticed.

"You *have* learned something from the duchess. Something valuable. Out with it, my child, I haven't all day."

"I . . ." *Think of something,* Cinderella urged herself. *Anything.*

But all she could think of was the truth: the king was planning to abdicate.

The duke inhaled in frustration before softening his

tone. "Come, my dear, it's all right. Sit down, sit down—I've frightened you, haven't I?"

He ushered her toward one of the plush chairs across from his desk, but Cinderella remained standing.

"You can tell me. Do you not care about the kingdom? It is my duty to see to it that our country remains strong and safe. The king's sister spends a great deal of time lobbying with the common folk, and arguing against laws that the council has passed to secure the future of our people. If she has shared something with you, it is your duty to tell me. It is your duty to Aurelais."

He said it so convincingly that Cinderella nearly believed him. Nearly.

"Th-thank you, Your Grace," she stammered, "but all the duchess and I talk about are tea, my dog, Bruno, and what books she'd like from the library."

Following a long exhale, the Grand Duke folded his hands over his lap. "Is something troubling Her Highness? A physician was seen leaving her chambers yesterday."

Cinderella tilted her head. "I don't know. I didn't see him."

"I ask only out of concern," Ferdinand pressed. "Is something amiss with her health?"

The question seemed innocent enough. "Oh, no. She's fine," Cinderella responded. "But she has had some trouble sleeping . . . she takes a sleeping draught."

The duke leaned forward with interest. "Come again?"

"A sleeping draught," Cinderella repeated. More hastily, she added, "Every afternoon after lunch with the king. It's the same one His Majesty himself takes."

"No wonder he no longer takes tea with me," the Grand Duke muttered, stroking his chin. "Interesting."

It seemed like a common enough thing for a woman the duchess's age to do—and the king. She didn't know why it interested the duke so much.

"You needn't look so frightened, Cinderella. The duchess is a powerful woman, yes, but she has had a turbulent past, and I would not be surprised if she harbored deep resentment toward her brother—and toward me and my late father."

"But why?"

"There was an incident, you see. . . ." The duke frowned, as if he'd remembered something that tasted sour. "There was an incident revolving around the duchess that endangered the kingdom, and it is my duty to see nothing like it ever happens again. Genevieve is not to be trusted. Understood?"

"Yes, Your Grace."

"Very good," he said. "You've done well, Cinderella. Very well. If you learn anything else of note, come find me at once. You are dismissed."

Not needing to be told twice, Cinderella left the room, breathing a sigh of relief once she was alone.

What an odd man, she thought. For the life of her, she couldn't imagine why he had looked so surprised to find out the duchess took a sleeping draught. At least it was better than his knowing the *real* truth—that King George was planning to pass the throne to his son.

Or that *she* was the mysterious princess everyone was searching for.

The duchess was already awake when Cinderella arrived to draw the curtains and help the lady out of bed.

Forgetting her place and entirely too aware of the Grand Duke's interrogation, Cinderella asked, "Are you feeling well, Your Highness?"

"Now there is an impertinent question," huffed Genevieve. "Didn't you learn it was improper to ask a lady about what ails her?"

"My apologies, Your Highness, but I thought—I was hoping I might be able to help you."

"Hah! There's nothing you could help me with," Genevieve said, stirring the sugar into her tea.

"Why can't you sleep?" asked Cinderella, concerned. "Nightmares?"

The duchess scoffed. "You truly wish to know?"

"Yes."

"Well, it isn't any of your business, girl. End of discussion."

Startled by the duchess's sharp tone, Cinderella bowed her head to show she understood.

"I'll be taking supper with my brother today. Be sure to have an extra pot of tea prepared for when I return, with a plate of shortbread. I'll need extra nourishment for tomorrow morning. Charles suggested the most ghastly hour for a tour of the kingdom."

Cinderella's heart skipped a beat. "Prince Charles?"

"Do I have any other nephews named Charles I'm not aware of?" The duchess wrapped the shawl over her shoulders and reached for her walking stick. "All these girls swooning over my nephew. I hope you aren't one of them."

"I wouldn't be eligible, Your Highness," Cinderella said, swallowing the lump that suddenly formed in her throat.

"All because of some silly laws that my silly ancestors made. The world is changing, Cindergirl, and anyone—I do repeat, anyone—can make something of herself if she puts her mind to it. Oh, to be young today!"

"You think a servant could become a princess?"

"My husband came from a family without wealth, but he was smart—and practical. He was a shrewd businessman, and became one of the richest men in Aurelais. Anybody can become anything, so long as they put their minds to it." She eyed Cinderella. "Hard work and fortitude, Cindergirl, is what will get you ahead. Not swooning over my nephew."

Cinderella hid a smile. "Yes, Your Highness."

"Good. Besides, you wouldn't want him anyway. He's been so melancholy over that idiotic princess with the impractical shoes. He doesn't even know her name."

Cinderella bit her lip and subconsciously reached out to rearrange the flowers before her. While it warmed her heart that the prince was still searching for her and had declared that he'd fallen in love with the girl he'd danced with at the ball, she couldn't forget how he hadn't recognized her outside the banquet hall.

Her stepmother's words echoed in Cinderella's head. *Look at yourself—you are nothing. An orphan and a servant. Who would want you? Certainly not His Royal Highness.*

"I blame my brother for young Charles's romantic notions. George was always the sentimental sort, a believer in love at first sight. That would explain the ball." Genevieve sighed. "Having Charles pick a bride in such a way, having all the women parade themselves about the palace. Love doesn't happen like that. Love takes time. George used to have more sense when the queen was alive."

"What was the queen like?" Cinderella asked.

"She was as kind as she was beautiful—far too good for my brother." Genevieve chuckled. Then her expression darkened. "She died far too young. . . ." The duchess's voice trailed off, and she quickly composed herself. "Anyhow, at this rate, the only way to find this mystery maiden of his would be to hold another ball!"

Cinderella pretended to study the flowers she'd arranged so she wouldn't have to meet the duchess's eye. "But that isn't happening, is it?"

"Of course not." Genevieve made a face. "Imagine, holding another ball simply so Charles can find this glass slipper maiden. What a ludicrous idea! Though now that you mention it, I'd better talk some sense into George before *he* comes up with such an idea. Wish me luck. If we are all to have some peace in this castle, I will need it."

"Good luck," Cinderella said faintly.

After the duchess left, Cinderella sank onto the plush carpet. She'd gone from "orphan" and "nobody" in her stepmother's eyes to "this glass slipper maiden" in everyone else's.

Who was she now? She was still a servant, albeit one for the royal family—and she received wages for her work. It was a respectable job, one many would dream of, one she was proud of, and yet . . .

"I'm not happy," she whispered. She said it again, louder this time. "I haven't been happy, not in a long time."

What a strange relief it was to finally admit that to herself. After years of wearing a smile for her stepmother and stepsisters, of pretending to be content to work in their household lest Lady Tremaine kick her out onto the streets, her heart couldn't heal itself over a mere week or two. It would take time.

Meeting the prince *had* made her happy, but that happiness had been fleeting. She needed something real for herself. A purpose.

Closing the duchess's door softly behind her, she allowed herself a long exhale. She had something in mind.

Chapter Thirteen

Ferdinand, the Grand Duke of Malloy, straightened the scarlet sash draped over his torso and flicked a speck of dust off his sleeve. Given that this nonsensical search for the maiden with the glass slipper was all but finished, he hoped he could get the prince to listen to reason.

Doubtful. But he would certainly try his best.

The morning was slowly aging, bright white light filtering in from the palace's arched windows.

After straightening his collar, Ferdinand turned to Charles's attendant, whose profile bore a striking resemblance to the young prince's. "What are you waiting for, squire? Announce me."

The sure-footed young man marched to the side and

knocked thrice on the prince's door before opening it. Then he cried, "Your Royal Highness, the Grand Duke."

Ferdinand was surprised to find the prince leaning against a marble pillar, his face to the sun-filled window, reading some nonsensical philosophy book. Ferdinand couldn't make out the title occupying the royal's attention, but before Prince Charles had left the palace for his studies at the Royal University, he had spent most of his time avoiding his tutors and playing pranks on the staff. To see him absorbed in a scholarly book so early in the morning surprised Ferdinand—and worried him.

The prince's years away had changed him, his exposure to greater Aurelais clearly giving him ideas about how the monarchy needed to change. Ideas like welcoming commoners in the council, or rewarding merit over class, or taxing the nobles to distribute wealth among the poor. Ideas that Ferdinand knew he wouldn't agree with.

"Ahem," began the Grand Duke.

The prince flipped a page, absorbed in his book.

A muscle twitched in Ferdinand's jaw. *These young people are so rude these days,* he thought. *So easily distracted.*

Still, the duke made no motion that he was irritated, and instead plastered on a smile. Heaven knew that any ambitious man who wanted the king's ear needed to master schooling his features into an expression of placid obsequiousness. And by God, he had.

Besides, he was aware the prince was frustrated with him for failing to find the maiden who could fit the glass slipper. Indeed, after he'd declared to the king that the search was futile and over, Charles's expression grew so lost and forlorn Ferdinand could hardly imagine the youth as a suitable sovereign. Over the past three days, the prince had become obsessed with finding the girl—so obsessed that he'd ordered the cursed shoe encased in a glass box, to be displayed outside the palace in case the girl should come riding by and see it one day.

A ludicrous idea. Ferdinand had almost laughed aloud when he heard it. The king's money was obviously better spent building defenses or encouraging relations with the neighboring kingdoms, but upon realizing the prince was serious, Ferdinand did not dare voice his opposition. He was too wise for that.

Let the boy lose credit in the council's eyes. Let the council see, as Ferdinand did, that Charles was completely unsuited for the throne. In the meantime, the Grand Duke would orchestrate his own schemes.

Beginning with this morning's visit.

He swept a bow. "Your Royal Highness, thank you for agreeing to this audience with me."

"What is it?" said the prince, his gloom-ridden eyes only briefly flitting up from his book to meet the Grand Duke's.

"Your Highness, I understand that you are disappointed in my service." Ferdinand's words tasted sour, so he lifted his tone an octave lest the ill flavor seep into his voice. "I wished to apologize for failing to find the maiden with the glass slipper."

"Apologize?" The prince's tone was harsh. "Somehow I doubt that's the only reason you're here."

"Come, Your Highness, I realize you are distraught—at me, and at this entirely harrowing episode. . . ." Ferdinand's voice trailed off. Truth be told, it was most harrowing for *him*. Even now, days after his search had concluded, when he closed his eyes, all he could see were ladies' feet. All he could hear were the strident cries: "It's my slipper! It's my slipper!"

Feet everywhere—it was the stuff of nightmares. Big feet, little feet, toes and heels and calluses and ankles . . .

He broadened his smile. "Can we not let bygones be bygones?"

His plea did little to soften the prince, but Charles at least put down his book. "What is it you want?"

Ferdinand drew a breath, the deep sort he always took before saying something important, something that needed to be said without pause. "Your father and I wanted to impress upon you a reminder that you are the crown prince, Your Highness, the only heir to our luminous kingdom. As such, it is your duty to consider marrying for the good of your country and your people—"

The prince pounded his fist on the table. "I don't want to hear any more of this."

"But, Your Highness," Ferdinand persisted, "it would please your father. He has been rather distraught lately, in private—so as to not worry you."

Charles hesitated. "Distraught over what?"

Aha, now he had him!

"The Princess of Lourdes is quite a beauty," said Ferdinand instead, unrolling one of several portraits he had brought. "And I hear the princess of—"

"Distraught over what?" interrupted Charles. "Ferdinand, if you are using my father as a ploy for me to marry a girl of your choice . . ."

"Sir, I would never!"

"Then I'll hear it from my father himself. I do not need advice from you."

"This is an opportunity for you to serve your country, Your Highness," Ferdinand said soothingly. "Aurelais is not as strong as it once was. You must consider the future."

"I'll consider it when I hear it from my father's lips, not yours."

Ferdinand's mouth clamped shut. When he spoke again, his voice was thin and tight. "As you wish, Your

Highness. Now if you'll excuse me, I understand when I've been dismissed."

The duke made a stiff bow, then stormed out of the room.

"These young people," he muttered when the prince could not hear. "They will be this country's ruin."

His teeth gritted, Ferdinand continued down the palace halls, growing more agitated by the minute until he reached his offices.

The first thing he did was pull up Dr. Coste's report on the king's health.

There has been little change in His Majesty's well-being. He has made a full recovery from the rheumatism he suffered this past winter, and any variation in his health—such as his recent poor sleep—may be attributed to stress. I have taken into account your concern and suggestion that His Majesty reduce his activity, but Your Grace may be pleased to know that at this time it is not necessary for him to relinquish his appearances with the Royal Council. Rather, such stimulation may improve his condi—

Ferdinand crumpled the note in his fist. Stress! What did these bumpkin physicians know? It *was* time for His

Majesty to cease attending the council; King George had long since stopped adding any value to the meetings, anyway.

And now His Majesty refused to take tea with him after dinner. "Who knew I'd sleep better without listening to you prattle on and on about policy? Go speak with Charles instead. He's been eager to become more involved with the council."

Charles, indeed!

The prince's return from university had thrown a wrench into Ferdinand's plan, painstakingly constructed over months and months. Now, if the king were to suddenly retire, Charles would be poised to take over. And given the prince's evident dislike for him, there was a good chance he would have Ferdinand stripped of his power as the king's most trusted adviser and confidant.

That absolutely could not happen. And he would see that it didn't. If nothing else, the Grand Duke was a man of carefully laid plans. His rise in court had been in part by the grace of his family name, but it had also taken years of meticulous engineering and carefully made alliances for him to gain the respect of the Royal Council.

He would have to accelerate his plan. But how would he go about it without drawing suspicion? His evening teas with the king had been perfect, allowing him to slowly erect the foundation for his scheme, but that was no longer an option. Besides, the time for action was upon him. Ferdinand drummed his fingers on the table.

Recent poor sleep, the physician's note had said. Was it true that the king was taking a draught to aid his slumber? That could provide just the opportunity he needed.

Genevieve's new girl had all but inadvertently revealed critical information. *She takes a sleeping draught,* the maiden had said. *The same one as the king.*

A sleeping draught was an unimportant revelation, one somebody else probably wouldn't have accepted from the girl as reasonable payment for installing her in the palace.

But after years of careful observation within its confines, Ferdinand had learned that, more often than not, what seemed the most insignificant pieces of information could turn the tides in his favor.

And he had a feeling that this one would play into his hands favorably, indeed.

Chapter Fourteen

Charles sighed, relieved when Ferdinand finally left. He had never liked the man, and since returning home from his studies, his dislike had only intensified.

For the life of him, he could not understand why his father placed so much trust in the Grand Duke.

Perhaps some things are meant to be mysteries, he thought wistfully, *like the identity of the girl with the glass slipper.*

Charles balled his fists at his sides. He hated the possibility that Ferdinand might be right about the search being pointless.

A quiet knock on the door interrupted his thoughts.

"Your Highness?" spoke his attendant, Pierre.

"What is it?"

"Your aunt, the duchess, sir. She awaits your company in the South Courtyard."

Charles hadn't forgotten, but he *had* lost track of the time. He had been doing that often lately.

"Please fetch my hat and my university jacket," he told Pierre. After a pause, he added, "On second thought, I'll bring them myself."

His university jacket, as he called it, was an ill-fitting double-breasted coat he'd worn every day when away from the palace—and he loved it. It was the only garment he owned that did not have gold buttons or epaulets, or fabric so white it looked like it'd taken an army of laundresses to press clean. It lay neatly folded on a wooden bench beside his writing desk, surrounded by two stacks of books precisely piled to obscure its location.

He threaded his arm through each of the lightly frayed sleeves. To his amusement, the holes in its lining had been patched with scraps of silk, and its worn wool had been pressed and cleaned. At least he had managed to stop the seamstresses from replacing all the buttons or trying to hide the old tea and coffee stains!

He'd won it from a classmate on a bet that he couldn't go one hour in town without being recognized as the crown prince of Aurelais. He'd made it sixty-five minutes before someone finally bowed.

Now it was one of his most prized possessions, and he wore it whenever he wished to not be recognized. Which, to be fair, was essentially all the time.

Charles ignored Pierre's raised eyebrow and headed for the South Courtyard. He had promised to take Aunt Genevieve for a ride through Valors that morning, but he hadn't promised to give the tour as the crown prince. No, today he'd simply be Charles, her nephew.

He had a feeling Aunt Genevieve would understand the way his father did not. *Could* not. That was why when she had asked him to take her into the city, he couldn't refuse.

Of all the royal coach house's carriages, Charles commissioned the most ordinary one for the day's tour, the one he and his father took when they didn't want to draw attention on the road. It was plain as any merchant's coach, bearing no flag with his family's royal crest, and no coat of arms painted on the doors.

Sure enough, Aunt Genevieve was already seated inside, her tiara sparkling in the wan morning light. She waved her fan when she saw him.

"You seem to have inherited your father's punctuality," she said dryly. She looked him up and down. "And the stable hand's sense of fashion."

"Good morning, Aunt Genevieve," the prince said in

greeting. He darted a glance at the empty seat beside her; part of him had almost hoped she'd brought her attendant so that he might have a second chance at meeting her. But his aunt was alone. Of course she was alone!

So why had his heart skipped a beat in anticipation of possibly seeing that girl with the blue eyes again?

Quickly, he recovered himself and bowed. "My apologies, Aunt Genevieve. It seems I've kept you waiting again."

The duchess clicked her tongue. "It's becoming quite the habit with you, Charles. First my welcome lunch, now this. I have half a mind to go back inside and catch up on my sleep." She waited for her threat to sink in. Before Charles could respond, she continued, "Luckily, it's a beautiful morning for a ride out into Valors, and I've already dismissed my girl until lunch."

Charles cocked his head slightly, tempted to ask where her attendant had gone.

"Come on, get inside. The sun isn't getting any younger, and neither am I."

With a smile, the prince obediently entered the carriage and signaled for the driver to take off.

As the coach lurched to a start, his aunt grabbed the side of her seat and snapped her fan closed. "Tell me, was it your idea to fetch me in this gourd of a coach, or your father's?"

"Mine, Aunt Genevieve. I thought we might see more of the city if we weren't recognized. If you are uncomfortable, we can change to a different coach."

"No." To Charles's surprise, his aunt doffed her tiara, tossing it aside. "Always scratches my head, anyway. Besides, if you're going to be dressed like a commoner, I am certainly not going around looking like a duchess."

Charles leaned back, hiding a smile. No wonder he'd always liked his aunt.

"Look at you, my boy." Genevieve patted his shoulders. "Such a strapping young man. You must have gotten your good looks from your mother. Heavens knows they weren't from George."

The prince laughed in spite of himself. "I've missed you, Aunt Genevieve."

"I've missed you, too." The angles of her face softened as she considered her nephew. She inhaled. "Funny, I left the palace because I didn't want to live life strung up like a puppet, and now that I'm back I lament not visiting more. I've missed too many years with my favorite nephew—"

"Last I recall, Aunt, I am your only nephew."

The duchess crossed her arms and gave him a stern look. "Much as I am fond of you, Charles, this tardiness is rather unbecoming of the future king." She raised her hand before he could explain. "I've heard from palace gossip that you're in a lovelorn state. Lovesickness is no excuse for dis-courtesy, do you understand?"

"Yes, Aunt Genevieve. I'm sorry. Truly. It's just that . . . I feel lost. Like I've met the one person who's meant for me, and she's vanished."

At his confession, she softened further, her features melt-ing into a smile that rounded out her cheeks and reminded him faintly of his father.

"What's so special about this girl?" she asked, leaning slightly forward, her eyes taking on a mischievous sparkle. "Inquiring minds wish to know—tell me about her, Charles. You could have the hand of any lady in the kingdom, any lady in the world, even. Why are you so set on this one? Rather rude of her to take off so suddenly!"

Charles hesitated, surprised by how relieved he was by his aunt's questioning. He hadn't talked about *her* to anyone—not about his feelings, anyway. Maybe this was what he needed to help sort out his thoughts. To get out of the haze that had clouded his mind ever since the ball.

"Any other girl would only want to marry me to become a princess," he replied finally. "She . . . she didn't even know I was the prince."

At that, Genevieve wrinkled her nose. "Plenty of ladies pretend to be ignorant, Charles. It's a coy game that they play—"

"Not her," Charles insisted. "Not her." He tugged at one of the buttons sewn onto the tufted cushion against his back. "There was something so sincere about her, so kind. I didn't even get her name. I'm beginning to worry that she was nothing more than a dream."

"Dreams don't leave behind glass slippers," said Genevieve sensibly. "For that matter, who would think to wear glass shoes, let alone to a ball?"

"I told you," said the prince, "she's different."

His aunt sighed. "You are hopeless, Charles. I see there's no talking you out of this, so let's talk about something else. I take it your studies went well."

"Well enough," he replied absentmindedly. "I did find it refreshing to study philosophy, history, and diplomacy instead of protocol or dancing."

While his aunt chattered on about how her husband, Arthur, had been a lecturer once at the Royal University, Charles gazed out the window. On his way home a week ago, he'd marveled at how little his hometown had changed. The oak trees, the wide pastures skirting the countryside, the rows of brick houses and the estates inhabited by the minor nobles, the winding road to the palace. Yet how different they seemed.

He couldn't place his finger on it, but he saw more now. He noticed the people as well as the land. Surely, what he had learned during his university courses had trained his mind to be that of a learned and knowledgeable king, but there was more to ruling than that.

The prince signaled for the carriage to slow down.

"What is it?" asked his aunt, startled by the apparent change in plan.

Charles opened the door, escorting his aunt into the town. It was still early, and no one paid him a second glance, but Genevieve was starting to get a few stares. They couldn't stay out long. "I spent almost my entire childhood behind the palace walls. Going to the university was the first time I got to see the rest of the world."

"What did you see?"

As they turned the corner, wending down a curved path, Charles spoke softly. "Poverty. Our people, starving. Orphans and beggars without anywhere to go." The prince reached into his trouser pockets and took out a gold coin. "I see it in the capital now, too. I'd never noticed before."

He placed the gold coin by a sleeping mother and child, wishing he'd thought to bring food as well. But it would have to do. It was only a start. Once he gained his father's confidence, he would do more. Much more.

When they returned to the carriage, his aunt watched him thoughtfully. "Going away did change you."

"I heard rumors, Aunt Genevieve, that your husband

cared deeply about improving conditions for the poor. That my father sent him away for it. Why . . . why would he do that?"

"That wasn't the reason your father sent him away," said Genevieve abruptly. "I don't want to talk about it—it's better left in the past."

"Forgive me, Aunt."

"If anyone should be seeking my forgiveness, it's Ferdinand, not you."

When she wouldn't elaborate, Charles gently changed the subject. "The Grand Duke isn't exactly in my good graces, either. He wants me to marry the Princess of Lourdes. I would consider it if I truly thought we were in danger of war. But I fear his real motive is to expand Aurelais's power to Lourdes."

Charles continued, "My father and I should be looking to improving this country for our people, not enlarging our territory. Times are changing. While I was at school, I would slip into town occasionally, unnoticed, and observe the people. How it surprised me to see them unhappy, some of them barely able to afford a roof over their heads, others begging on the streets. There were riots, too—riots against the nobility that Ferdinand denies ever happened. If the council won't address the problems arising within our own country, then I must."

"What would you do about it?" said Genevieve quietly.

"That is the difficult part, is not it?" confessed the prince. "I'll make enemies of powerful men like the Grand Duke, and the people will dislike me by nature for being the head of the regime that oppresses them. But I want to help them. Truly, I do."

"Your father and mother were blessed to have you as a son," Genevieve said. "They tried for many years to have a child, you know."

Three brothers and two sisters had died before him. Charles had never met any of his siblings, and the physicians had pleaded with his mother not to try for a sixth child, citing her health and her age. She had persevered, but in giving birth to Charles, her health had suffered.

A familiar wave of guilt overcame Charles, and he turned to the window, sucking in a gulp of air.

His aunt touched his arm. "Your father only wants the best for you. He doesn't want you to be alone."

"I understand, but I just returned home. I don't know why he's in such a rush for me to marry."

Genevieve hesitated, then she drew the windows closed and lowered her voice. "George plans to abdicate."

The confession sent a jolt through the young prince. He blinked back his surprise. "What?"

"I've already said more than I should have. He will tell

you himself, when the time is right." She frowned. "Best to keep this to yourself, Charles. I don't trust the Grand Duke. Lord knows what he'd do with this information. The transference of the crown always brings about a period of uncertainty and unrest. It wouldn't be above the duke to take advantage of that and rally the lords to take more power for himself. "

"I would dismiss him before that ever happened."

"It wouldn't be that easy. Ferdinand has great influence. The nobility trust and revere him."

"He's a manipulator. Every time I try to tell Father so, he won't believe me."

"You must not blame your father. Ferdinand has been his friend longer than you've been alive. Forty years of ruling Aurelais will exhaust any man, and the Grand Duke has taken advantage of that." Genevieve's expression turned grim. "The point is, you must surround yourself with people you trust."

"I trust *you*, Aunt Genevieve."

"I'm even older than your father," she said gravely. "Neither of us will be here forever."

Charles perched his arm on the carriage door and looked to the horizon, punishing himself with a glance at the sun. He blinked away the sting in his eyes. "You're right. But I worry that I'm . . . I'm not ready. I worry I'll *never* be ready."

"What does your heart tell you?"

"I don't know."

"Don't know?" She paused, and when she next spoke, her tone was gentler: "I heard you promised to marry the girl who fit this so-called glass slipper. A rather rash declaration, was it not, Charles?"

The prince sighed. "Father and Ferdinand wrote the proclamation. I didn't have a choice. . . . Besides, what was I supposed to do, Aunt Genevieve? Let her go?"

"I'm not trying to lecture you, but any girl could have fit that shoe. *Any* girl."

"I wouldn't care whether she were a princess or a scullery maid," Charles said fiercely. He already knew the Grand Duke's opinion, and he didn't need a second person haranguing him that the girl he'd fallen in love with could be "a mere commoner."

"That is not what I meant." Genevieve clicked her tongue, deliberating over how to explain. "Fitting a glass slipper is not a sign of character or of compatibility. Surely you must know every eligible maiden in the kingdom dreams of marrying you. A girl might cut off her toes simply to fit the glass slipper. Making a promise like that could have doomed you to a union with someone you didn't love, someone just pretending to be the girl you met."

"I see what you mean, Aunt Genevieve." Charles bowed

his head. "That was Father's idea, but I agreed to it. It was foolish of me. I understand that now."

"Love has a way of addling our wits." Genevieve tilted her head. "You take after George in that regard. He was very much in love with your mother, you know. She wasn't a commoner, yet she was certainly on the diminutive end of minor nobility. My parents didn't approve of the match, but George raised all hell to be with her."

"I didn't know."

"To this day, your father is a romantic." Genevieve gave a tight smile. "Funny, until then, my parents always considered *me* the rebellious one."

Charles had heard stories about his aunt when she was young. How she once stole his father's trousers and traipsed across the royal lawn in them, an act that had distressed his grandmother so much that she nearly had a stroke. How she'd once made a slingshot out of a gold necklace and shot pearls at her tutor for suggesting she wasn't as bright as the future king.

Since her last visit, his father rarely spoke of her, but when he did, it was always with a sort of bittersweet sadness. The prince didn't know what had passed between the king and his sister, and he didn't dare ask.

"Were you unhappy, Aunt Genevieve?"

"No, no. On the contrary, I liked my husband very

much. But I married him for a chance to get away from the palace and all this." She gestured at the tiara she'd tossed to her side. "I married him for freedom, for a chance not to have my life laid out for me. Few kings and queens have had the luxury of marrying for love. You're lucky your father is giving you that chance."

"I know."

"Then?"

The young prince's brow knotted, and he clutched the side of the carriage door. "It's like she vanished completely, as if she never existed. No one knows who she is, and no one's ever seen her before."

"It is strange that she will not come forward," Genevieve allowed. "You said she didn't know you were the prince?"

Charles thought back to that night, remembering how—moments before she took off—she'd exclaimed that she hadn't met the prince. "Yes, and she vanished soon after I tried to tell her."

"I'm sure she knows by now." Genevieve reopened her fan and batted it at herself. "Perhaps we *should* have another ball."

"Please, Aunt Genevieve, be serious."

"I do not usually enjoy such spectacles myself. Heaven knows they're a tremendous waste of money and time." She paused. "But sometimes your father does have a spark of wisdom in him. The last ball was open to every eligible maiden in the kingdom. Do you understand the importance of that, Charles?"

"I hadn't thought about it," he admitted. "Not until recently."

"Ferdinand must not have been pleased about that, I can assure you. The villagers have few opportunities to mingle with nobility. Men like Ferdinand do not allow it." She let out a resigned sigh. "Another ball may well be the solution. Maybe your girl will make another appearance."

"I doubt it. I fear she's vanished for good."

"People don't just vanish," said the duchess. "Mark my words, if she has any sense in her at all, she'll be at the ball. And if *you* have any sense in you at all, you should make sure she's the right one for you, not just because she fits a silly slipper. We'll make it a masquerade."

"I'm afraid I'm not following. Why a masquerade?"

Genevieve clasped her hands. "Because, my dear nephew, even if this girl is as wonderful and kind and beautiful as you say, I want you to be sure you're in love with her and not a pretty face. What do you say?"

"What choice do I have?" said the prince with a sigh. But he managed a smile at his aunt. "My father did always say you were wiser than he."

"Did he now?" Genevieve said with a twinkle in her eye. "That just may be the smartest thing he's ever said. I'll be sure to remind him of it."

She opened the window of the carriage to wave outside at the people. "Besides, your father hasn't officially welcomed me back to court. He owes me a party."

"Won't he be suspicious, given you hate parties, Aunt Genevieve?"

"I wouldn't count on your father remembering that. In any case, it would be nice to be presented before the court again, to remind my old enemies that I'm still well and alive."

Bemused, Charles shook his head at his aunt. "Then I'll do it. But only to welcome you to the kingdom. It's been so many years since I've seen you."

"Oh, good. It's rather gauche to suggest a ball be held in one's honor, but I'll have a word with your father. I used to be quite good at making him think my ideas were his own. You'll see. That girl of yours will be there, too—I'm sure of it."

Charles hoped she was right.

Chapter Fifteen

The duchess had instructed her to be back before lunch, so Cinderella walked briskly, making for the Royal Library.

She'd visited a few times now, but always to acquire books for the duchess; she'd never gone for herself.

The library was in the southern wing of the palace, at the end of a long hall that displayed not only paintings but also an eclectic collection of royal art: porcelain vases, sculptures of birds and trees, finely woven tapestries, jeweled trinkets.

She wandered down the corridor, skimming the paintings on the walls. There were plenty of the king and the late queen, and far too many of a man who looked like an older version of the Grand Duke—the current duke's father, she presumed. Most of his portraits looked newer than the others, as if they'd been planted on the walls to replace what had been there before.

She soon came across a portrait of a young, unsmiling Prince Charles, mounted on a magnificent stallion.

"You look so serious," Cinderella said to his portrait, her shoulders shaking with humor. But her laughter soon died. The artist had also somehow managed to capture the depth in Charles's warm eyes. He couldn't have been much older than seven, the age the duchess had said he'd been when he lost his mother.

A bittersweet mix of emotions stirred inside Cinderella, but she pushed them aside as she entered the library.

"What books should I seek?" she wondered aloud, unable to contain her excitement. "One of those pirate adventures Her Highness can't seem to get enough of reading? Or a book on gardening—or art? I would *love* to paint a portrait of Mama and Papa one day . . . then again, it's been so long since I've sat with a good history book. The palace library should have plenty of books on how the royal gardens came to be, or on the palace's architecture, or—"

Magic, it suddenly came to her. If there was a place for her to learn more about it, and the tumult her fairy godmother had alluded to, it would be here.

"More tomes for Ginny, eh?" The librarian, Mr. Ravel, pushed his spectacles up on the bridge of his nose and continued reading whatever was on his desk. "If she keeps this up, we'll need a cart to haul back all her books once she leaves. Well, what is it today?"

"I'd like whatever you have on the history of magic," said Cinderella.

Mr. Ravel's eyes flew up from his page. "Excuse me?"

"I said, I'd like—"

"Yes, yes, I heard the first time." Mr. Ravel threw a quick glance over his shoulder; he looked worried someone might hear. Then, glowering at her, he whispered harshly, "Does Ginny think I'm hiding something from her? I told her I gave the duke all I could before he was exiled. Everything else was destroyed: the paintings, the books, everything."

This wasn't at all what Cinderella had expected to hear. "Destroyed? But why?" She swallowed. "Because it's forbidden?"

"Obviously, you dimwit child!"

"But why . . . why is it?"

He scoffed. "I suppose you're too young to remember its perils—always praying that our prince or princess wouldn't be cursed at birth by a dark fairy. The council spent years working to ban magic, and we are all better for it."

The speech sounded rehearsed, like something Mr. Ravel was *supposed* to say. "What would happen if a fairy were to sneak back into Aurelais and use her magic?"

"She would be executed, most certainly!"

"Executed!" Cinderella cried. "But magic can do so much good. Why would the king—"

"Shhh!" the librarian cried. "Enough with the questions. We shouldn't even be discussing this. Are you trying to get me dismissed? Tell your mistress I value my position here, and I don't want to hear about this ever again."

"Yes . . ." Cinderella said, stricken by the librarian's outburst. "Yes, sir."

"Good. Now if there is nothing else—oh, hello there."

A group of young girls entered, distracting Mr. Ravel as Cinderella slipped into the library. Once she lost herself among the stacks, she let out a sigh of relief.

So it was true: magic *was* forbidden.

Did that mean Lenore had put her life in danger by helping Cinderella go to the ball?

Cinderella's thoughts spun wildly, trying to make sense of it all. She had so many questions.

She spent the next hour searching the library for vestiges of the mysterious magic archive. But as Mr. Ravel had warned her, everything was gone. Which only made her wonder—why was magic so dangerous that there weren't even books about it?

Tired and about to give up, Cinderella suddenly remembered the mysterious note she'd seen in the book she'd borrowed for Genevieve.

We must bring magic back. Maybe 36 ships and 47 pirates can help. —Art

The numbers had to mean something. Thirty-six ships and forty-seven pirates . . . Could they be shelves and books in the library? And art . . . Could she find a clue in the art history collection? It was worth a try.

"Besides," she murmured to herself, "if there used to be fairies in Aurelais, then they couldn't have gotten rid of *everything*. There has to be something—maybe a book on painting or sculpture that refers to magic."

Unfortunately, even as she pored over the books in the art section, she couldn't find anything. Shelf thirty-six, book forty-seven was a volume on medieval needlepoint. Shelf forty-seven, book thirty-six was a tome on painting without color. She was about to give up when she returned to the fiction section where she usually borrowed novels for the duchess. If she couldn't find something for herself, she could at least bring Genevieve a new book.

As she scanned the shelves, she wondered whether the thirty-six might have been eighty-six. After all, the note had been old and smudged . . . there! Book forty-seven on shelf eighty-six caught her eye. It was nearly the last book in the collection, a slim volume wedged between two thicker ones.

The Historical Tapestries of Pirates.

Her heart jumped. "That doesn't seem to belong here."

The edges of the spine were singed, many of the pages ripped out. But as Cinderella closed the book, about to give up, she heard something flutter inside the book's spine. Carefully, she looked inside, and pried out a tightly wrapped scroll.

Art read a label on the parchment. It was fragile with age, and it crinkled under her fingertips.

No, it wasn't parchment at all, but a page from an adventure novel, much like the ones the duchess read. A note was written in the corner:

I'll meet you at the fork in the tunnels tomorrow at noon. Ferdinand intends to destroy it. —Ginny

Could this note be from Duchess Genevieve? And the note in the other book she'd found—*Art* . . . That was the name of her husband, Arthur!

Cinderella reread the note over and over again, unable to believe what she'd found. Was it the Grand Duke who'd had the magical archives destroyed? Had he aided his father in the ban?

Slowly, the pieces came together. Magic must have caused the animosity between Genevieve and the Grand Duke—was it the reason the duke had asked Cinderella to spy on her?

Before she could seek more answers, footsteps

approached, and Cinderella sprang up in alarm. As quickly as she could, she rolled up the note and returned it to the book.

"Cinderella! What are you doing here?"

It was Louisa and two other seamstresses—Cinderella recognized Gisele and Victoria from Blooms and Looms—followed closely by the royal librarian.

"I . . . I was just getting some books for the duchess."

"You!" cried Mr. Ravel. "You aren't allowed to be moseying about the royal archives. I thought you'd left—"

"I'm finished," Cinderella said quickly.

"So are we," said Louisa, grabbing Cinderella and her friends by the arms. "Thank you for your help!"

Once the girls raced out of the library, Louisa gave in to a fit of giggles. "Did you see how upset he was? 'You aren't allowed to be moseying about the royal archives.'"

"And the way he latched on to us the whole time!" Victoria added.

"As if we were going to steal his precious books."

Cinderella laughed, too. "Why were you three in the library?"

"The head seamstress asked us to compile some designs for a dress for Duchess Genevieve. She's going to have a welcome banquet at some point, so we need to be prepared in case she wants a gown made for the occasion."

"Cinderella, you work for her. Maybe you can help us."

"I could," she mumbled as they passed the hall of portraits once more. Except this time Cinderella's eyes picked out the faded sun lines on the brocade wallpaper, a telltale sign that some paintings had come and gone. The frames for the former Grand Duke's portraits were more ill-fitting than most—and she thought of what Mr. Ravel had said about the destruction of all paintings about magic. What must have been in this hall before? Portraits of fairy godparents to the royal family, perhaps?

"Cinderella?" Louisa said, tapping her shoulder.

"Sorry, my mind was elsewhere."

"I've noticed," said her friend dryly. "You have a habit of disappearing into your daydreams."

"She'll want to wear something black," Cinderella said. "She doesn't talk about him often, but she's still in mourning for her husband."

"You think so?" said Gisele. "I would have thought she'd be glad he died. He was the reason she left the palace in the first place."

"Do you know why he was banished?" Cinderella asked.

Victoria shrugged. "Something about a disagreement with the king."

"There's an unwritten rule not to speak of it," said Louisa, glancing over her shoulder to make sure the guards couldn't hear. "My father used to attend the Duke of

Orlanne . . . back when I was a little girl, but he's never said anything about what happened. Not even Aunt Irmina will talk about it."

"Why not?" asked Cinderella.

"Let's just say there are spies all around the palace . . . and people have been dismissed for less."

While the seamstresses changed topics back to what Duchess Genevieve should wear to her welcoming banquet, Cinderella listened only half-heartedly.

She had a hunch the so-called "spies" were the Grand Duke's. Now that she'd begun to piece together the past: his role in banning magic in Aurelais and his fraught relationship with the Duke and Duchess of Orlanne, she would have to be especially careful about what she said the next time he called for her.

And ensure he never found out about her fairy godmother.

Chapter Sixteen

Ferdinand did not appreciate Genevieve's unexpected appearance in the Center Court Stateroom. At least she had had the decency to wait until the council had dissolved, but the precious time after the meeting was when he best had the king's undivided attention and could swat away any untoward ideas his rivals in court might have tried to put in the king's head.

They exchanged glares as she stepped inside, her eyes glittering like the sharp emeralds studded on her tiara. A smug simper rested on her face.

Good heavens, how he despised that woman.

However, Ferdinand knew better than to show it. He stretched his lips wide, smiling until his cheeks ached. "Why, Your Highness. We were not expecting you."

The king's head bobbed up, his bewildered expression echoing Ferdinand's sentiments.

"Five minutes is all the time I require," Genevieve said, waving her fan at the duke with unconcealed distaste.

A thick wave of perfume assaulted his senses, and he coughed. "I beg your pardon. His Majesty and I have business to discuss. We have much to review about the council meeting, and—"

"And your sovereign could use a break after hours of listening to the ministers row and bicker with you," Genevieve finished for him. She turned to King George, who was struggling to stifle a yawn, his eyes hooded with fatigue. He did indeed look like he could use a rest.

But Ferdinand would rather die before he ever yielded to the Duchess of Orlanne. "I am afraid that is not how it is done. As the Grand Duke, I—"

"As the king's *sister*, I must insist. I have urgent affairs to discuss with my brother. *Family* business."

At that, George raised a thick eyebrow in curiosity. "Out, out," he said, tilting his head at Ferdinand to leave the siblings alone.

"But, sire, there is the matter of our treaty with—"

"That can wait. Later, Ferdinand."

Hiding a grimace, Ferdinand bowed and turned on his heel, walking slowly and defiantly for the door. Once it closed on him with a resounding thud, he pulled on his mustache angrily.

That woman!

What right did she have to claim the king's attention? She'd been away for years; now she expected to waltz back into court and usurp his hard-earned position? That was not how it worked.

He gave the guards by the door his most authoritative glare, and they immediately looked to the other direction as he crouched by the keyhole, hoping to catch what Genevieve was telling the king.

Alas. The harridan had the cunning to keep her voice low. He couldn't make out a word.

Waiting was agony. He watched the seconds tick by on his pocket watch, then gave up and reached into his pocket for a handkerchief.

"Drat, where is that blasted thing?" he mumbled, checking pocket after pocket. While he searched, his fingers looped through a hole in one of his pockets, and he cursed. He'd have to send it to the seamstresses for mending.

The door behind him opened, and Genevieve sailed out. She looked insufferably pleased with herself.

"My brother will see you now."

Ferdinand rose, straightening the tassels on his epaulets with a quiet grunt as he strode back into the stateroom.

Inside, he found the king still in his chair, toying

with two porcelain figurines of a boy and a girl. Perfect. Ferdinand wanted to pick up where they'd left off: the topic of Prince Charles's marriage.

At last finding a handkerchief, Ferdinand began polishing his monocle. "As I was saying, sire, before we were interrupted, I am simply trying to do what is best for the kingdom."

"My son getting married is what's best for the kingdom."

"I agree. But he needs to marry the right girl."

"Bah, the right girl. All this talk of bloodlines! What does it matter who he marries, so long as they make each other happy?"

The Grand Duke frowned. "Surely you don't mean that."

"It's time to throw another ball," declared the king. "A masquerade ball, so that way Charles will forget this mystery girl."

"Sire, you just threw a ball!" Ferdinand said, his frown deepening. Already his mind was reeling over what costs another ball would entail, and all his careful work balancing the budget. He would have to change the king's mind, and quickly—once George was set on something, the stubborn old man wouldn't let it go. "If it's the prince's future you're concerned about, why not consider my list of eligible princesses—"

"No more princesses. I don't have time for fiddling over

peace treaties and allocating dowries and such. If it's money you're worried about, think of how much we'll save on the wedding if we just have it right here."

"That's not what I meant, sire."

"Then what better time to throw another one? The wine's been opened, the floors already polished."

"But what . . . what will we say?"

"Say?" King George coughed, his thick white eyebrows knitting together. "I'm the king, aren't I? We don't have to say anything."

Ferdinand grimaced and crossed his arms. The king was being far too insistent about this idea. Usually he at least considered Ferdinand's suggestions. But ever since Charles had returned—and now Genevieve—everything was spiraling out of control.

"This is *her* idea, isn't it?" Ferdinand said in realization, unable to mitigate the irritation in his voice.

The king ignored him. "Indeed! What better way to welcome my sister to the palace than with a ball? And Charles gets another chance to meet his true love."

Ferdinand detected an elusive strain in George's voice, but he looked better than he had the past month. When his son had returned, so had the bloom in his cheeks and some of the vigor in his personality. Certainly, his stubbornness.

Ferdinand would bide his time. Carefully.

In the meantime, he had more important issues to press. "Perhaps, sire, we'd be better off trying to arrange a marriage for the prince with the Princess of Lourdes."

"An arranged marriage? You remember how that turned out for Genevieve. Also, the Lourdes royal family is unbearable."

"Yes, but I'm sure the prince will see reason once we explain."

"Bah, reason. Does a young man pining for a girl with a glass slipper sound like someone who is prone to reason?"

"No, sire, but—"

"And didn't you doubt that my plan would work? If it worked once, it can work again." King George clasped his hands together and rubbed them. "All we have to do is create the right mood, invite the right girls."

Ferdinand's brow furrowed. "But why a masquerade?"

"Genevieve has this idea that the boy will find true love better if he's not blinded by the girl's beauty." King George coughed. "Always practical, my sister."

"Sire, are you all right?"

"I'm fine!" barked the king. "Stop questioning me, and do what I ask."

Calm, Ferdinand. If the king is going to be dead set on Charles marrying, you must see to it that he selects your bride. A bride the council will thank you for choosing.

"I don't think that another ball is the answer. Give Charles some time, and he'll forget the girl. Then we can arrange a marriage for him with a proper princess from one of the neighboring—"

"The ball's been decided," interrupted the king. "This is your last chance, Ferdinand. Don't disappoint me again."

"Certainly, Your Majesty." The Grand Duke swept a bow, but as soon as he turned away from the king, he scowled. Things were not going as he had planned. Not at all.

When he returned to his chambers, Ferdinand sank into his chair and drummed his fingers on his desk. If the king wanted to be foolish and take Genevieve's advice over his, then more drastic measures needed to be taken. The duke needed to prepare for the worst: it stood to reason that when Charles ascended the throne, he would kick Ferdinand out of the council and replace him with some radical fool he'd met at university.

Ferdinand needed to cement his power, and now. If he could finagle Charles into marrying the Princess of Lourdes, her father would reward him handsomely, maybe even insist on making him ambassador to Lourdes. The council would laud him for being the engineer of such a desirable royal union: his legacy would be established, and his power impossible to undermine—even for Charles.

But first, Ferdinand needed an informed report from his sources within. No, "sources" wasn't quite right. He preferred to think of them as involuntary emissaries.

The first one he would call for would be that doe-eyed servant girl, Cinderella.

Chapter Seventeen

Cinderella had a feeling, as the Grand Duke peered at her through his monocle, that he was mildly displeased she did not fear him.

She had dreaded their meeting, to be sure, but she wasn't afraid of him and she wouldn't pretend to be. The only person she'd ever been truly afraid of was her stepmother, but those years with Lady Tremaine were over.

"Young lady, I see no point in beating around the bush. I have called you here regarding a matter of critical importance to the state." The Grand Duke drummed his fingers on the gilded desk. "Have you learned anything of value from Genevieve?"

Cinderella straightened in her chair, lifting her chin so she could meet his eyes. "I don't understand what you mean,

Your Grace. Mostly, I brush Her Highness's hair and help her dress. She doesn't talk to me about important matters."

"She does not *need* to talk to you. That is why I installed you as her personal attendant." The duke glowered at her. "You have every opportunity to eavesdrop on her conversations, read her mail, record her comings and goings. Why, when she was away with the prince, you should have been searching her room for indications of treachery!"

"Treachery?" Cinderella repeated with a frown. By that, did he mean *magic*? "Sir," she said carefully, "why would the king's sister be a traitor?"

The Grand Duke leaned back against a plush cushion, steepling his long fingers before answering. "Because of her husband! How else but for subterfuge do you think he obtained his fortune? It is no secret that the Duke of Orlanne passed Aurelais's secrets to our enemies, weakening us among our allies. All while giving King George poor advice that nearly ruined this kingdom."

"What sort of advice?"

"What does it matter? She married a traitor."

"She said she married a businessman," Cinderella said.

The duke's gaze intensified. "So she *has* been talking to you."

When Cinderella cringed, he leaned forward, his palms pressing against his desk. "She's trying to charm you the way she's charmed the prince. Yes, her husband was a wealthy businessman, one who nearly toppled the monar- chy with his treason. Everything she's told you is a lie. What else *has* she told you about her husband, my child?"

"Nothing," said Cinderella, determined not to say any more.

Ferdinand let out an exasperated sigh. "I shan't blame you for believing the best of her. A young, simple servant girl like you couldn't possibly begin to grasp just how con- niving Genevieve can be, so let me explain:

"When the Duke of Orlanne was young, he showed great promise, so much that King Philip, King George's father, invited him to Valors to be an adviser to the throne. The king even knighted him for being a visionary—and then he betrayed the crown."

Cinderella couldn't keep quiet any longer. "Betrayed the crown *how*?" She had to bite her tongue to stop herself from adding, *By supporting magic?*

"Why do you think Genevieve has lived outside Aurelais for all these years? It's because her husband surrounded himself with traitors who corrupted his good judgment, such that he tried to dethrone the king. He should have been executed, but your mistress was able to save him. But in doing so, she, too, was exiled from Aurelais. That is, until last week, when the king called her back to court."

The duke twirled his mustache, as if he knew he'd suc- ceeded in getting her attention and cooperation. "You will find out for me, Cinderella, why His Majesty has called her back. Should you succeed, I will see to it that your post in the palace is a permanent one. If you fail, well . . ." He paused for effect. "Are we clear?"

Cinderella pursed her lips, emotions warring inside her. The duke's threat finally *did* frighten her; she was beginning to feel happy here, and finally the miserable life she'd led before—where she'd forced herself to live in her daydreams to get through each day—was fading in her memory. But then again, how could she live with herself if she went from serving one tyrant to another? Even if she managed to hold on to her position with Genevieve, that would change once the duchess's visit was over. She would have to find another way to live eventually.

"I don't think I can do this," she said quietly. "Duchess Genevieve has been kind to me, and I will not spy on her."

The duke's expression darkened. He straightened in his chair, arranging his collar. "I see."

"Now if you will excuse me, Your Grace," said Cinderella, starting to rise, "I should return to—"

"Not so fast," he interrupted. "I advise you to reconsider my most generous offer, young lady. Lest your friend Louisa and her dear aunt suddenly lose their positions in the palace as well."

Cinderella went very still. "Louisa?"

"Yes," replied the duke, picking at his mustache.

"Though, why stop there? I'm sure she has mentioned to you that her father also works in the palace. He's a steward, I believe. What a pity it would be if his position were suddenly offered to a younger, fitter man. And her mother keeps a modest dress shop in the garment quarters, a store that struggles to pay its rent. Louisa was so kind as to bring you into the royal household, but that good deed may be her family's undoing."

He peered into his monocle, then wiped the lens on his coat before returning it to his eye. "I would suggest you consider your loyalties very carefully."

Cinderella's hands trembled at her sides. Everything was starting to sway and spin, and she gripped the end of the duke's table for support. She couldn't be the reason Louisa was dismissed.

"Well? Shall you reconsider?"

"Yes, Your Grace," she whispered.

His mood improved, a bounce returning to the clipped ends of his words. "Very good. Now see to it that you have more to offer the next time we meet. And remember, my dear, if you are caught in the act of investigating the king's sister, I unfortunately will not be able to come to your aid. So use caution."

Cinderella nodded mutely.

"I will summon you again in three days."

———

Three days.

Cinderella walked mindlessly, her feet automatically taking her back to the duchess's chambers. With every step, her heart hammered in her ears.

What should she do now?

The answer was clear. She didn't trust the Grand Duke, in spite of his sterling reputation as the king's trusted adviser. How could she help him, knowing he'd had a hand in exiling Lenore's kind?

But what about Louisa's job in the palace? Cinderella squeezed her hands into fists.

What will I tell him when he calls for me again? What will I say when he asks what I've learned about the duchess?

While on her way, she hurried through the portrait gallery, but this time she focused on the paintings of the duchess. The last one of Genevieve portrayed her and her husband, a studious-looking young man, and their three young children. It was the only portrait in the entire gallery with the Duke of Orlanne. His smile was warm, and tucked in his breast pocket was a lavender handkerchief, its color matching the fan in his wife's hand.

Lavender, like Cinderella's sash.

Craning her neck, she leaned closer to read the spines of the books painted behind the duke. Most of the words were too small for her to make out clearly, but she deciphered the word *enchantments* on one of the books. . . .

"Cinderella, Cinderella!"

Across the hall, Louisa hurried toward her. Her friend was out of breath, and her cheeks flushed with excitement.

"Aunt Irmina wants us back at Blooms and Looms right away. Something about an urgent announcement."

"What's going on?"

"It's only a rumor. But"—Louisa's hazel eyes glittered with excitement—"but they say the king is throwing another ball!"

Another ball? The news made Cinderella furrow her brow. Did that mean the prince had given up on searching for her? Did it mean he was seeking a new bride?

"You go ahead," she said, "I . . . I need to finish a few things for the duchess before I come."

Chin up, she told herself as Louisa headed back to the servants' quarters. *Who cares about another ball, anyway? You're here to make a new life, not mope over the prince.*

No matter how much she wanted to see him again.

Whatever the rumor was, whether there was to be a ball or not, Cinderella wouldn't give it a second thought. What mattered most now was finding a way to protect Duchess Genevieve and helping Louisa keep her job in the palace.

And all that depended on untangling herself from the mess she'd gotten herself into with Grand Duke Ferdinand.

Chapter Eighteen

On most occasions, Genevieve d'Orlanne would have been the last person Ferdinand wanted to see, but today he sought her out. He needed information, and he didn't trust that doe-eyed servant girl to get it for him soon enough. Luckily, he knew just how to needle the king's sister.

"I do not recall inviting you to tea, Ferdinand," Genevieve said, receiving him frostily.

"I'll have coffee then, thank you." The Grand Duke snapped his fingers, sending the nearest servant into a frenzied dance to fetch a fresh pot.

Genevieve glared at him as he took the seat across from her. "That isn't what I meant."

His cup of coffee arrived promptly. Crossing one leg over the other, Ferdinand took a sniff before sipping.

"What do you want?"

"Blunt as always," said Ferdinand affably. "I must say, I'm pleased to find you haven't changed after all these years. I merely wished to have a conversation with you, Genevieve. It's been so long since you've been here at court, and with all the excitement over Charles's missing bride-to-be, I haven't had a chance to properly welcome you back."

Narrowing her eyes at him, Genevieve furiously swirled her spoon in her tea, creating a miniature tempest in the cup. "You, welcome me back? I can't imagine whose company I'd find more venomous—yours, or a viper's."

"I have never understood what happened to us," Ferdinand forged on. "We were friends once, don't you remember?"

"No, I do not."

"We might never have trusted one another, but we respected each other," he amended. "I sense, now, that most regrettably is no longer the case."

"I find it hard to respect a two-faced scoundrel. If only my brother could see you as I do."

Ferdinand blinked. "You wound me, Genevieve."

"That's 'Your Highness' to you."

"Let's not play a game of rank now. Else I'll remind you that it is thanks to me that you were permitted to keep your title."

"Thanks to you?" Genevieve scoffed. "Thanks to *you*, my husband died in shame. Thanks to *you*, my children were banished from Aurelais and robbed of their birthright."

"It could have been much worse," replied Ferdinand smoothly. "Few get to spend their exile on an estate provided for by the king. And lo, now you've returned and most have forgotten the degree of your treachery. Even the king, it appears."

She was struggling to keep her composure; Ferdinand noticed how taut her cheeks had become, how the pulse in her neck thickened and throbbed. She peeled off her glove one finger at a time, her voice flat and wooden when she spoke next. "If you are trying to blackmail me, Ferdinand, go ahead. I don't care what anyone at court thinks of me. Least of all, my brother."

"Not even your nephew? Your influence on young Charles is unacceptable. He doesn't understand what a threat your beliefs are to the future of this nation."

To her credit, she barely flinched. "You dare to imply that I don't care about Aurelais? My family has ruled this country for centuries. My ancestors tilled and founded this nation with their blood and tears before yours first arrived."

"I'm not the only one. You've been away from court for far too long, and yet now you frolic back to the palace and resume your position as the king's sister? Why now, Genevieve?"

The duchess set her teacup on its saucer with a sharp clatter. "Why don't you ask the little spy you've planted in my household?"

Ferdinand choked on his coffee. Promptly reaching for his handkerchief, he blew his nose, then faced Genevieve, his posture stiffening. "Just what do you mean?"

"Don't try to be coy. I know my attendant is one of your spies."

"That innocent-looking creature?" Ferdinand spluttered, pretending to be offended. "She looks like she's barely spent a day out of the countryside. I wouldn't bother."

"Yes, that's precisely why you picked her. But unfortunately for you, she's sharp enough to see you for what you are—a wolf in sheep's clothing. And she isn't afraid of wolves."

He raised a thick eyebrow. "Isn't she now? Where is the young lady, anyway?"

"*Cindergirl* is at the library, fetching a new novel for me."

"A book?"

"Yes, Ferdinand. Unlike you, I have hobbies other than scheming and conniving."

"Yes, I quite remember. Yours are more in the line of deceit and treason."

ELIZABETH LIM

"Why, you!"

She'd stepped into his net, but he needed to proceed carefully if he was going to ensnare her. He clasped his hands together and rested them on his lap. In his smoothest, most all-knowing tone, he said, "After all these years, after publicly swearing you'd never return, there must be a reason you've come back."

"I heard my nephew had come back from university. I wanted to see him."

He didn't believe her, not for an instant. King George's sister was a skilled deceiver, and her denial was too quick.

"You and I both know that is untrue." Ferdinand paused deliberately. "You forget it is I who have the king's ear, *and* the council's trust. I am aware His Majesty is planning to pass the throne to Charles. That's why you're here."

The barest of flinches flickered across Genevieve's face, but Ferdinand caught it. No matter how she denied it now, he had gleaned the truth.

She pressed her lips tight. "I am here to help Charles find a wife."

"He needs to marry a princess," said Ferdinand. "Preferably a princess of one of Aurelais's neighboring kingdoms—such as Lourdes. King George has ruled for forty years. No matter what kind of sovereign Charles turns out to be, the transition between reigns will be difficult.

We must strengthen our position by allying ourselves with Lourdes so that our enemies do not pounce on any perceived weakness."

"Aurelais has been at peace for nearly half a century," Genevieve said calmly. "What makes you think all of a sudden we have enemies that are eyeing our territories?"

"We have been at peace because my father was vigilant, and I have carried on his task of safeguarding this kingdom from the likes of men such as your husband, who would open our gates to evils such as magic and . . . and . . ."

"A more powerful middle class?" said Genevieve snidely. "You seem rather sore, Ferdinand. The people are gaining more power, with or without magic."

"The riots will be contained. They are but a trifle compared to the chaos and instability magic would have brought. Fairies consider themselves above the law, what with their unnatural abilities and bringing aid to those they deem good and worthy."

"Yes, but if the fairies happen to bless princes and dukes, that's all right."

"A hierarchy of rank brings about order. Peasants don't deserve fairy guardians waving their problems away with magic wands."

"I think you had better leave."

The Grand Duke pretended not to hear her. "You and your late husband might as well have cursed Aurelais's future when you put the idea in the king's head to send the prince to university."

Genevieve hissed at the Grand Duke. "Cursed Aurelais's future? What century do you think you live in? Times are changing."

"Yes, which is exactly why we must remain vigilant. Mark my words, Charles is young and idealistic, and these ideas he's picked up—of 'strengthening the country from within' and 'empowering the people'—will bring ruin to Aurelais. Just as your husband nearly brought ruin to this monarchy."

Genevieve clenched her teeth. Her narrow face had grown tight with anger. "You've overstayed your welcome, Ferdinand. Your coffee is cold."

"Quite so. Quite so." In his most cordial tone, he said, "I look forward to the party tomorrow night, Your Highness. Good day."

He bowed, but she refused to acknowledge him.

Just as well. She would be so angry for the rest of the day she'd want to do nothing but avoid him. While Genevieve was deciding on napkin colors and music selections for the masquerade tomorrow, he would make a few arrangements of his own.

Arrangements that would ensure the future of this kingdom, and most important, his position in it.

Chapter Nineteen

Cinderella had to squeeze her way into the servants' quarters. So many girls had gathered, excitedly chattering, that she could hardly make out Louisa waving to her from the other side of the hall.

"Another ball! Can you believe it?"

"That only means more work for us. There's no chance Madame will let us attend. She wouldn't even let us go to the first one—"

Cinderella moved faster, threading through the crowd toward Louisa and wishing she could shut her ears. She would have loved to drown in her daydreams. Every snippet of conversation she caught was about the prince:

"I hear he's looking for a new bride."

"So he's given up on the girl with the glass slipper?"

Darting away before she could hear an answer, Cinderella instantly berated herself. *What do I care if the prince is looking for a new bride? I don't have any claim on him.*

"Attention!" rang Madame Irmina's voice. "I have an announcement."

All rumbling amongst the servants ceased. The women quieted, lining themselves against the walls to hear what their mistress had to say, and Cinderella hurried to Louisa's side.

"Many of you may have heard already, so this will merely be a confirmation." Irmina drew a deep, dramatic breath. "There is to be another ball. Tomorrow night."

"Tomorrow night?" many of the girls repeated, unable to believe it. "But we just—"

"No buts. By the king's command, it is to be even grander than the one before it. Unfortunately, you know what that means."

"It means we'll be staying all night at the palace," someone protested. "Polishing the silver and mopping the floors."

"Your duty is to the crown," said Irmina harshly. "Anyone who objects will see themselves with a double shift and half pay for the rest of the month." She scanned the girls, one thin eyebrow raised as if daring anyone else to complain. Then she let out a breath. "Now I know this is unexpected and will mean extra obligations for all, but if it is any consolation, the ball will be in honor of Her Highness, the Duchess Genevieve d'Orlanne—and it is to be . . . a masquerade."

A masquerade in honor of the duchess? Cinderella's attention reeled.

Had Duchess Genevieve changed her mind about suggesting a second ball to the king? She hadn't said anything about a ball welcoming her to Aurelais—certainly not at such short notice. Then again, the king's sister had been irritable and curt ever since the night before. Cinderella wondered what could have upset her.

"You look like you just ate a piece of bad cheese," Louisa said, elbowing Cinderella in the side.

"I do?" Cinderella asked faintly.

"You ought to be relieved. As the duchess's attendant, you don't have to help with the cleaning, or the sewing, or the cooking. Only dressing your mistress to the nines, obliging her every whim and fancy, and helping her scour Valors for the perfect mask to go with her hair."

It took Cinderella a moment to realize her friend was joking.

Louisa touched her shoulder. "I've heard the duchess can be difficult. Let me know if you need any help with anything."

"She isn't so bad," Cinderella replied. When Louisa gave her an incredulous look, she insisted, "Really."

"Before any of you get any ideas," continued Madame Irmina, "understand that anyone who is found sneaking off into the ball will be discharged immediately." Her gaze swept across the room. "I will not be as forgiving as I was the last time."

"Aunt Spoilsport," Louisa muttered. She turned to Cinderella, whispering, "Don't worry, we'll find a way to go."

"I don't plan on going."

"What?"

Before Cinderella could reply, Irmina announced, "You are all dismissed." Then she spun to face the two girls. "Except you, Cinderella. A word."

Cinderella blinked, unsure of what she could possibly want.

"Ahem," said Irmina, looking pointedly at Cinderella until she glanced down and realized her sash was crooked. Irmina waited until it was fixed before continuing, "You've lasted longer than I expected, and it appears Her Highness actually finds you a competent royal attendant. I have determined that you may stay—at least for the duration of Her Highness's visit."

"Oh, thank you!" Cinderella clasped her hands together

and nearly hugged Louisa's aunt. It wasn't a permanent position, but it was a start. She'd continue to earn wages, and if she saved wisely, she might even be able to open a shop one day, like Louisa's mother.

"Don't thank me." Madame Irmina didn't smile, but she didn't frown, either. That was a start, Cinderella supposed. "You do your job, and you don't cause any mischief. Eyes to the ground and ears tuned to the bells, understood?"

As if on cue, the duchess's call bell tolled, clattering loudly against the wall.

"Now, off with you. Make the duchess happy so she doesn't give my girls any extra work before the masquerade."

"I'll try," Cinderella promised, buoyed by Madame Irmina's newfound trust in her.

Unfortunately, when Cinderella returned to the royal apartments it appeared the duchess was not in a better mood.

"There you are," huffed Genevieve. "I thought I'd have to send a search party to get you."

"I'm sorry, ma'am. Madame Irmina called us for a staff meeting."

"I didn't ask for an explanation. Only that you be prompt."

Cinderella's shoulders fell. Whatever rapport she had established with the Duchess of Orlanne seemed long forgotten; for whatever reason, the king's sister was preoccupied by something that greatly vexed her.

"It's getting late, and there is much for you to do before tomorrow."

"Will you need a gown fitted, ma'am?" Cinderella asked as she tidied up the spread of teacups and empty plates scattered around Genevieve's sitting room.

"A gown? Whatever for?"

"For the ball tomorrow night. Madame Irmina told us it was to be in your honor, so I thought you might want to try on your gown in advance—"

"Not now, Cindergirl. I will tell you when I need a gown fitted. You do not decide."

Thinking it would be wise to change topics, Cinderella said, "Did you have an enjoyable ride out into town yesterday?"

She almost added "with the prince," but she bit her tongue.

Genevieve powdered her nose, then snapped the compact shut. "What did *you* do during your morning off, Cindergirl?"

"Me?" she stammered. "I . . . I went to the library."

"What for? I didn't ask for any books."

"For myself, ma'am." Cinderella bit her tongue. Much as she liked the duchess, she didn't dare tell her she'd been trying to learn more about magic to help her fairy god-mother. "Now that I'm working in the palace, I wanted to learn more about Aurelais's history, and about the people in the portraits I've seen in all the halls."

"Bah. My family is hardly worth reading about."

"Is that what's been bothering you, ma'am?"

"What's bothering me is my own business. Let me be. No, wait." A sigh. "I'm not rankled at *you*."

Is it the Grand Duke? Cinderella wondered. But she didn't dare ask.

"I would have thought that after ten years the palace would have changed. Honestly, had I known that everyone here was still churlish and narrow-minded, I would never have come. Even George . . . oh, he's been cordial enough to me and I to him, but we've been dancing around our past, as if it never happened."

"Maybe you should talk to him about it."

"I should." She gave a morose smile. "But pride has always been my strong suit, you see, and George's, too. I don't even remember who started the argument, not that it matters. Thankfully, Charles is more like his mother. He will make a fine husband and father one day."

Cinderella's heart quickened a beat, but she said nothing.

"One day soon," added the duchess. "George is eager

to have his son wed. Maybe tonight Charles will meet someone."

Cinderella looked up at the duchess. Summoning her courage, she asked, "Do you think the girl with the glass slipper will return? Do you think she . . . *should* return?"

The duchess wrinkled her nose. "If you ask me, it'd be best if my nephew never saw that girl again."

The words stung Cinderella. Yet how could she blame the duchess? To her—to *everyone*—the identity of the elusive young lady dressed in a moonlight-blue gown and glass slippers, who had riveted the entire ball and captured the heart of the prince, was a mystery. And the greater puzzle was why she—Cinderella—had vanished, leaving the prince heartbroken.

Even Louisa was fascinated by the runaway princess. Fascinated, and also incredulous.

"She must be very rich and very powerful," she'd said one evening while Cinderella was helping her finish some mending in the servants' quarters. "Who else would run away from a chance to marry the prince of Aurelais?"

"Maybe she isn't either of those things," Cinderella reasoned. "Maybe she was just a regular girl—like you or me—who stumbled upon the chance of a lifetime to go to a royal ball."

"Regular girls like you or me don't have a gown so fine,

especially not one that fits so perfectly," said Louisa sensibly, taking a seamstress's point of view.

"Someone could have given it to her."

"Ha!" Then Louisa tilted her head, considering. "Let's imagine you're right. Let's say she's a common girl like us. Maybe she fled because she was afraid."

"Afraid?"

"It'd be the only reasonable explanation. Say the prince fell in love with me . . . I'd be thrilled beyond all measure, but well, I'm not so naive as to think it would amount to anything. A prince marries a princess, not some palace seamstress."

Cinderella couldn't think of a response, so she'd simply nodded, her neck wooden as her head bobbed up and down.

Only she knew the truth. She'd fled because of what her fairy godmother had told her: that magic only lasted so long and her magnificent clothes and carriage would become rags and a pumpkin upon the stroke of midnight.

Then again, more than once she'd wondered what would have happened if she had stayed past midnight. Would Charles have accepted her, or would the sight of her in rags have mortified him?

Maybe Louisa was right and she *had* been afraid. Maybe she didn't want to know the answer. It was better this way, keeping the prince as a cherished memory. She needed to protect herself; she'd experienced enough heartache to last a lifetime.

She returned her attention to the duchess, who had dipped into her armoire, flipping through the many fine garments she had brought to the palace.

"Everyone is inordinately obsessed with this girl," said Genevieve, unaware of the thoughts spooling in Cinderella's mind. "Another reason to hold a second ball. Charles needs to move on and forget this spineless glass slipper lady."

"Spineless?" Cinderella echoed, heat rising to her cheeks. "Why do you think she's spineless?"

"A girl who runs off on my nephew must be hiding something."

"What if she didn't know he was your nephew?" asked Cinderella carefully.

Genevieve lifted a skeptical eyebrow. "Even so. A potential princess of Aurelais cannot afford to have secrets. The court would eat her alive if she were anything less than perfect. Trust me, *I* would know. She must be a model of courage, grace, and virtue. A princess who runs off like that and refuses to come forth is not a paragon of any of the three."

"I'm sure she had a good reason."

"Believe what you wish," said the duchess, withdrawing a deep emerald gown from her closet. "Have the collar mended before the masquerade. I don't need a fitting—I've been wearing this dress since before you were born and it still fits."

As she folded the gown into a small trunk, Cinderella hesitated. "Do you think the prince loves her?"

"I think he's in love with the idea of her," replied the duchess flippantly, her words echoing Cinderella's fears. "If she were to return to the ball, I am certain he would propose marriage, but that's only because George is forcing him to."

Forcing him to? Cinderella's ears began to ring uncontrollably, the words repeating over and over in her head. She sucked in a breath to calm herself. "What . . . what do you mean?"

"My brother is the one behind the royal proclamation— and the ball. George is in such a rush for Charles to find a wife that he vowed my nephew would wed the girl who fit the glass slipper. Honestly, from what I know about this girl, I don't think that such a union would be good for Charles, or for Aurelais."

Cinderella's hands, clenching the sides of the trunk, shook, and she had to fight to keep her voice from trembling. "I see. Then let's hope she doesn't appear tomorrow."

With the hastiest curtsy she could manage, Cinderella hurried out of the room, ignoring the duchess's call, "Cindergirl, I wasn't finished with you!"

———

Cinderella needed to breathe. Everything felt suddenly hot, and she desperately needed some fresh air, needed to clear her mind of what the duchess had told her.

Her heart ached with disappointment, and try as she might, she couldn't reason it away the way she had whenever her stepmother hurt her. This was new, deeper than the sting of when Charles hadn't recognized her in the palace.

To learn that the entire ball had been a ruse to find Charles a wife, that he had all but been *forced* to choose someone. No, that wasn't the surprising part. That wasn't the *hurtful* part.

What hurt was that Charles had picked her simply because he had to pick *someone*. And now, if there were another ball, he'd choose the next girl who caught his eye. Maybe she had taken their connection that night for granted . . . but had he never cared about her in the first place?

Of course, there was the fact that he hadn't recognized her. Days later, the pain from seeing him spin away from her and disappear down the corridor, as if she were a perfect stranger, was still fresh.

Cinderella's head throbbed, and she clutched the trunk holding the duchess's dress tighter.

Did *she* care about *him*? She'd thought she did, but how

many young men had she met while under her stepmother's charge? None.

The prince was the first. He'd been so charming, listening to her attentively as if she were the most important person in the world and not a servant to be ordered about or treated with callous contempt. His easy smile and warm eyes had won her over, and now here she was, still thinking about him.

Maybe she was naive to expect he felt the same as she did—that they had shared something special. Truth be told, it would be foolish of him to marry someone he'd only met once. Besides, she knew nothing about being a princess. And she'd spent enough years under her stepmother's pitiless eye; she didn't need to spend the rest of her life under her entire country's.

Cinderella stopped at one of the windows, pressing her hand against the cool glass.

Outside, the gardens beckoned. Bathed under the cloak of moonlight, they were breathtaking. The hedges rustled under the dim lamplight, swaying to an invisible symphony, and the marble pavilions shone white as pearls.

It was late enough that no one would be passing through now. Perhaps she could cut across and make a short detour before heading to her room. Being outside would help her think clearly again.

After a long breath, Cinderella pulled away from the window, making for the two doors leading outside to the gardens. She waited for the guard to open them, but he met her gaze with a penetrating glare.

When she tried to enter the doors, he stopped in front of her.

"What is your business here?"

Cinderella blinked, unsure why the guard had taken such a sharp tone with her. "I wanted to walk out into the gardens back to the servants' quarters."

The guard peered at her as if she'd uttered the most foolish thing he'd ever heard.

"Servants are not permitted to access the royal gardens, not without express permission."

Cinderella took a step back. "So the entire garden is off-limits, even to the staff? But it's even larger than the palace."

"The palace is not yours to roam," the guard admonished. "There are rules to respect. Traditions to honor."

Cinderella raised her chin, but she knew it was no use arguing. Without another word, she turned away and continued to her quarters, her heart even heavier than before.

Being around nature had always lifted her spirits. She had grown up helping her mother tend the flowers in their garden, which had once been the pride and joy of the family estate. But after her stepmother had fired her father's staff to save on expenses, the entire yard had fallen to disarray.

"Who has any use for a garden?" Lady Tremaine would say. "The flowers can't be sold. Let them die."

Cinderella had tried as long as she could to maintain the garden, rising before the sun to nurture her mother's rose-bushes and tulips. But one morning, she'd found the entire garden trampled by Lucifer.

Back then she'd blamed it on the cat. But now she knew better. Knowing how much her mother's garden meant to her, Lady Tremaine must have let Lucifer loose on the flowers. By the time Cinderella discovered what he had done, the garden had been destroyed, and Lady Tremaine had ordered Cinderella to clean up the "dirt." The very next day, her stepmother had a brick path laid over the area so that another garden might never grow there again.

The memory still stung, even after all these years, and Cinderella pushed it away. Her stepmother didn't deserve another second of her time, not even in her thoughts.

Before long, she'd returned to her room. Setting aside the duchess's gown, she sat on her bed to give her tired feet a short rest. Work in the palace wasn't half as strenuous as it had been at home with her stepmother and stepsisters, yet Cinderella hadn't been sleeping well.

There was so much she'd missed during her unhappy years with Lady Tremaine; now that she was free, there was so much she wanted to do. There was so much she *could* do. She wanted to see the world and to help others who might have felt as lonely and trapped as she had. She didn't want to have to force herself to smile anymore just to bear each day; she wanted to find out what truly made her laugh, what truly made her happy. She wanted to get to the heart of things—to find the truth, instead of turn a blind eye.

She drew a deep breath then, wiping the tears from her cheeks, and got up from her bed. Duchess Genevieve must be wondering what had happened to her.

Cinderella faced her reflection in the mirror. "I'm not alone anymore. I have Louisa, the girls from the palace, even Duchess Genevieve . . ."

Then why am I still crying?

Because every time she dared hope for something, for some glimmer of happiness, it slipped her grasp, almost like stardust. Whenever she reveled in something of her father and mother's, Lady Tremaine sold it—or destroyed it. When the Grand Duke was searching for her to bring her to the palace, Lady Tremaine locked her in the tower. When she had finally dared hope someone might care for her, it turned out to be part of a larger ploy.

Could any happiness she found actually last beyond midnight?

As she splashed her face, trying to wash the redness

from her eyes, a shadow flickered behind her. A warm light swelled from the darkness, so bright it illuminated her entire room.

Startled, Cinderella turned around, only to find her fairy godmother waiting behind her.

"Fairy Godmother!" she breathed, embracing the older woman.

"There, there." Lenore stroked her hair. "I heard you crying, and I felt . . ." She revealed her wand. "*It* felt your sadness. Why the tears, my dear?"

"Nothing," said Cinderella quickly. When Lenore raised an eyebrow, she sighed and explained, "I found out the ball was just a scheme for the prince to find a bride. And now there's going to be another one."

"Isn't that wonderful news? You can see him again."

She swallowed, a hard lump lodged in her throat. "No, I'm not allowed to go. Besides, I don't want to. It's just a silly ball, and I . . . I want to leave that part of my past behind me."

"What makes you think it's a silly ball?"

"I have a job in the palace," Cinderella continued without answering. A touch of pride edged her voice as she said, "And I'm free of my stepmother to lead my own life. I wouldn't want to run into her again."

Lenore's shoulders softened. "My child," she murmured, "you needn't fear her."

"I know, but . . ." Cinderella pursed her lips. She didn't want to talk about her stepmother anymore; she had so many questions for her fairy godmother. "I have another dream, too. One to help people. Like you."

"Like me?"

"You told me that magic was forbidden, and when I went to the royal archives, the librarian said that everything to do with magic has been destroyed. Oh, Fairy Godmother, what happened all those years ago? What happened to magic . . . and to you?"

Lenore sighed, taking a moment to gather herself. Then she looked at Cinderella with a sad glimmer in her eyes. "When I was your age, there were many fairies in Aurelais. Good ones, mostly—we fairy godparents were once emissaries to the human world, using our magic to help keep the peace across kingdoms. But there were a few rotten fairies, ones that caused mischief with their curses and dark magic. Because of them, the people of Aurelais started mistrusting us as a whole. The situation became so dire that they began hunting us, and killing us." The fairy godmother swallowed visibly, and Cinderella reached out to comfort her.

"I didn't know," she said.

"You couldn't have. The king's council has done its very best to wipe magic's existence from the entire country. Most people have already forgotten what it was like."

"Did everyone have a fairy godmother like you?"

"Not everyone," she replied. "But your grandmother was good to me even when others began to hunt my kind. She sheltered me so I could stay in Aurelais, and when she gave birth to your mother, I swore to repay her kindness by watching over Gabrielle and becoming her godmother—a connection that is not forged lightly. Sadly, as things grew worse, I had no choice but to leave. When I finally gathered enough courage to return, Gabrielle was all grown up, with a daughter of her own."

"Is it dangerous still? Should you be here? I don't want you to get in trouble, Fairy Godmother."

"Oh, child." Lenore laughed sadly, not quite answering the question. "I owe your family so much. . . . What I regret most was not being here when your mother needed me."

Cinderella held her breath as her fairy godmother went on.

"You meant everything to Gabrielle. After you were born, I thought she'd finally achieved her happily ever after. I'll never forgive myself for that mistake. For thinking I could find some new goddaughters and godsons in other kingdoms, and they could replace your mother in my heart."

"It wasn't your fault," Cinderella said gently. "You were forced to leave."

"I was a coward," Lenore said. "I was afraid of losing my wand. It becomes like a part of you, magic. And we fairies had decided long ago to leave, or else risk losing our wands . . . or worse. So, we left. *I* left even before magic became illegal. Others were not quite so lucky, forced to leave their homes—their loved ones—with no plan in place. "

Lenore removed her hood, letting it settle over her shoulders. "Years later, I sensed something was amiss with my Gabrielle. I borrowed enough magic to make a quick trip back to see her. And lo, upon my return I learned your mother had fallen gravely ill. I arrived the day your father took you away so you wouldn't catch her sickness. I stayed with her as long as I could, but there was nothing I could do. And for the first time, I could understand why so many resent my magic."

"Why?"

"Because magic can only aid someone's fate, not change it."

Cinderella's chest tightened. "And my mother's fate was to . . . to . . ."

"Yes, my child. I'm afraid so." Lenore turned aside to wipe away the moisture from her eyes. "After Gabrielle passed away, I was so grief-stricken that I did not visit your father's household for many years. I convinced myself it was just that—the inevitable sorrow that follows a loss—which explained the shroud of darkness emanating from your household. Too late, I learned that it was so much more.

I blame myself now for the years you endured under that awful woman."

Her stepmother.

Cinderella inhaled. She clenched her fists, anger stirring inside her when she thought of all the years she'd endured under Lady Tremaine's cruelty. And all the years her fairy godmother must have endured because of the country's twisted thoughts about magic.

"It was not your fault," said Cinderella, taking her fairy godmother's hands in her own. "You've already done more for me and my family than we could ever have asked for. I am in a better place now."

"Yes," said Lenore quietly. She shook her head. "But remember, happiness isn't just a smile. You can't force it to come true."

The words made Cinderella's heart ache. "I wish I'd realized that earlier."

Lenore squeezed Cinderella's hands. "Do what makes you happy, Cinderella. That is what I want for you. That was what I was hoping to help with when I first came to you. Go to this masquerade ball with your new friends, put on a pretty gown, and dance the night away. Sneak out into the royal gardens and drink tea under the moonlight. Get lost in the streets of Valors and spend some of your wages on something that'll make you happy to look at every morning.

Even the small joys are worth cherishing, and they will lead you to greater ones."

"I want to help *you*," said Cinderella. "I want magic to return to Aurelais."

Lenore shook her head sadly. "That would take a miracle."

"You once told me miracles take a little time."

"Perhaps not this one."

Cinderella wouldn't give up. "Why does the Grand Duke hate fairies so much? Why did the king exile you from Aurelais?"

"That is a story for another time, Cinderella." Her godmother patted her shoulder and then, with a flick of her wand, began to vanish. "Focus on your own happiness. Find your own miracle."

"But—" Cinderella started.

Lenore stopped her with a sad smile. Then the fairy godmother touched her forehead to Cinderella's and disappeared.

Chapter Twenty

The next morning, Cinderella couldn't stop thinking about her conversation with Lenore. But, of course, duty called, and she knew the seamstresses would be busy preparing for the night's masquerade, so she shuttled Duchess Genevieve's gown to Louisa for last-minute alterations at an early hour.

When she entered the workroom, she stifled a gasp. There were fabrics strewn across the floor, mannequins half dressed, and ribbons tangled in knots, spiraling from their spindles. In the thick of it was Louisa, so harried she barely noticed Cinderella's presence.

"Where is everyone?" Cinderella asked.

"You mean the other seamstresses?" Thread dangled from Louisa's mouth, and her fingers were covered in thimbles. "They're at fittings. Is that from the duchess?"

"She needs the collar repaired." Cinderella passed her the gown. "Why are you the only one here?"

"I have to stay. All the lords need their uniforms pressed, and the ladies need their gowns hemmed and bodices cinched. It goes on and on." Louisa rubbed her eyes with the back of her hand. "I'm the most junior, so I'm stuck with the cleaning and the mending. At this rate, I'll need eight pairs of hands to finish before the ball."

Cinderella glanced at the array of lavish finery. Some of the dresses flaunted the high empire waists that had been the fashion during the earlier part of King George's reign, but a good majority of the gowns sported natural waists and puffed sleeves, with chokers and headbands to match. The style looked familiar. . . .

"I see you've discovered 'the mysterious princess effect,'" said Louisa dryly.

Cinderella spun to face her friend. "What?"

"Seems the girl with the glass slipper has set off a new trend."

Heat rose to Cinderella's cheeks. "You mean they're trying to dress like *her*?"

"Yes, but I don't think it'll help the prince notice any of them." Louisa rolled her eyes. "Not when he's so hopelessly in love."

The sarcasm in her tone made Cinderella blink. "Then why bother?"

"Why not?" Louisa shrugged. "They're rich, so what's another ball gown to them? A lottery ticket, a chance to win the prince's heart. I almost can't blame them—can it even be love if they've only met once? That's stuff made of fairy tales—'and they lived happily ever after.'" Batting her eyelashes, Louisa fanned herself with the sleeve she was working on, then pretended to faint in her chair. She bounced up. "Real life doesn't happen that way. In real life, you learn that Prince Charles gets terrible onion breath after dinner every night, that he has hairy warts all over his back, or that he dislikes dogs."

"I hope he doesn't dislike dogs," said Cinderella, not knowing whether to smile or frown.

"Aren't you the romantic?" Louisa laughed. She stabbed her needle into the pincushion and began folding the garment she'd just finished. "Fine, maybe not. But I don't believe in love at first sight, do you?"

"I think it happens."

"The king probably agrees with you. The seamstresses have a bet going on that the real point of this whole new rigmarole is finding the prince another bride."

Cinderella picked up a puddle of pink satin, fixing her stare a little too hard on its soft folds. "Doesn't everyone think that?"

Louisa shrugged. "Who can keep up with these royals?

I certainly can't. Last night, I didn't arrive home until well after midnight, and even then I was up helping my mother sew until dawn." She picked at one of her bandaged fingers. "She's been flooded with dress requests for the masquerade."

"I could help," suggested Cinderella, picking up a pair of light blue trousers from one of the baskets.

"Don't you have to assist the duchess?"

"It's early. She's still asleep for now."

"All right, then take care of these." Louisa practically tossed a pair of trousers at her. "It's an urgent order. I'll work on the duchess's collar."

Cinderella claimed one of the three-legged stools in the corner and laid the pants on her lap. There was a note pinned to one of the legs that the left pocket needed to be mended.

That would be easy enough. Cinderella reached for a needle and a spool of thread in a matching blue. As she tugged at the trouser pockets, a few handkerchiefs and an empty snuffbox fell out. Cinderella carefully put them aside and resumed her work only to find there were yet more hidden pockets in the trousers. One held an empty vial.

"Whose are these?" she asked, turning them inside out.

"I don't know. They don't usually tell us who the

garments belong to, unless it's a member of the royal family. Such pockets are commonplace enough." Louisa grinned slyly. "Nobles need all sorts of hiding places for their fans and secret love letters."

"Secret love letters? You're joking, aren't you?"

Louisa laughed. "What do you think the nobles do all day? They don't have to toil for their wages like we do."

"The king works," Cinderella reasoned, "and so does the Grand Duke." *If you call spying and scheming "work."*

"True, but the rest of them busy themselves with balls and gossip." Louisa sighed, staring longingly at the duchess's gown. "And beautiful, beautiful dresses."

A strand of pearls had fallen off the trimming on one of the sleeves, and Louisa stroked her chin, studying how she should begin her work. "The lace on this alone costs a fortnight's salary. Can you imagine owning a gown so beautiful?"

She took the sleeves and tucked the dress under her chin, letting the skirt fall over her legs with a swoosh. Cinderella did the same, holding up the trousers and pretending to be a young lord.

"Miss Louisa, would you do me the honor of a dance?" She bowed with a flourish, and Louisa curtsied; then the two girls danced to an imaginary waltz.

"You know, you look a little like her."

Cinderella tilted her head. "Hmm?"

"The runaway princess. Has anyone told you that? A couple of the girls from Blooms and Looms have mentioned it."

Cinderella's mouth went instantly dry. Her throat constricted—could she trust Louisa with the truth? "Well, I . . . um, I—"

Thankfully, at that instant, the door burst open and the two girls immediately rushed to the nearest chairs. In stormed Madame Irmina, heaping another basket of clothes by the ones already next to Louisa.

"I see I was wrong about you," Irmina said, frowning at Cinderella. "I reward you with a permanent position in the palace, and the first thing you do is stir up mischief with my niece! Disappointment always abounds when it comes to these new young hires."

"No, no, Madame Irmina," said Cinderella. "I was just dropping off Her Highness's gown—"

"Then she was helping me with some of the mending. Truly, Aunt Irmina."

"I hope so," Irmina replied, still frowning. "You girls better get back to work. There's a ball tonight, and both your jobs are on the line."

When she left, Louisa erupted into laughter. "That

was close. Did you see how cross she looked?" Louisa pretended to fan herself. "I think she isn't happy unless she threatens at least one person's job a day, old Aunt Spoilsport."

Cinderella smiled. "She's not so bad. Compared to my stepmother, your aunt's as gentle as a mouse."

At the memory, Cinderella's amusement faded. She lowered her gaze so Louisa wouldn't ask about her past and resumed work on the "urgent" trousers. Now that the pockets had been emptied, Cinderella quickly checked the material, especially the white stripes on the pant legs, for stains. As she finally began to sew, something rustled against her ankle.

"What's this?" she murmured to herself, removing several scraps of paper from yet another one of the hidden pockets. The papers had gone through the wash, smearing the ink, and while the writing was small and neat, it was barely legible. Cinderella glanced at the scraps to make sure they weren't anything important, but the only words she could vaguely make out were *concoction* and *pain*. Not knowing what to do with them, she crumpled them into her pocket to throw away later.

Louisa tilted her head at her. "You know, everyone says the duchess is such a terrible mistress, but you don't seem to be that afraid of her."

"I'm not," Cinderella admitted. "I've seen real cruelty, and the duchess is not even close. She can be difficult, but her heart is in the right place. Besides, she likes Bruno, and since adopting him, she's been kind to me."

"Maybe, but I think there's more to it than Bruno," determined Louisa. "You just seem so cheerful, Cinderella—cheerful yet sad. I don't know how to explain it, but I bet people find it difficult being angry with you. I wonder if that's why the duchess likes you so much. Even Aunt Irmina does, even if she won't admit it."

"I find that hard to believe," said Cinderella dryly. The trousers were finished and she held them up, checking her handiwork. She had reason to be proud, and she moved on to the next garment. A rack of coats stood by one of the windows, and Cinderella wondered whether any of them might be the prince's.

What was he doing now, she wondered. Preparing for the ball—and a new bride?

"You mentioned that most of the nobles busy themselves with gossip and balls," she said, in as casual a tone as she could muster. "Is the prince like them?"

"Prince Charles? Oh, no, no, he's nothing like that."

"What . . . what do you know about him?"

Louisa dipped her needle into the sleeve she was working on, then tied a finishing knot. "Not much. He's been away at the Royal University for years. All I know is he wasn't happy about the ball."

"Why not?"

"It's all rumors, of course. But the king threw the ball the night the prince returned and invited every eligible maiden to attend. The prince didn't have an inkling that it was happening until the night of, and everyone said he yawned during the introductions. I wouldn't blame him—he must have been so tired from his journey home! A couple of the girls slipped out for half an hour to watch—they think he was about to leave entirely until he met the runaway princess."

Cinderella wished everyone would stop calling her a princess. "Did you see her?"

"Only at a glance." Louisa laughed. "My fingers were sore from all that sewing for the ball, so I left just as she arrived. I thought she was just a tardy noble. I could kick myself for missing all the fun." She gave Cinderella sidelong glance. "But I'm going to stay longer this time."

"What about what your aunt said?"

"I'll be careful, and I'm not the only one who's sneaking out. After two parties in quick succession, who knows when the next one will be?" Louisa rifled through the basket Madame Irmina had left and fished out a dress. It wasn't as sumptuous as the gown with the pearl trimming she'd danced with earlier, but the color matched her hazel eyes. "Look, the perfect gown just happened to land at my feet."

"It's beautiful," Cinderella breathed.

Pressing the dress against herself, Louisa grinned. "You heard my aunt: this basket's for next week. No one will miss it." She tilted her head thoughtfully. "If I tuck in the bodice a little, and add some lace to the sleeves . . . it'll be just right for the ball. Will you come with me? It'll be more fun if we go together."

"Oh, I couldn't. I can't risk it . . . I need this job." Cinderella trained her gaze on the sleeve she was repairing. "I don't have an aunt who'll protect me if I get in trouble."

"Just for an hour?" Louisa pleaded. "Everyone's invited, technically. Even us. Madame Irmina can't fire us for that, no matter how much she wants to. She didn't fire the girls who slipped out last time."

"But . . ."

How could she tell Louisa that *she* was the mysterious princess? A part of her *did* want to go to the ball, even if the prince didn't recognize her—just to spend time with her new friends.

But a part of her also worried that her stepmother would be there.

"My stepmother," Cinderella finally admitted. "You asked if I had a home to go back to. I don't, but I do have a family." She stared at her hands. "My stepmother . . . she'll be looking for me."

Sensing something was wrong, Louisa set down her work and sat beside Cinderella. "You sound afraid of her."

"She wasn't good to me." Cinderella swallowed, remembering. "My papa was lucky in his work and made a small fortune as a merchant. When he first married my stepmother, he helped her pay off her first husband's debts. After he died, she took over the household, but she didn't have any interest in taking over his business. Instead, she squandered the money on jewels for herself and dresses for her daughters. Times were difficult, and she had to dismiss most of the help. 'Cinderella, we must all do our part,' she told me. 'My daughters are delicate creatures, but seeing as you are so strong, you must help with the housework for now.'

" 'For now' became ten years. Along with the housework, I did the sewing and the mending, the cleaning and the cooking . . . I even took care of the chickens and the cows."

"You were a servant for your family," said Louisa with a little gasp.

"It wasn't so bad," Cinderella began, but as soon as she said it, she realized that wasn't true. It had been *terrible*; she'd just tried not to acknowledge it.

"Not so bad?" Louisa said. "That sounds *horrible*." She scooted her stool closer to Cinderella's and lowered her voice. "So you ran away. What made you finally decide enough was enough?"

Cinderella pursed her lips, an ache rising in her chest. The truth hurt. "She wanted to sell me."

"Sell you?" Louisa's eyes bulged.

"She hired a man to take me away from Aurelais." Cinderella clutched her skirt, recalling the terrifying night and her harrowing escape. "Someplace so far I wouldn't be able to come back."

Horror etched itself on Louisa's face, and she squeezed Cinderella's arm.

"It's all right," said Cinderella, but her voice trembled as she spoke. "That's how you found me on the road. . . . I jumped out of the coach and tumbled onto the street. It was raining hard, and Bruno and I didn't have anywhere to go."

"You're safe now," promised Louisa. "You won't ever have to go back."

Cinderella nodded mutely and started to reach for another garment to sew, but Louisa kept her hand on her arm.

"I can't promise tonight's masquerade will erase what awful things your stepmother's done to you, but it will be a start. Don't let fear of my aunt be what's keeping you from going to the ball. She acts tough because it's her job, but she's soft at heart."

"Really?"

"If she catches us at the ball, we might get extra chores . . . but it'll be worth it for a night to remember. She was young once, too, though it's hard to imagine."

Cinderella chuckled. "Was she a troublemaker like you?"

"Mama says she was worse! How she ended up in charge of Blooms and Looms is a miracle." Louisa clasped her hands. "If you see your stepmother at the ball, tell me and we'll leave right away. Friends watch over each other."

That made Cinderella smile. She couldn't remember the last time she'd had a true human friend. It'd been years since she'd had someone her age she could talk to.

It would be nice to go with Louisa. Cinderella pursed her lips, considering. And besides, while she was there, she could see what the Grand Duke was up to. Perhaps she could discover something useful for either the duchess or her godmother.

"You know what?" she said slowly. "You're right. I will go."

Louisa clapped her hands with delight. "Do you want to meet at sundown?"

Her spirits buoyed, Cinderella smiled at her friend. "Yes."

"I'll come to your room," promised Louisa. "I have the perfect dress in mind for you."

Chapter Twenty-One

Dusk fell swiftly, and as the rumbling of carriages arriving outside the ballroom pierced the palace's usual calm—reaching even Cinderella's ears as she outfitted the duchess in her royal accoutrements—she grew more and more anxious.

"You keep looking out the window," rebuked Genevieve. "Are diamonds falling from the sky, or is there some other reason I am unworthy of your attention?"

"Neither, Your Highness," Cinderella replied, chastened.

With a frown, the duchess examined the chignon Cinderella had arranged. "Hmm. It'll do. But good heavens, you certainly are distracted this evening. You've missed a button." Genevieve lifted her chin so Cinderella could refasten the back of her collar. "You're jumpy as a catfish, girl, and you're not even the one being welcomed back to court!"

Unable to deny it, Cinderella bit her lip.

"What is it?" persisted the duchess. "Are you planning to sneak into the ball?"

"Is it sneaking if all the eligible young ladies in the kingdom are invited?"

Genevieve arched an elegant eyebrow and bent to stroke Bruno's ears. "That was the last ball, Cindergirl. This one is expressly by invitation only. That way if any young lady decides to dash off, Charles will at least know her name."

As if he understood the duchess's barbed remark, Bruno sank deeper into his cushioned bed. Cinderella wished she could do the same.

"I was only going to go for an hour with a friend. I've never—"

"No more." Genevieve held up her fan, silencing Cinderella. "I do not want to be an accomplice in your illicit outing. I'm sure Madame Irmina has given you girls her fair warning about sneaking out to the ball."

"She has," Cinderella said. A twinge of panic riddled her nerves. "Ma'am, I—"

"I said I don't want to hear it." The duchess sprang from

her seat, gliding toward a ribboned box that Cinderella had brought to her chambers earlier.

"Open this," she ordered Cinderella.

Carefully undoing the ribbon, Cinderella lifted the box's lid. Inside were three masks. The duchess removed two, holding them up.

"I had these made for the masquerade, but the shopkeeper was overzealous and sent me too many. I only need one." Genevieve laid the masks side by side on the table. The green one was decorated with peacock feathers accented with violet and indigo gems, and the white one resembled a swan; its feathers were opalescent, with a band of black velvet around the eyes.

"They're beautiful," Cinderella said admiringly.

"Take them. One for you and one for your friend."

Cinderella drew a sharp breath, surprised by the duchess's offer. "I couldn't."

"Take them, Cindergirl. That's an order." Genevieve pushed the masks into her hands. "If you're going to break the rules, do it properly—and with style. Besides, they don't go with my gown."

Cinderella brushed her fingers over the swan mask's delicate feathers. "Thank you, Your Highness."

"No need to thank me. Just make sure when you report to work tomorrow morning you have your head out of the clouds. Off you go. My nephew will be here to escort me to the ball any moment now."

At the mention of Prince Charles, Cinderella's heart skipped a beat. Part of her wanted to encounter him again, and part of her dreaded it more than anything.

"Yes, ma'am." She curtsied. "I hope you have a grand time."

The clock struck eight as Cinderella hurried back to her room, where Louisa, already dressed for the ball, was waiting.

"You look beautiful!" exclaimed Cinderella.

"Keep your voice down," whispered her friend, though she beamed at the compliment. "Aunt Irmina's still upstairs." Then Louisa twirled, showing off her olive-green gown and the gold trimming she'd added to its cuffs. "Wait until you see yours."

"I've got something, too. Look what the duchess gave us." Cinderella opened the hatbox, and Louisa's eyes widened.

"They're exquisite," she breathed, picking up the swan mask. "This will go wonderfully with your dress."

Louisa stepped aside, lifting the pale pink gown draped over Cinderella's changing screen. Its fluted sleeves shimmered with tiny crystals overlaid upon the gossamer silk, and the skirt, dappled with gentle threads of silver, seemed to dance off the candlelight against the wooden floor.

"How did you—"

"One of my mother's customers ate too many oysters and fell ill," explained Louisa with a mischievous glint in her eye. "Won't hurt anyone if you borrow her dress for a few hours."

"I couldn't possibly—"

"Yes, you could. Mama's already agreed to let you have it for the night. You're not allowed to refuse."

Touched, Cinderella pressed the gown's soft silk to her chest. "I guess in that case . . ."

"Hurry and put it on before Aunt Irmina gets back."

Eager to comply, Cinderella slipped behind the changing screen. The gown was still warm from having been pressed, and the ruffles tickled her collarbone as she slipped it onto her body.

"I had a feeling it'd be just your size." Louisa surveyed Cinderella with an approving eye. "But it's missing something. A shawl maybe, or a necklace."

A necklace. Cinderella opened her dresser drawer for her mother's beads. "Will this do?"

"Oh, that's very nice," said Louisa. "The perfect finishing touch."

While she clasped the beads around her neck, Cinderella

glanced at herself in the mirror. The pink dress was elegant and understated, its shape slim and formfitting—unlike the billowy skirts on the ball gown her fairy godmother had conjured for her. That suited her just fine. She wasn't going to the masquerade to catch the prince's eye.

Or at least that's what I keep telling myself. The thought slipped into her mind before she could stop it.

Cinderella took in a deep breath, trying to relax all the tension gathered in her shoulders. Her toes wriggled in her shoes. No glass slippers this time; her shoes were made of leftover scraps of satin and, for good measure, she'd added a band over the ankles so they wouldn't fall off.

Then again, she wasn't planning on having to dash off at midnight this time.

A touch of wistfulness came over Cinderella as she and Louisa arrived in the ballroom. It was just as magnificent as she remembered: a crystal chandelier hung from the ceiling, reflecting brilliantly upon the marble floor, making it seem like she was walking among the stars.

She scanned the room, searching first for the Grand Duke and then for her stepmother. No sign of Lady Tremaine and her daughters.

With a sigh of relief, Cinderella adjusted her mask, the feathers tickling her cheeks as she tied it tight behind her hair.

"Are you sure no one will recognize us?" she asked Louisa.

"I'm certain. Stop fretting!"

Cinderella fidgeted with her mask one last time and inhaled. There was no need to worry. They had taken a secret entrance into the ballroom, one used most frequently by the servants who served the king on his private balcony, so no one had seen them arrive. Not to mention the mask! There were so many people—all wearing masks—that even if her stepmother and stepsisters were present, chances were slim they'd recognize her.

She swept her fingers against the marble balustrade, her shoes sinking into the plush carpet as she and Louisa descended one of the ballroom staircases. Last time, she'd been so caught up in the moment that she barely had time to absorb and admire her surroundings.

How foolish I was, she thought. *I didn't even know he was the prince! I didn't bother wondering why the orchestra started playing the moment we began to dance, or why there was no one else on the floor with us.*

She wouldn't be so foolish anymore.

The orchestra had begun a waltz, the violins swelling into a lilting melody, but there was to be no dancing until the duchess made her appearance.

"Why does everyone keep looking to the door?"

Cinderella asked, but she knew the answer as soon as the words left her.

"Everyone is waiting to see whether the lady with the glass slipper will show up tonight. The entire household is betting on it."

"What do you think?"

"I have fifty silver aurels on it." Louisa's eyes glittered behind her mask. "What about you?"

"I . . . I don't think so."

"Come on, some of the girls are over by the buffet. Smart idea to get some nourishment before the dancing starts!"

Cinderella had started to follow Louisa when, out of the corner of her eye, she spied the Grand Duke perched on a private balcony beside a portly elderly man, speaking in hushed tones as his companion observed the assembly with a pair of binoculars.

Could that be the king? she wondered. Given the older man's uniform, pinned with so many medals it weighed down his shoulders, it had to be.

She touched Louisa's shoulder. "Why don't you go first? I want to explore a little."

"Shall I come with you?"

"No, I won't be long. I . . . I just want to catch a glimpse of the king."

"Don't take too long." Louisa shot Cinderella a sly

smile. "Our kingdom's most eligible bachelor will make his appearance with his aunt soon. You won't want to miss that."

Louisa spun away and missed the deep flush that colored Cinderella's cheeks at the mention of the prince.

Composing herself, Cinderella pursued her mission of spying on the Grand Duke and returned to the secret door through which she and Louisa had entered. Located in one of the ballroom's many anterooms, it looked like an ordinary wall panel, marked only by an ivory knob in the center. Inside was a network of narrow tunnels that Cinderella didn't dare explore lest she get lost. After retracing her steps, she cracked open the door a hair, just in time to hear the duke say:

"If I may say so, Your Majesty, I saw the young prince with your sister. They were riding into the city yesterday morning, and since then, he hasn't been himself."

"What are you trying to say?"

The duke took out his monocle and wiped it clean with a handkerchief. "As I've been trying to tell you, your sister's influence on the prince concerns me. Fortunately, I have invited the Princess of Lourdes to attend—"

"I do not want to hear this, Ferdinand. Just let me have my hour's worth of peace and quiet."

"But you must listen, sire." The duke lowered his voice,

and Cinderella couldn't make out his next words, but the color suddenly drained from King George's face.

Oh, no. Cinderella swallowed hard. The duke must have discovered what Genevieve had been trying to hide from him—that the king was planning to abdicate.

Her heart hammering in her ears, she dared open the door a fraction wider.

Her suspicion was verified by the king's next words: "Does Charles know?"

"He will not have heard it from me."

"Do you think he *should* know?"

A long, deliberate pause. "No."

Before she could hear more of their conversation, the king disappeared behind a curtained partition, and from the top of the ballroom staircase, the royal crier announced, "The Duchess Genevieve d'Orlanne, sister of His Royal Majesty, King George-Louis Philippe, honorable and beloved sovereign of Aurelais."

Brass fanfares trumpeted across the chamber, startling Cinderella, who quickly exited the secret panel to join the rest of the guests in greeting the duchess.

The Duchess of Orlanne had donned a black mask with silver whiskers, and she descended the staircase regally, fluttering a matching fan with feathers so long they nearly brushed against the carpet. At her side was Prince Charles, wearing a white mask that covered the upper half of his face.

As the fanfare faded, the orchestra resumed its incidental music until the prince and the duchess reached the dance floor. Then a slow triple beat emerged from the orchestra's lush harmonies.

Cinderella watched the prince dance with his aunt, hiding a smile. The harsh angles that typically lined the duchess's mouth eased away, and Cinderella saw a trace of the cheerful, mischievous young duchess from the portrait gallery.

Then, as they danced, Genevieve whispered something in the prince's ear. Cinderella flinched, having a strong feeling the duchess was telling him to forget "her."

Tearing her gaze from the dance floor, Cinderella wove through the crowd to look for Louisa, but she didn't see her friend by the buffet.

"Her relationship with the king was never a good one," murmured a lady blocking Cinderella's path, "but she was best friends with the queen. After Her Majesty passed away, she and King George had a terrible row and that was the end of that."

"I heard it had to do with her husband. He was one of those ruffian intellectuals—even got himself in jail once, remember? The king had to create a new territory to knight him so it wouldn't be so disgraceful for Genevieve to marry beneath her. You'd think she would have been more grateful."

"Well, who knows what happened between them? It was all very hush-hush."

"Married to that traitor, I would be, too! Maybe we'll find out now that she's back."

The conversation flustered Cinderella. She didn't know what bothered her more: their spiteful words about the duchess's past, or their disdain that her husband had been a commoner.

Both, she decided, finally spying a way around the noblewomen.

Behind her, the prince's dance with his aunt came to an end, and polite applause rolled across the room. Then, as soon as it was considered tasteful, every eligible lady in the ballroom pushed her way forward, batting her fan to get the prince's attention.

Cinderella backed into a corner so the waves of eager young women wouldn't trample her as they rushed forward. Jewels glittered and a mix of rich perfume and desperation filled the air. Every lady parading past the prince was attractive in her own way, be it a lovely face or a stunning gown. If the prince was looking for a new bride, he had hundreds to choose from.

Stop thinking about it. That's not your concern anymore.

The problem was she didn't see Louisa anywhere. She had started toward the back, where the buffet and a chocolate fountain awaited, when she noticed the Grand Duke had detached himself from the king's side and was now speaking with a young woman wearing a tiara.

Who was he speaking to?

Before Cinderella could investigate further, three flamboyantly dressed women paraded across the ballroom. Though they wore masks, Cinderella would have recognized those auburn ringlets, those black curls, and that tight gray bun anywhere—but the familiar blue and green feathers, the blue-gray shroud, and the haughty, upturned noses only confirmed it. A tide of panic washed over her.

It was Lady Tremaine—and her daughters.

Chapter Twenty-Two

Blood rushed to her head as Cinderella ducked behind one of the ballroom's towering flower arrangements. Only after the count of three did she dare glance back at her stepmother and stepsisters.

Good, they hadn't seen her.

Catching her breath, she edged along the table and searched the area for Louisa.

She did say she'd be by the food, didn't she? thought Cinderella, stepping back for a better view of the buffet. Her heel landed hard on someone's shoe, and she spun around, horrified as the stranger let out a quiet gasp of pain.

"Oh, pardon me!" she exclaimed. "I'm so sorry—"

The stranger's mask slipped off, and Cinderella's knees dipped instinctively into a crouch, her fingers reaching out to catch it before it fell. The string hooked over her thumb, and in triumph, she held out the mask to the stranger.

"Here—" she began.

Her breath caught in her throat as she looked up. It was the prince!

He had changed his clothing in an apparent attempt to go incognito, doffing the ivory jacket with gold epaulets for a simple blue coat with bronze buttons. But she would have recognized that face in any outfit.

"Thank you kindly," said Charles, also half crouched. He started to rise to take the mask from her, but she was so startled to see him that she dropped it, and this time it fell to the ground.

Her hand leapt to her mouth. "I'm sorry," she uttered quickly. "That was clumsy of me."

Thankfully, the prince laughed. "I'll get it. It seems to have a mind of its own."

Prince Charles picked up his mask and pressed it against his face, quickly tying the string behind his head. Then, as he rose, he finally looked up and into her eyes—

And he let out a quiet gasp. "It's you."

Her heart skipped a beat. What should she say? What should she do? Her legs were frozen in their spot, and if not for the table behind her, she was afraid she would have stumbled over her own two feet.

"It's you," Prince Charles repeated in wonderment, his expression softening. He cleared his throat, a distinct rush of red coloring his ears as he realized he was staring at her. When he spoke again, his voice grew even gentler. "I thought I recognized your voice. I . . . I hoped I would see you again."

Cinderella could have sworn the room was floating, and she with it. The glowing chandeliers swam around her, their lights blinking like stars.

He hadn't forgotten her. He recognized her. And moreover, he seemed happy to see her.

Her lips parted. He was waiting for her to respond, but what could she possibly say? How could she explain why she'd left the other night, and why he hadn't been able to find her?

He hasn't asked you for an explanation, she chided herself.

"H-hello," she said, hoping he wouldn't hear how her heart hammered. The simple greeting instantly made his face brighten, and she wondered whether he could have possibly worried the same—that *she* had forgotten him.

"Hello," returned the prince.

Before he could say more, a server appeared with a tray of fresh glasses. Charles gestured at it, and as he offered her a glass of water, his hand trembled slightly—the only sign that he was as nervous as she was. "Were you . . . thirsty?"

Cinderella smiled shyly. "No, thank you. I was just looking for someone. A friend."

"A friend?"

"Yes. She came to the ball with me. But I think she might have made her way to the dance floor."

Charles set the glass down. "Let me accompany you there to find her—and selfishly steal a dance for myself if I may."

Yes, she wanted to say. She desperately wanted to dance with him, to talk with him, to get to know him better. And yet . . . the duchess's words haunted her.

I think he's in love with the idea of her.

Well, the same could be said of Cinderella, too, for what did she know of the prince?

Nothing. After one kiss, you were imagining yourself his bride. It's a good thing the Grand Duke never asked you to try on the glass slipper. You would have fallen into a dream with a harsh awakening.

No good could come of their meeting. She was a servant in the palace, he the only heir to the throne of Aurelais. Maybe if she made an excuse to leave, she could run back to the servants' quarters and pretend this had never happened.

Then, right as she'd gathered her resolve, a smile lifted Charles's warm brown eyes, and she melted.

"Cat caught your tongue?" he prodded softly. "Or are you looking for the prince?"

His gentle teasing set her heart at ease.

"Your Highness, I apologize. I didn't—"

"Don't bow, and don't apologize." His words carried no trace of admonishment, only relief. "You have no idea how glad I am you're here."

Rather bashfully, he extended his arm for her to take. "It seems for once the Grand Duke's done me a favor."

"What do you mean?"

Prince Charles gestured in the Grand Duke's direction.

"He's searching for you," Cinderella murmured, stating the obvious, still not understanding. "He doesn't look happy."

"See that girl behind him?"

Cinderella craned her neck to look. Yes, the same young lady with the tiara she had noticed earlier.

"I was hiding in the corner of the ballroom, trying to dodge Ferdinand's ploys to have me dance with her. If not for his scheming, I might never have seen you again."

Cinderella's blush deepened. She stared at her hand, resting comfortably on the prince's arm. "It looks like they're waiting for you," she said quietly.

"And *I've* been waiting for you," replied Charles. He gestured at her mask. "A swan. It suits you."

"I didn't have many choices. It was either a swan or a peacock."

The prince leaned closer, speaking softly. "Swans were my mother's favorite birds. She used to tell me that once they fall in love, they stay in love forever."

A fanfare pierced the ballroom's din—and Cinderella's thoughts. "Announcing the Princess Marie of Lourdes."

A young man dressed like the crown prince of Aurelais bowed to greet the princess, and Cinderella whirled toward the prince, blinking back her confusion. "But you're here."

The prince laughed. "Pierre was kind enough to exchange clothes with me for the night. I must say, having a loyal attendant who looks like me has come in handy." He gestured at the young man in the white mask standing stiffly beside the king's throne as introductions were made. The princess was clearly waiting for him to ask her to dance, but Pierre stifled a yawn instead.

"He's doing too good a job of impersonating me," said Charles, amused.

Dozens of ladies surrounded the fake prince, and even from the outskirts of the ballroom, Cinderella could hear them crying, "Your Highness! Do you remember me?"

"Poor Pierre."

"I think he rather enjoys it," said Charles wryly. "Anyway, I'll make it up to him. For now, let's take advantage of our disguises, shall we? Would you do me the honor of a dance?"

She touched her mask nervously. Hundreds of guests filled the ballroom, their faces blurred by candlelight. Cinderella scanned the crowd for her stepmother and stepsisters, but she couldn't find them.

Stop worrying, she told herself. *Enjoy the moment.*

"You aren't still worried that you've forgotten how to dance, are you?" Charles smiled. "I know for a fact you haven't."

Cinderella blushed, surprised he had remembered their conversation from the first ball. Still, the joke relaxed her, and she smiled back at him. "No, I'm not."

Then she took his arm, letting a whirlwind of excitement sweep over her as they began to dance.

Was she imagining it, or had the music suddenly gotten more lush and romantic? The violins seemed to swoon with her every step, or maybe she was simply happy. Happy to have found Charles again, to have this second chance with him.

She wanted to get to know him. It had become apparent that she hardly knew anything about him other than what *everyone* knew about the prince: that every morning he rode his horse across the palace grounds, that he had been close to his mother, that he didn't enjoy attending royal balls.

But where to start? Their conversation now certainly wasn't stilted, but she was forcing herself to be polite and on her best behavior. Was it because he was the prince, and now she couldn't help being more nervous and thus more ceremonious than before?

"What's on your mind?"

He sounded tentative, as if he were worried she'd run off again.

She smiled shyly at him, becoming all too aware of how her heart skipped when their eyes met. It was like they were meeting for the first time. The night could stretch as long as it needed to this time; Cinderella did not have to be back by midnight. She had no magic spell to worry about, and knowing her stepmother and stepsisters, they were too busy fawning over and following the imposter prince.

And yet . . . there were hundreds of people in the ballroom. The music swam in her ears, the murmurs of other dancing couples buzzing. Over the prince's shoulder, she finally spied Louisa waving at her from the edge of the floor. Her friend had found her own dance partner, and she winked at Cinderella, mouthing, *Who is he?*

Flustered, Cinderella pretended not to understand, and she turned to the prince. "Could we . . . could we walk through the gardens again?" she asked. "It was so lovely the last time."

"I rather enjoyed the walk myself," said the prince. "It'll be good to get away from here. It's hard to talk over the music."

Soon the ballroom glittered behind them, a silvery dome beyond the labyrinth of rose-studded bushes, leafy hedges, and marble fountains.

A cool breeze tickled the back of Cinderella's neck, gently rattling her green beads.

"My mother would really love it out here," she sighed.

"Do you still help her tend her garden?"

"No, she passed away years ago."

"I lost mine at a young age, too," said Charles. He removed his mask, slipping it into his coat pocket.

"I remember," Cinderella said softly. Though everyone had loved the gentle queen—and no one more than the prince—their mothers had died in the same year, and Cinderella recalled wondering if everyone in the town was wearing black to mourn her mama. "My father used to tell me that my mother was in heaven with the queen. He had a feeling they'd become friends, and they would watch over each other. That helped a little, to think that she was in a good place."

"Were you very lonely without your mother?"

"Yes," Cinderella admitted. "We did everything together when she was alive. She'd take me out to the gardens to play on our swing. She could name every bird in the sky and paint them, too. We were supposed to travel Aurelais together and collect flowers from every city, then paint them once we returned home." She swallowed at the memory, one she had long forgotten until now. "Papa used to tease us for always being lost in our imaginations together. I still have a bad habit of falling into my daydreams." Before he could ask her more, she said, "Were you . . . lonely?"

"Yes, but you wouldn't have thought so if you'd been there. I was always surrounded by people. Tutors, advisers—everyone sought to shape how I thought because I'll be the future king. There was no one I could really . . ."

"Talk to?" Cinderella finished for him.

Charles smiled. "Exactly."

"I understand. Better than you know."

Shadows flickered across the manicured bushes, and a chill swept over Cinderella. "What was that?"

"I don't know." Creeping up toward the bushes, the prince surveyed the area. He grimaced. "The Grand Duke again, I'd wager. He must have talked to Pierre and gotten suspicious." He stood. "Let's get away from here. Why don't I show you more of the grounds?"

Cinderella nodded. "I'd like that."

Little by little, her nervousness faded, and she laughed when the prince told her how he used to run into the garden when he was a little boy, chased after by his tutors.

"I loathed my history lessons," he confessed. "All the tutors always trying to impress upon me that I was related to these great kings, all of them with the same names. Always a variation of George, Louis, Charles, and George again. At least it made my exams easier." The prince chuckled. "I must be boring you."

"You're not," she assured him. "Though history was my favorite."

Her father had hired tutors for her, but soon after he had died, her stepmother had put an end to her education. Sometimes, when she had to dust the library, she'd pore through the books on the shelves when no one was looking. Her stepmother had sold off the valuable ones long ago, but Lady Tremaine recognized that books looked impressive to the few guests they had to the house, so she'd kept them as decoration—at least until she caught Cinderella reading them.

"My father traveled often when he was alive," Cinderella explained, "and he used to bring me curios from all over the world and tell me their histories. I loved it."

"Then maybe you'll appreciate this," Charles replied as he directed her through the endless maze of marble stairs and pruned hedges. They soon found themselves before a glorious fountain of angels, illuminated by a constellation of silver lanterns and surrounded by a coronet of swans with wreathes of ivy over their elegant necks. Water tinkled steadily from the sides, like soft percussion against the wind's song.

"This fountain was commissioned by my great-grandfather," said Prince Charles. "Aurelais had just ended a twenty-year-long war with its neighbors, and he had this fountain made to celebrate peace, but also to remind us of the bitter costs of war."

Cinderella brushed her fingertips against the water, its gentle ripples tickling her skin. "Like the fountain in the city center! My father used to take me there when I was young." She folded her hands over her lap. "I haven't been back there in many years."

"I'll take you one day. Though I have to confess, I don't get a chance to visit the center of the city much. It is not easy to go around without being recognized."

"But you have Pierre," Cinderella joked.

"Pierre can only fool so many. Unfortunately, he doesn't have much luck with my father or the Grand Duke." He gently guided her away from the fountain. "There's something else I want to show you."

They walked through the gardens, the lilting music

from the ballroom growing softer and farther away. Whenever he thought she wasn't looking, he stole a glimpse of her, his lips parted.

"It's been a long time since I could talk to anyone this way," he confessed. "Without feeling like I was . . . different."

"What about at the Royal University?" As soon as the question left her lips, Cinderella blushed, realizing she'd revealed how much she'd asked about him. "I mean, I heard that you'd been studying away from the palace for several years."

A grin widened on Charles's face, his eyes brightening so much Cinderella swore they shone. He took a deep breath. "Even when I was a child, I never had many friends at school. All the boys were ordered not to offend me and to always agree with what I said. I used to beg my father to send me abroad and give me a different name, but he always refused.

"He didn't understand that I simply wanted to fit in. When I arrived at the university, I tried enrolling under a false name, but it was no use. I could have said my name were Peter the Pauper and everyone would have still known who I was. I could have never set foot in the classroom or opened one of my textbooks and still have passed every course with honors."

"So you made no friends?"

"I had a few," he said. "But even then, we weren't close." His gaze met hers, and there was such tenderness in his warm brown eyes that Cinderella wished time could stop so she could memorize the way he was looking at her. "I don't feel that way with you. I feel like I've been looking for you my entire life."

His confession sang in Cinderella's ears, the intensity of his words arresting her in her place. "I know the feeling," she whispered.

A chime punctuated the end of her words, and she instinctively looked up the clock tower. It was midnight.

She lurched, giving in to a momentary flare of panic before remembering that the time didn't matter. She didn't have a magical curfew—no coach that would turn into a pumpkin, no horses that would turn back into mice, and no glittering ball gown that would turn into rags at the stroke of twelve. She could stay out all night if she wished.

Finally, they arrived at the end of the garden, and not far from the entrance of the palace, a glittering glass box atop a marble pedestal awaited.

"This is what I wanted to show you," Charles said, unlocking the box and lifting her lost glass slipper. "I believe this belongs to you."

Cinderella held the shoe close, treasuring it. "I wanted to bring the other slipper to the duke when he was searching for me, but it shattered, and I worried . . . I worried I'd lost the only keepsake I had of the most wonderful night of my life in years. I thought I'd never see it again. I thought I'd never see *you* again."

"You'll never have to worry about finding me ever again. I promise." Charles gestured at the slipper, then at a nearby bench. "May I?"

With a shy nod, Cinderella returned the slipper to him. A soft breeze swept past her mask, and she lifted it, letting the cool wind temper the heat in her cheeks.

Neither of them had made a move toward the bench, and Cinderella, ignoring the sudden swoop in her stomach as she realized Charles was staring tenderly at her, sprang onto her toes and kissed his cheek.

When she let him go, the prince rocked back on his heels dazedly, clutching the glass slipper against him as if he feared he'd drop it. "What was that for?"

"A thank-you," replied Cinderella, smiling at the confused but happy-looking prince. "For reminding me that not all miracles have to end at midnight. I'll explain—"

Charles drew her close, and her voice drifted.

"I'll explain . . . later . . ."

As he bent forward to kiss her, trees rustled, and the click-clack of heeled shoes stomped nearby. Cinderella lifted her head, distracted by the sound. Voices—in the near distance—rose above the ripple of fountain water in strident tones. "There she is! Anastasia, Drizella—follow me."

Cinderella immediately lurched, untangling herself from Charles's embrace. Her vision reeled; the moon became watery, the hedges a haze of green.

Panicking, she twisted away from the prince, but his fingers were laced with hers, so gently she could have pulled hers away . . . but she didn't just yet.

"What is it?" he asked. "What's the matter?"

What's the matter? The familiar words echoed inside her. It was the question he had asked before she'd fled from the last ball.

She faltered, not knowing what to say, not knowing how to explain.

Charles bent to retrieve her mask, which she must have dropped when he kissed her. He held it out to her in both hands, but when still she wavered, confusion knit itself in the prince's brows. Confusion—and hurt.

"Hurry, girls!" Lady Tremaine's voice cut through the garden.

Remorse burned in her throat. The thought of hurting him again tore at her. But she couldn't risk an encounter with her stepmother. She wanted to tell him who she was— she'd meant to, but she'd thought they would have more time. Now she recognized her error, and it was too late.

"I'm sorry, but I—I . . . I have to go."

"Wait, please." Charles held out the mask to her. "I . . . I don't even know your name."

"It's Cin—"

"Your Highness!"

At the sound of her stepsister's shrill call, Cinderella panicked and drew away her hand from the prince. The mask slid from her fingers, falling into the pond beneath the bridge.

And, for the second time, before he could stop her, she rushed down the stairs.

Chapter Twenty-Three

Her heart thundering in her ears, Cinderella dashed across the royal gardens, making for the servants' quarters. Even when Drizella's and Anastasia's shouts had faded, she didn't stop.

Follow the clock tower north, Louisa had instructed her, *then make a left at the purple tulips.*

Cinderella trained her eyes up at the clock, its iron hands ticking minutes past midnight. By the time she reached the purple tulips, she was out of breath, her lungs tight with exhaustion. The entrance to Blooms and Looms was just ahead, the sentries she'd encountered when she first arrived still standing guard.

"Look, it's the new girl. Trying to get back before Madame Irmina does her curfew check?"

"Y-yes . . ."

He chuckled. "You're a bit late for that, I think. Luckily, you're not the only one who sneaked out—"

Cinderella's eyes widened. "Did Louisa . . . ?"

"Got off with a warning from Irmina hours ago. She's gone home already."

"Oh." Relief swept over her.

"Don't worry," said the guard kindly. "Irmina won't discharge you for going to the ball. If she did that, she'd have not a soul left working for her. But I would expect a stiff talking-to in the morning."

Cinderella offered him a faint smile.

Shuffling into her room, she took off her borrowed dress and flung it over her chair. Then, burying her face in her hands, she collapsed onto her bed.

The moment she'd heard her stepsisters, her first instinct had been to run away. But should she have stayed? She could have explained things to him before dashing off. Or at least told him her name.

It doesn't matter. It's best he doesn't find out who I am . . . a maid in his own home.

And why not? she countered herself. *Am I afraid he'd never want to see me again?*

Cinderella shook her head, hardly able to believe that she was wrestling against her own feelings. *No, I'm not. Because he isn't like that.*

She clenched her fists, remembering how he hadn't recognized her when she'd worn her palace uniform. A cord of bitterness knotted in her throat.

Sooner or later, he would find out who she was. For all she knew, her stepsisters had recognized her and told him already.

Would Charles have her dismissed from the palace if he knew the truth? Would he ever want to see her again?

Lady Tremaine's words rang in her head over and over. *An orphan and a servant. Who would want you?*

She gritted her teeth at the memory. Knowing her stepmother, she'd tell the prince that Cinderella was a thief and a liar, a troublemaker who deserved to be sent away for good.

No one's come for me, she reasoned, curling up against the wall tiredly. Her hands went up to her neck, clutching her mother's beads. *They didn't see me. They only saw the prince.*

Uncertain what tomorrow would bring, she finally closed her eyes, drifting along the edges of her dreams until sleep finally claimed her.

"Get up, get up!" cried Madame Irmina, rapping on her door.

Cinderella sprang up from her bed. The green beads rattled over her chest, and she quickly stuffed them into her pocket before greeting Louisa's aunt.

Irmina scowled at her. "Amelia has taken ill, so we need an extra serving girl at breakfast this morning. That means you, Cinderella."

Cinderella's gaze flew up. "Me? Serve the royal family breakfast? I couldn't. I—the duchess is waiting for me—"

"Well, you'll have to deal with two shifts, won't you?" Irmina said, crossing her arms. "And, for not being in bed by curfew, I've a list of extra tasks for you after breakfast. Now hurry up and change. I expect you in the main hall in five minutes."

Five minutes later, harried footsteps pattered outside her door, followed by another knock.

"I'm the worst friend," Louisa cried. "One of the valets last night told us Madame Irmina was about to do her curfew check. I couldn't find you."

Cinderella swallowed. This wasn't the time or place to tell her about the prince. Already her head was throbbing with panic over what she'd do when she had to serve him breakfast.

I'll keep my head down, she said, inhaling. *And I'll hide behind the other girls if I have to. He won't see me.*

"Cinderella?" said Louisa. "Are you listening?"

"It's all right," she assured her friend quickly. "I can handle the extra work."

Together, they assembled in the main hall, along with a dozen other girls who'd stolen out to the ball.

One by one, Madame Irmina doled out their punishments. When at last she reached Cinderella, her mouth thinned into a tight, disappointed line. "When I set rules, I expect them to be followed. That goes especially for new hires such as yourself. Here I was starting to think there might be some hope for you."

Cinderella felt heat rush to her cheeks.

The bells chimed for the serving maids to get to work, and Madame Irmina threw an apron and Amelia's orange sash at her, then pushed a tray into Cinderella's arms. "Once you finish serving breakfast, report here immediately for the rest of your extra tasks."

"The dress is in my room," whispered Cinderella to Louisa as she tied on the orange sash. "I'll bring it to you after I'm finished with the breakfast service."

"Follow me." Madame Irmina grabbed her by the sleeve, dragging her toward the kitchen. She motioned at a large tray sitting on one of the shelves, heavy with jams, a porcelain teapot, teacups, pastries, and silverware, all meticulously arranged.

"Bring that into the royal hall," said Irmina. "And for the love of God, don't drop it!"

Cinderella was more than up to that task, at least. Years of balancing trays—one in each hand for her stepsisters, and one on her head for her stepmother—made short work of one platter.

She picked it up easily and wove into the line of servants carrying breakfast into the royal dining hall.

Keep your eyes down, she warned herself, but it was impossible to follow her own advice. The first thing she did when she entered the dining room was search for the prince.

Her eyes picked him out easily; he sat to his father's right, his fingers clutching the thin handle of his teacup. Though he wasn't drinking.

Seeing him, her stomach flipped. She couldn't face him again, not so soon after the masquerade the night before. What would she tell him? How would she explain her running away—for the second time? Worse yet, how would he react upon learning that she was a servant in the palace? In front of his father . . .

And the Grand Duke.

Fighting the urge to duck behind a column, she fell slightly out of sync with the other servants processing into the hall. She hurried forward to catch up, and her mother's beads clattered in her pocket. She'd forgotten to leave them in her room. No chance of doing that now; it was too late. Besides, she had other things to worry about.

Chin up, she reminded herself. Maybe he wouldn't recognize her in her uniform. After all, he hadn't the first time.

Just serve the food quickly, then leave.

The king sat at the head of the table. To his right was

the prince, and to the left was the Grand Duke, tying a napkin around his neck in preparation for his meal.

"The Princess of Lourdes was most distraught," the duke was saying. "Most distraught indeed. She was an honored guest of Aurelais, and imagine my mortification when I brought her to be introduced to the prince, only to find out it was his attendant!"

"Charles, what have you to say for yourself?" said King George sternly.

When the prince did not reply, Ferdinand threw his hands up in the air. "Sire, this is a national embarrassment. It'll be the doom—"

"She was there," interrupted Charles finally.

"She?"

"The maiden with the glass slipper?" Ferdinand raised an eyebrow. "Well, why didn't you say so? Where is she now?"

Charles stared at his cup of tea.

"She got away again, didn't she? A rather peculiar young lady, I said so before. I'll say it again to remind you, Your Highness. A girl like that is unfit to be a princess—"

"I won't have you slandering her," cut in the prince. "You don't know her."

"*No one* knows her, Your Highness," returned the duke smugly.

So, Cinderella thought with a quiet breath, *he isn't angry. He's still looking for me.*

The king was quiet during the exchange. As Cinderella approached them with their breakfast, he reached over to the fruit bowl for an orange.

The duke shifted the bowl closer to the king. "Let me help you with that, sire."

"Hmm? Oh, thank you."

Charles frowned. "You seem preoccupied, Father."

The king cleared his throat, but his voice still came out thick and hoarse. "I'm starting to think Ferdinand might have a point." His expression became melancholy, thick white eyebrows folding downward. "I'm not going to be here forever, my boy. I want to see you happy before I go."

"Father, please . . ."

"No more looking for this girl. This afternoon, we'll meet to discuss your betrothal to the Princess of Lourdes."

Cinderella swallowed and focused on setting the breadbasket on the table, along with the accompanying jars of strawberry jam and orange marmalade, and dish of butter— all as quickly as she could. Her last task was to serve the tea; then she could finally leave.

Keeping her head down, she leaned forward to fetch His Majesty's cup so she could refill it. As she bent, her green beads slipped out of her apron pocket and fell into the pot of tea on her tray with a resounding splash.

Cinderella froze. An apology tumbled out of her mouth, but the words were incomprehensible, even to her. As she regained her senses, she reached for a napkin to dry the king's setting, but Madame Irmina—coming out of nowhere—beat her to it.

Irmina batted her away, deftly inserting herself to clean the mess Cinderella had made. "Cinderella!" she admonished, then went on, "My deepest apologies, Your Majesty. The girl is new, and rather clumsy."

If the king replied, Cinderella couldn't hear it. She backed behind a marble column, hoping the prince was too busy listening to the Grand Duke's speech about the Princess of Lourdes's "effervescent beauty and incomparable grace" to pay any attention to her.

The seconds stretched, but before long, Madame Irmina had cleared the royal table and the entire incident appeared forgotten.

"What are you gaping at?" Madame Irmina whispered harshly as she passed Cinderella on her way out of the dining room. "Get back in the kitchen."

"The—the necklace." Cinderella didn't see it—or the king's teapot—on Madame Irmina's tray. "It was my mother's."

"You can get it later." Shoving Cinderella behind her,

Irmina grumbled, "Hurry now, you're making a scene. It's already bad enough that you've disrupted His Majesty's breakfast—"

Cinderella didn't hear the rest of what Louisa's aunt said. The entire time, she'd told herself not to look at the prince. But in a moment of weakness on her way out, she glanced at him . . . to find him staring at her, his mouth agape.

She darted her eyes away, rushing out. She could only guess what he was thinking. How she wished the earth would swallow her whole.

She heaved a sigh of relief once she made it back to the kitchen. A silver platter with a steaming pot of tea and a slim vase of fresh orchids awaited her. "The duchess will take her breakfast in her chambers."

Cinderella fetched the tray and hurried on her way. She had scarcely made it out of the kitchen when her eyes widened in shock.

There he was—Prince Charles, asking one of the serving girls where she was.

She started to turn away, but the prince was too fast. He caught the edge of her sleeve and gently touched her arm.

"Stay, Cinderella. Please, stay."

"You know my name?"

"Madame Irmina spoke it when you dropped this"—he lifted her mother's necklace into view, unwrapping it from an ivory napkin—"into my father's tea." A sheepish grin spread across his face. "I was in such a rush to catch you, I didn't get a chance to clean it properly. It should be dry, but it might still smell like raspberries and lemons—this morning's tisane." He bowed slightly, taking her hand and pressing it to his lips. "Cinderella."

She blushed, drawing her hand away and retrieving her mother's necklace. The beads were still warm from the tea, and she flinched, remembering how astonished Charles had been to see her serving him and his father at breakfast. "You should go back. They'll be missing you."

"What's the matter?"

"I'm . . . I'm not a princess, Your Highness," she blurted. "Or a lady. I'm just—"

"The girl I've been waiting for my entire life?" said Charles. "First, please—don't call me Your Highness."

"But—"

"It's Charles. Just Charles."

"Pri—" Cinderella sucked in a breath. "I mean, Charles."

Charles. The name settled on her tongue, and Cinderella's cheeks warmed. How easy it was to call him by his name, and what a difference it made.

"Cinderella," he said, smiling. " 'Equal in step, equal in heart. For always.' "

"That's beautiful."

"It was my parents' promise to each other. And now, mine to you. If you'll have me."

If you'll have me. Cinderella could hardly believe it. The prince was asking her to be his bride. His bride! She tried to find any trace of uncertainty in his eyes, but all she saw was warmth and sweet promise. It certainly did not look as though he were being forced to ask for her hand.

Happiness bloomed inside her, warming her from head to toe. Being with him, that ache of loneliness she had suffered for so many years would ease away. She'd have a new family, a new home.

Still, she hesitated. It was one thing to hope for someone who'd love her. For years, she had closed herself off from the idea of a new family in order to protect herself. But now that the chance had come . . . Cinderella wrestled with it. With all of it. Marrying the prince meant she'd become a princess. She wouldn't just join any new family—it'd be the *royal* family.

She'd spent so much of her life pretending: in her father's chateau, that she was content to be her stepmother's servant, that she could live the rest of her life there and be happy simply dreaming and wishing. Even at the ball, she'd pretended to be someone she wasn't. Would she be pretending again if she married Charles—pretending to be a princess?

"People wouldn't accept me as your bride," she whispered.

"They'll accept you if I tell them to." He took a deep breath. "Trust me."

"I do, but . . ." She lingered on her words, wondering how she'd tell him about her fairy godmother and how she had come to the first ball. Wondering how she could explain the confusion and uncertainty knotting inside her now.

"But?"

"I think I need some time." She took his hand, covering it with hers. "It isn't a no, Charles, but I've only just left my home. . . . There's so much I'm still learning. And there's someone—a friend who needs my help." Her voice drifted. She wanted to ask him about Lenore, and whether he could help bring magic back to Aurelais, but she wasn't sure how to put it into words.

"I understand," said the prince. If she'd disappointed him, he hid it well. "Take a few days. Take as much time as you need. In the meantime, I'll ask my aunt to release you from your duties—"

"No, don't do that."

He raised an eyebrow.

"I don't want your aunt to know just yet," she explained. "I'll tell her when I'm ready. Besides, if I leave, Madame Irmina will have to send a new girl to attend her. Your aunt

won't be pleased that she'll have to train yet another attendant, and all the servants will have to draw straws. . . ."

"Then I will not speak to her." Charles looked down
at their clasped hands. "But while you're making up your
mind about me, may I come find you? I want to get to know
you better, and you to know me." His eyes wavered, so
hopeful Cinderella couldn't help hiding a smile back.

"All right, but . . ."

"What is it?" he asked.

The prince was close enough that she could see the
stray crumbs of his breakfast still on his lips, and a smudge
of marmalade on the side of his mouth. Holding up the corner of her apron, she dabbed at his lips.

"It wouldn't do for a prince to return to breakfast with
jam on his face," she said, wiping away the marmalade. The
tips of her fingers accidentally brushed against the bend of
his lips, and a shiver raced down her spine.

She darted her fingers away, forgetting she was holding her apron. Its folds landed over Charles's chest, and she
instinctively reached out to fix it. But as her hand hovered
just over the prince's heart, so close she could feel his pulse
beating unsteadily against her fingertips, she flattened her
palm against his chest.

And, as if it were the most natural thing in the world,
she brought her mouth to his.

It was a kiss even sweeter than their first, and Cinderella was glad she had set down her tray, for she surely would have dropped it this time. She stood on her toes, gently pushing Charles a hair's breadth away, so she could whisper:

"This isn't a dream, is it? You, here with me . . . that we've found each other?"

"The sound of my heart in my ears would have woken me up by now if it were." Charles kissed her fingertips, holding them close to him. "I thought it was you—that time in the portrait gallery—when I first saw you wearing Aunt Genevieve's sash. I should have known. I should have found you then."

Cinderella held her breath. "You'll never have to worry about finding me ever again," she said softly, quoting him. "I promise."

They kissed again.

But in their exhilaration, she and the prince made one mistake. Neither of them saw the Grand Duke hiding in the opposite corner, taking in every word of their romantic interlude.

Chapter Twenty-Four

Ferdinand was most perturbed by what he had witnessed. All this time, the maiden with the glass slipper had been *her*.

Cinderella.

Ferdinand had *thought* she looked familiar. What an idiot he'd been to recruit her to spy on Genevieve. Now the girl knew far too much. And if Charles had his way, she would become princess of Aurelais—and then, one day, queen.

"The servant becoming a royal," he muttered to himself, hardly able to believe it. "This is even worse than I feared. It will doom the kingdom."

Displeasure darkening his expression, he twirled his monocle. The prince couldn't possibly marry a servant. The people were already getting ideas; the youth especially no longer had the same respect for rank and breeding—just yesterday, in the western countryside, there had been a riot against the local lord, a riot Ferdinand had worked hard to conceal from the king. And in the east, a band of young revolutionaries had demanded that the king allow commoners to serve on his council—imagine!

If Charles married Cinderella, who knew what the people might do?

Who knew whether the monarchy would survive?

Straightening his back, he tidied the folds of his jacket, dusting imaginary dirt off his sleeves out of habit. He was about to return to his duty at the king's side when he stole another glimpse at the prince and his newfound bride.

They were still talking, their heads bent close like a pair of purring lovebirds. The public display of Charles's affection nauseated him, and normally he would have turned away from the sight in distaste. But then the maid's pale knuckles twisted at the cloth of her apron, even while she smiled at the prince.

A clear sign something was amiss. Given Ferdinand's long experience working with subterfuge and deceit, he was positive she was hiding something, something she desperately wanted to confess to the prince.

Ferdinand frowned. Could it be that she felt guilty for working with him, the Grand Duke?

No, in the height of romantic love, court intrigue and the machinations of espionage wouldn't be on this simple peasant girl's mind. It had to be something else.

The duke had always had a strong sense of intuition; it was what had gotten him so far in his position. He had a feeling that whatever the prince and his bride were discussing, it would be useful to hear.

He inched closer to the couple, tilting his head to catch what they were saying.

"I didn't mean to leave," Cinderella began. "But well, you see, I didn't have a choice. I . . . I had to go because . . ." Her voice trailed off, and the duke leaned forward, nearly tripping over his own shoes.

"Because of what?" asked Charles.

Yes, because of what? Ferdinand echoed in his thoughts.

"Because of my fairy godmother. It was her magic that helped me to the ball, and she warned that at the stroke of midnight, everything would be as it was before."

"You have a fairy godmother?"

Fairy godmother! Confounded by the possibility that magic was involved, Ferdinand knit his thick brows. No, it couldn't be—all magical beings had been banished from Aurelais years ago. His father had seen to that. Magic had brought chaos to every kingdom it touched, what with uncontrolled and uncontrollable fairies casting spells and curses. That magic might have somehow returned to Aurelais was terrifying news.

"Strange," murmured Charles, "I haven't heard anyone talk about magic in a long, long time. I'd almost forgotten about it."

Ferdinand crouched, tiptoeing yet closer to the corner of the wall. Fearing he might have misheard the girl, he held his breath. He needed to listen closely to what she said next.

"Yes," replied Cinderella, staring nervously at her hands. She looked up at the prince. "All of it was magic—the dress, the carriage, the horses. It all vanished."

"But not the slippers."

"No, not the slippers."

"And not you."

"Not me." A pause. "You see, that's why I was in such a hurry to leave. It sounds silly now, but I didn't want . . . I didn't want you to know that everything you saw was a spell cast by my fairy godmother. That my carriage was really a pumpkin, the horses really four mice. And my gown, nothing but rags."

"I wouldn't have cared."

"I suppose I was afraid." Cinderella swallowed. "It'd been so long since I had actually talked to someone—I was afraid you wouldn't accept me. I was afraid that if I stayed, I'd care about you too much, and it'd make going back to my old life impossible."

Cinderella looked up at the prince, her voice soft. "Do you believe me?"

Charles tilted her chin toward him, his expression so tender Ferdinand wrinkled his nose, repulsed. "Yes, I believe you."

Carefully, Ferdinand crouched backward and stood. He had heard all he needed to.

Lo and behold, it was *sorcery!*

That explained why his men hadn't been able to find her. Who would have guessed to chase a pumpkin drawn by four mice?

Ferdinand clenched his fists at his sides, remembering his abject embarrassment when he'd had to report to the king that the maiden had vanished. He hadn't been able to understand it, either: how would a young lady in a coach manage to elude dozens of trained guards—then disappear without a trace for days?

But now all the pieces of the puzzle had come together.

He had to hand it to the girl; she *was* charming. The loveliest young lady at the ball. And no wonder, with a fairy godmother at her side!

Ferdinand grimaced. He would have to proceed very, very carefully. If this Cinderella girl had a magical accomplice, then she was a danger to the kingdom, a threat to all.

Even more so, because Charles clearly was in love with her.

Ferdinand had to tell the king right away. But first, he needed to ensure the king would be on his side. These days, now that Charles had returned, that was increasingly unlikely. Well, Ferdinand would take drastic measures to make the king agree. Even if that required some magic of his own.

A visit to his trusted pharmacist would do just the trick.

Chapter Twenty-Five

At last, Duchess Genevieve retired for her afternoon nap, and Cinderella tiptoed out of the bedchamber and quietly shut the door.

Behind her, Bruno nipped at her ankles and let out a low woof.

"Her Highness is asleep." She placed a finger on her lips. "Be good now. I'll be back soon."

After filling Bruno's water bowl, Cinderella tore off her wig and undid her apron. She needed to freshen up in her chambers before meeting Charles, but attending to the duchess as well as taking over Amelia's chores had taken all morning and afternoon. It was already past four.

After bidding goodbye to Bruno, she raced for her

quarters. Well, servants weren't exactly permitted to *race* across the palace, but Cinderella did her best. Her heels clicked at a brisk tempo against the wooden parquet, her steps a steady counterpoint to the unsteady beat of her heart. She hadn't known her heart could dance, but here it was, beating in a maddening rhythm that thrummed in her chest and buzzed in her ears.

It didn't slow as she changed in her room, so filled was she with the idea of a fresh start. And as her mind whirled, she realized there was one person she wanted to tell—one whose life could change just as much as hers.

"Fairy Godmother? Lenore?" Cinderella whispered as she looked into the mirror. There was no answer. Perhaps the fairy had borrowed too much magic and could not get to her. Cinderella went on, hoping her godmother could hear her from wherever she was. "All is well now—between the prince and me, but I haven't forgotten about you. I'm going to tell Charles about the ban on magic. Once he hears more about the situation, I know he'll confront the Grand Duke and talk to his father about reversing it."

Cinderella paused, gently touching the mirror with her fingertips to seal her promise. Then she made her way out of the servants' quarters, ready to meet the prince. She did not know what the afternoon would bring, but she had more hope in her heart than she'd had in a very long time.

She was just rounding the hallway with the portraits when she heard it—a familiar voice calling her name.

Cinderella. Cinderella.

Startled, Cinderella came to a stop. The gallery was empty. . . . Where was the voice coming from?

"Lenore?" she whispered. "Is that you?"

The painting to her right shimmered. It was one she had noticed before—of Genevieve and Arthur—and the voice seemed to be coming from the volume under the Duke of Orlanne's arm, with the obscured title, *Enchantments.* . . .

"Yes," whispered her fairy godmother. Her voice was tremulous and faint. "My child—"

"Did you hear me earlier? I have such wonderful news. About Charles." She blushed. "I mean, the prince. He knows it was me at the ball, and he . . . I think he cares for me. He'll help you, I know it."

"Oh, my dear, I know you think you've solved it, but . . . perhaps you need to know more about what happened. Why magic is forbidden."

Cinderella drew closer. She couldn't see Lenore, but the outline of a pearly white wand glimmered from the spine of the painted book. Her godmother was there. "I'm listening."

"Years ago, when the queen was born, all the high fairies of Aurelais blessed her with gifts: beauty, charm, grace, kindness, wit—and lastly, selflessness. As she grew up, she brought joy to everyone who met her, most of all to the king. But there were those who sought to take advantage of her kindness, the Grand Duke's father being one of them.

"One winter, a terrible fever spread across the kingdom. Out of the goodness of her heart, the queen sent all the royal physicians to look after the people. There weren't enough doctors, so on some days, she went, too. Then things worsened, and the fever took her."

Cinderella drew a sharp breath. "Poor Charles."

"It was a dark time," Lenore continued. "The Grand Duke's father took advantage of the king's grief. For years, he'd been threatened by the power fairies possessed, by the influence we could have on the court. He took advantage of the growing distrust and fear already rampant in the kingdom against our kind. He blamed us for making the queen too kind, too selfless. Rallying those who were already rounding up and executing fairies, he hunted the high fairies who had blessed the queen and destroyed their wands. The king, distraught, listened, and he forbade magic in Aurelais and banished all fairies, warning that if we ever returned, not only would our wands be broken, we would be imprisoned for life." Her voice deepened. "That is why we have been living in exile."

"Oh, Lenore," Cinderella whispered. "I'm sorry."

"I tell you this only so you are careful, my child," said her godmother. "There are those in this castle who are very content with the way things stand—the present Grand Duke being one of them. I have heard that he has taken up his father's causes with gusto."

"What about the Duke and Duchess of Orlanne?" Cinderella asked. "I found something in the library that I think they wrote to one another years ago, about trying to help."

Lenore smiled sadly. "The Duke of Orlanne did his best to fight the ruling, and he lost much of his support in the council doing so. He and the duchess warned many fairies when the Grand Duke would begin his hunt."

"The duchess is back now," said Cinderella. "She could help. And the prince . . ." Cinderella couldn't give up the idea that things could be different—for all of them.

Lenore's voice brightened slightly. "The prince's love is what you deserve, my dear. But the duke will be suspicious of you once he learns of Charles's affections. Even more so if you start talking about magic. Be happy, and keep yourself safe. Do not interfere."

"But Fairy Godmother, I—"

The grandfather clock at the end of the hall began to chime, cutting off Cinderella's reply. She glanced back, making sure no one else had entered the hall.

They were still alone, but when Cinderella turned back, the painting had gone still.

"I'm going to help you," she promised.

Charles was waiting for her in the glass conservatory before the garden entrance. He started when their gazes met, lurching slightly forward and nearly tripping over his shoes. Cinderella chuckled, and the prince's eyes filled with mirth.

"I'm sorry to keep you waiting," she began. Her voice trailed as she remembered what Lenore had said about his mother. She wanted to ask him about magic, but Lenore's warning to be careful was fresh on her mind. She'd wait until they were outside of the palace and out of range of the duke, with his "ears" everywhere.

"I got a little sidetracked in the gallery."

"And here I thought Aunt Genevieve was the one keeping you," Charles teased.

"She did give me a few extra chores," said Cinderella, grateful when he didn't ask if she had told the duchess yet that she was his intended bride. "I don't think she's very happy with me right now—I brought her the wrong type of tea three times."

She blushed sheepishly, and as his smile widened, her stomach gave a pleasant flutter. She smiled back at him. "I guess my mind was somewhere else."

"I've become quite familiar with the feeling," confessed Charles, gesturing at his clothes. "I might have put this shirt on backward twice today."

"You?" she said playfully. "I assumed you had a valet who dressed you. Maybe two."

"Since the day I was born," replied Charles in a serious tone.

"Really?"

"No." He chuckled. "I am quite capable of dressing myself. Sometimes, I worry it's the only thing I'll be capable of."

Though he tried to hide it, a note of melancholy colored the prince's last words.

"You sound worried," said Cinderella softly.

"I am," Charles murmured. "So much has changed. It's funny, the thought of one's parents getting old. When we're children, they worry so about us. Now I feel like things have reversed, and soon I'll be expected to take on his responsibilities. I don't know if I'm ready."

Before Cinderella could reply, Charles brightened and gestured at the garden doors. "But we've lingered here long enough. Come, there's so much I want to show you."

"Where are the guards?" asked Cinderella. She'd been nervous about coming to this part of the castle, half expecting the guards wouldn't permit her outside. But she hadn't come across a single one.

"I dismissed them. As of today, anyone in the palace is welcome to enjoy the gardens."

Cinderella's eyes widened. "Do you mean that?"

"By royal decree of the crown prince." With a flourish, Charles stepped aside, revealing a new sign he'd posted on the glass door.

"'By royal command,'" Cinderella read, "'every person in the palace, whether a member of the royal household, a guest of His Majesty the King, or a retainer of the crown, hereby shall be permitted access to the royal gardens.'" She clasped her hands, mustering her enthusiasm. "It's very nice."

But something was still missing, and it showed on her face.

"What is it?" asked the prince.

"Every person in the palace," she repeated. "Why not anyone in Aurelais—or anyone at all?"

"Surely not anyone can walk into the palace," said Charles, confused.

"Valors doesn't have a public garden," Cinderella explained, "and the palace . . . one of the reasons I dreamed of going to the ball was because I spent all my life staring up at it. Opening the gardens would give everyone a glimpse of the palace—of their ruler. Even if it was just *part* of the garden."

"You have a point. I'll bring it up with my father—how is that?"

Her smile widened, and that was all the response he needed.

Taking the prince's outstretched arm, Cinderella stepped through the double doors into the gardens. It was nearly sundown, and a soft glow bathed the flowers.

"This way," Charles said, gesturing at a wooden bridge over a pond. "When do you have to be back?"

"To the duchess?" Cinderella repeated. "I hope she doesn't mind my telling you her naps are usually an hour long."

"Then that's just enough time."

"For?"

"A surprise," replied the prince, guiding her through a garden of fluted lilies. Across the lilies was a pond, its waters a vibrant green from reflecting the trees around it. In the center of the pond swam two elegant white birds, their long necks curved toward one another.

"Swans!" Cinderella breathed. She leaned against the bridge's rail and gazed at the pair of swans gliding across the pond.

At her side, Charles rested his elbows on the bridge. "They're here every evening before sundown. Sometimes, during sunset, you can see the light dapple their feathers. Look."

Rays of golden light stroked the swans' wings, which shimmered against the still waters.

"I used to come here whenever I could to watch them," said Prince Charles. "I'm certain it's been the very same pair of swans for years. When I saw them, I'd feel a little less lonely."

"How happy they look," mused Cinderella, watching as the swans took flight, their feet skidding across the pond before they soared into the sky. "Free to come and go as they please."

She watched them weave through the clouds until they finally disappeared.

"What are you thinking about?" asked the prince.

"Once they fall in love, they stay in love forever," Cinderella murmured, repeating what he'd told her at the masquerade. "My parents had a love like that. Always laughing together, telling each other stories, and dancing with me in the middle. My mother was the one who taught me how to waltz. And to sing."

Cinderella started for one of the trees on the other side of the bridge. "There used to be a swing in the family garden, one hanging from a sturdy oak tree—just like this one. Mama would sit on it and sing about the sweet nightingale perching on the branches above her. Sometimes, she'd put me on her lap and my papa would push the two of us toward the sky. When I got older, birds used to sit outside my window, too. The same ones every day. I'd listen to them before starting my chores."

"Your chores?"

Cinderella faltered. She hadn't meant to bring up that aspect of her past, but she trusted him enough to tell him the truth. "Yes . . . after my father passed away, my stepmother dismissed the household staff to help make ends meet. Her stepdaughters took my bedroom and my clothes, and I . . . I became their servant." She placed her hand on his, anticipating his reaction. "It's in the past now. I'm happy, and I'm definitely not lonely anymore. I have Louisa—she's the first friend I've had in years, aside from my dog, Bruno, and the mice in my stepmother's house. And now I have you."

Charles entwined his fingers with hers. "My parents didn't have any other children," he mused, "and Father was always busy in meetings with the council. I didn't have many friends, but I encountered a few wise professors, and I learned to love my studies—I spent hours every day in the library. Books became my friends because I didn't have real ones."

"I loved reading, too," said Cinderella wistfully. "My parents used to have a beautiful library." She omitted the fact that her stepmother had sold off many of the books. "There'd be stories about the countries around us. I'd forgotten most of them until now. It's easy to forget how vast the world is, and how little of it I've seen. I've . . . I've never even been outside the capital."

"Then I'll bring you," Charles promised. "I'll take you

all around the world. We'll tour all the neighboring king-doms. Together. But I have to warn you, traveling as royalty isn't as grand as it looks."

"You mean, it's not thirty courses at every meal and ser-vants waiting on you hand and foot?" Cinderella teased.

"Not always. Everything is always planned out for you. You don't get to choose where you want to go or what you want to do. But you do get to learn more about the world, and see lots of operas and ballets."

Cinderella covered her mouth, hiding a laugh. "To any-one else, that would sound wonderful. Especially the ballet. I haven't been to see one since I was a little girl, but I can easily do without the thirty-course meal and the servants."

Prince Charles grimaced. "I'm sounding spoiled, aren't I?"

"You grew up being told how to act. What to wear, what to say, where to go, and what to eat. I understand that. . . . It wasn't so different for me."

He took her hand. "It is silly feeling sorry for a prince. But up until now, I never had a choice in anything. Before I left for school, the only time I left the palace was when I was out with my father on official business. Even when I did go out, I saw only a sliver of Aurelais. I should have gotten to know my country. I'll have to rule Aurelais one day, and everything I do will be scrutinized by my council and my people. If there's one freedom I'm determined to have, it's to choose who I love and marry."

The warmth in his words made Cinderella's stomach flip. Strange, they'd only been together for a few hours at most, yet how familiar he was becoming to her.

She looked into his eyes, suddenly feeling bold. "I want to go everywhere with you. Whether we get to choose where we go, or not." She brightened, an idea hitting her. "Louisa and I sneaked away to go to the masquerade—*we* could dress up as merchants when everyone's sleeping and slip out." She grinned. "See the real Aurelais, as you say."

"You mean it?" Charles asked. When she nodded, he clasped her hands, bringing them to his chest. "Let's start tonight. I'll try to get Aunt Genevieve to dismiss you early for the evening. Meet me by the coach house? I have some-place I want to bring you."

The coach house wasn't far from the stables, which Cinderella often passed on her morning walks with Bruno after she'd brought the duchess breakfast. She hadn't paid much attention to it before; it was where the royal carriages were kept. There had to be over a dozen carriages, each with gilded trimmings along the doors, fine velvet uphol-stery, and thick blue flags.

She didn't see the prince anywhere, or any attendants.

"Charles?" she called out.

No answer.

The coach house was empty.

Cinderella walked toward the stables, wondering where the prince could be. He'd told her to wait outside the coach house on the path, but—

There, at the very end of the road, was a carriage that had none of the royal finishes. It was plain, with faded white paint peeling along the edges, and open windows instead of glass panes or curtains. In the driver's seat was a shadowy figure she couldn't make out in the dim lamplight. The wheels grumbled against the gravel path and the horses nickered.

The carriage stopped, and Cinderella gasped.

The driver was Charles!

Setting down the reins and climbing down from his seat, he looked at her sheepishly, the slightest pink tinge coloring his cheeks. A driver's cap covered most of his black hair, and he wore a twill coat that was ever so slightly too boxy and large. But for his face, he was almost unrecognizable.

"I encouraged everyone to take the evening off," he explained, even though she hadn't asked for an explanation. He seemed nervous, which was oddly comforting.

She was nervous, too.

Don't be silly, she tried to reason with herself. There was nothing to worry about, and he knew who she was—a commoner, a former servant in her stepmother's house—and he didn't care in the least. So why was her heart racing?

Because she was finally spending time with him—as herself instead of as the maiden with the glass slippers or the princess with the mask. And also because she still needed to ask him about her fairy godmother, and whether he could help her return to Aurelais.

Unaware of her thoughts, Charles gestured at the carriage. "I hope you don't mind."

"Of course not."

He started to open the door for her, but Cinderella shook her head. "I'm sitting with you—in the driver's seat."

"It's chilly out," he protested.

She grabbed one of the blankets from inside the coach. "Then I'll wear this."

Gathering the folds of her skirt in her hand, she climbed up to the carriage box, ignoring Charles's extended hand.

"It's rather high. Are you sure you don't—"

Cinderella plopped onto the seat and grinned down at him. She held out her hand to him. "Do *you* need help getting up?"

Returning her grin, the prince took her hand, and she helped him up to the driver's box. It was a tight and narrow space, made for a single driver and barely large enough to fit them both without their knees grazing one another's and their arms so close they were practically linked, but Cinderella didn't mind. Maybe she hadn't needed the blanket after all—the warmth of his presence next to her was enough to make her cheeks burn.

"Where are we going?" she asked after he prodded the horses to begin moving.

"It's a surprise."

"Another surprise? You're spoiling me."

"Once all of Aurelais knows who you are, we won't have the luxury of going out."

"Maybe it won't be so bad."

"Perhaps," he allowed. "But after word spread at school that I was the prince, everyone began asking me for favors for their family or avoiding me. Some of the students even hated me."

"Hated you? For being the prince?"

Charles's jaw clenched, and he nodded. "I don't blame them. Many people think the nobility holds too much power, too much wealth. Things have changed, Cinderella, but not enough. And they won't, not when men like Ferdinand are in charge."

"I thought your father was in charge."

"My father cares deeply for the people, and the country . . . but as he's gotten older, I think he's lost sight of how to rule Aurelais. Too much time with the Royal Council, listening to men who eat with golden spoons and sleep on goose-feather pillows. It was different when my mother was still alive."

"How so?"

"He loved her dearly, but they didn't always get along. Father has an explosive temper, you see, and he's stubborn as a bull. He and my mother would argue fiercely over how to govern Aurelais. She wanted him to focus more on the people rather than on pleasing the council. I remember during one argument she called him a child for letting Ferdinand and the council influence his decisions instead of listening to his heart. I want to be a king who listens to his heart." He sighed. "There I go, talking about politics when we should be talking about you."

"I want to hear it," Cinderella said, gazing at the city below them. Thousands of lamplights glittered beneath the hill, twinkling like a constellation of stars. "Aurelais is my home, too. I've spent too many years trapped inside my stepmother's home, not knowing what's been happening around me."

"Then you will," promised the prince. "But tonight is for us."

Along the outskirts of Valors, Charles stopped their coach before an open-air theater. "Here we are," he said nervously, tethering the horses to a nearby tree. "It's just a rehearsal, but I've heard the dancers are even better than the Royal Ballet's. I thought you might like it."

"I do." Cinderella marveled at the stage, a simple wooden platform surrounded by a crown of oak trees adorned with hundreds of candles. Half a dozen wagons and coaches were scattered across the field: other patrons who'd known about that night's rehearsal. Closer to the stage were benches and makeshift chairs, each seat filled by someone raptly anxious for the ballet to begin. The orchestra was much smaller than the one that had played at the masquerade the night before, but its music sailed on the wind, carrying clear and true to Cinderella's ears.

"The ballet tonight is *Dancing Princesses*," announced the conductor, before the overture began in earnest.

"Ohh," she breathed.

"You know the story?"

"You don't?" When the prince shook his head, she smiled. "It's about twelve princesses who sneak out to dance in a magical fairyland. Their father is so distressed about it he offers one princess's hand in marriage to anyone who will discover where they go each night."

Charles raised an eyebrow. "Is anyone able to solve the mystery?"

"You'll have to watch the ballet to find out," Cinderella replied mischievously. "It was one of my favorite stories growing up."

"Not anymore?"

"No. When I was a child, I loved pretending to be a princess in a castle, waiting for some curse to befall me and a handsome prince to break it. But as I got older, the feeling of being trapped was all too real. . . ." Her voice drifted. "After Mama and Papa died, things changed. I realized that real life isn't a fairy tale." She threaded her arm through his. "Sometimes, it's for the better."

"It's funny. I used to pretend to be sick so I wouldn't have to go to the ballet. And when I did go, I'd fall asleep. My mother would laugh to see me going willingly."

A flood of warmth radiated inside Cinderella's chest, and she teased, "Are you going to fall asleep tonight?"

"I have a wild guess the company will make a difference." He spread a blanket over their laps. Under the moonlight, their hands brushed against each other. "Besides, Father's royal box always smelled of stale cedar and politics. Both were very conducive to falling asleep."

A gentle breeze tickled Cinderella's nape, and she shivered as she inhaled the fresh air. No stale cedar here, nor the sweet undertone of perfume that usually pervaded the palace. She did catch a whiff of sugared nuts from a vendor closer to the stage, and the smell of horsehair. But she didn't mind.

"Politics doesn't have a smell."

"Oh, it does. I could never even hear the music because someone was always trying to get Father's ear."

"Someone like the Grand Duke?"

"It was Ferdinand ninety percent of the time," admitted the prince.

The mention of the Grand Duke made Cinderella's mood somber. She leaned forward, trying to relish in the music of the overture.

"Something's troubling you," Charles observed. "Tell me."

She bit her lip, glancing at the costumed ballerinas waiting offstage. A few of them were dressed as fairies. "Can I ask something of you?"

"You may ask anything of me."

"My fairy godmother told me that magic was once a part of everyday life here in Aurelais. But now she and her kind have been banished. I'd . . . I'd like to help her return."

"Then we shall," Charles promised. "I'm supposed to begin attending the council meetings shortly. I will bring it up the first chance I'm able."

Warmed by his answer, Cinderella started to reach for his hand, then hesitated. She didn't like the thought of keeping anything from him. "My godmother also told me that the king banished her kind because of . . . what happened with your mother."

The prince's brow knit with confusion. "What happened?"

"You don't know?" she said softly.

"She was sick—many in the kingdom were. She and Father sent me to the countryside that winter so I wouldn't fall ill."

She swallowed. "My fairy godmother said that your mother ordered all the royal physicians to leave the palace and treat those in need. That she joined them, and when she became ill . . . it was too late. The Grand Duke blamed her death on the kindness and selflessness that the fairies blessed her with when she was born. And then . . . he convinced your father to exile all fairies from Aurelais."

Charles's jaw tensed. "I never knew," he said at last. "Every time I asked my father, he refused to speak of her. Her death hurt him so much."

A couple of ladies sitting a row ahead turned to look at them.

Cinderella touched Charles's hand and lowered her voice. "I understand if you've changed your mind about wanting to help."

"No, I haven't. My mother was the kindest person I ever met, and there isn't a day that I don't miss her." Charles inhaled a ragged breath. "But from everything she ever told me about magic, I know that it doesn't make your choices for you. She would never have wanted my father to banish the fairies. She would never have let him unfairly persecute hundreds based on . . . on lies."

The prince turned to her. "Come with me to the next

council meeting. I'll do whatever I must to convince my father to change the law. You can ask your fairy godmother to testify—"

"No, it isn't safe for her. Not with the Grand Duke here. He was helping his father take advantage of yours back then. Surely he wouldn't want things to change now. But . . . *I* will advocate for her, if I can."

"Why am I not surprised that Ferdinand would have something to do with this?" Charles gritted his teeth before giving her a small smile. "Don't worry, Cinderella, we'll have a word with him."

Cinderella squeezed his hand. "Together."

"Together." Charles clasped her hand over his. The ballet was about to begin. "Now I want to tell you something. I promised to show you the world, but I can't promise we'll have many nights like this, with just the two of us."

"No royal guards watching and listening to everything we say and do?" she joked, but Charles's face was still sober.

"I thought about what you said—that Aurelais has never had a commoner for a princess." Charles squeezed her hand. "You will be the first."

Cinderella exhaled. This had also been weighing on her heavily. "I don't know the first thing about being a princess. How to walk or talk or—"

"Protocol and etiquette are overrated," Charles interrupted, trying to reassure her. "Who cares what fork should be used for asparagus or olives or oysters? Or how one addresses a baroness versus a countess? But if that's what worries you—all the rules can be learned. What can't be learned is the happiness your laugh brings to those around you or the way your eyes dance when you smile.

"It's no small thing I ask of you," he continued. "And I would understand if you changed your mind. Or if you need more time."

Trying to untangle the emotions and thoughts inside her, Cinderella fell quiet. All this time, what had kept her from readily accepting Charles's proposal? Fear that she wouldn't be accepted, fear that he had fallen in love with the idea of the girl at the ball, not her. Fear that she wasn't ready to make such a life-altering decision, not so soon after finally escaping her stepmother.

But perhaps she *was* ready. If she listened to the strongest emotions bubbling around her heart, they urged her to be happy. Wasn't that what Lenore had taught her? Wasn't that the point of it all? There were so many things they had no control over—the pride and machinations of others, disease, death. Shouldn't they hold on to happiness when they had it? Already in these past few days, she'd been happier with Charles than she had in years. The answer was simple.

"I'm ready," she whispered, her stomach fluttering as soon as the words left her.

Charles looked at her, the light in his eyes wavering. "Then—"

"Yes," she spoke over him. "I accept."

He drew her close, holding both her hands and bringing them to his lips.

Wishing this moment could last forever, she leaned against the prince's shoulder. At last, she knew.

So this was love.

Chapter Twenty-Six

To his dismay, Ferdinand was not invited to dinner. He blamed Genevieve.

Brimming with the information that magic had returned to Aurelais, he waited for the king to return to his chambers. But when the opportunity finally arrived, the guards at the door stopped him from entering.

"The king is asleep, Your Grace. He is not to be disturbed."

The duke sniffed. "I have important—*urgent*—news for His Majesty."

"We were given specific orders, Your Grace. I'm afraid I cannot let you pass—"

"This is important!" Ferdinand wedged himself between the guards, ignoring their protests and attempts to stop him, and barged through into the king's bedchambers.

"Your Majesty, Your Majesty," he cried, drawing the long velvet curtains that bathed the king's bedroom in darkness. He shook George's arm, hovering over him as the king stirred. "Sire, I have urgent news."

King George rolled over in his bed, then threw a pillow over his head. "Ferdinand? Confounded man, I asked not to be disturbed! Go away. That's an order!"

"But Your Majesty, the prince has found the mysterious maiden."

At the news, the king shot up on his bed. "This is cause for celebration. Quick, quick, the—"

"You'd best listen to my report, first," interrupted the Grand Duke, lighting the candle at the king's bedside.

"What is it? I don't have all day."

"It's the girl," said Ferdinand curtly. "It appears that your son, the prince, has uncovered her identity, and . . ." He paused for effect.

"And?" repeated the king. "From your tone, I'll take it you aren't pleased. Let me guess, she's a baroness. No, a merchant's daughter. A mysterious heiress?"

"She's a servant," Ferdinand said flatly.

"A servant." George leaned back, stroking his chin. A dry hacking sound escaped him, and Ferdinand couldn't tell whether it was a laugh or a cough. "Now that is unexpected."

Ferdinand struggled to conceal his frustration. The king was beginning to sound increasingly like his sister. "My question to you, sire, is what do we do about it? The prince is intent on marrying her, but as you know, this cannot be. She's not only a servant, but also an orphan."

"Why should that matter?"

Ferdinand threw up his arms. "Because the prince plans to ask for your permission to marry her."

"He has it."

Ferdinand's jaw went slack. That was wholly unexpected. "B-b-b-but . . ."

"Enough, Ferdinand. You wrote the proclamation yourself, didn't you?" King George shoved a copy of it in the duke's face.

"Said noble prince will, upon bended knee, beg, request, or if need be, implore said maiden that he be granted her hand in marriage. Whereupon should the aforementioned maiden look with favor upon his suit, then shall the happy couple pledge their troth . . ."

" 'And in due course,' " finished Ferdinand, " 'upon the inevitable demise of His Most Gracious and August Majesty, the King, succeed to the throne, there to rule over all the land, as king and queen of our beloved kingdom.' "

The inevitable demise.

Ferdinand's thoughts lingered on the phrase, and he recalled how he'd ignored it. It was a standard line, one that normally concluded decrees of such nature. Besides, reports from Dr. Coste always stated that though George's health was weaker than before, it was in no perilous state. Nothing was amiss. That *had* been as Ferdinand had wanted it.

But ever since that blasted ball . . . Now the wording snagged Ferdinand's attention.

It was he, the Grand Duke, who should rule Aurelais upon George's passing, not the prince and his *scullery maid*.

It would have been fine if Charles had the decency to marry one of the foreign princesses Ferdinand had selected, but a maid? And one with a fairy godmother?

As always, Ferdinand would have to take matters into his own hands. The king wouldn't understand how dangerous the girl was. He'd have to exaggerate her story, fabricate a background for her. A sorceress . . . yes, he would tell King George that the maid practiced dark magic. That, if anything, would get His Majesty's attention.

When the king wasn't looking, Ferdinand patted one of the side pockets in his trousers, making sure that what he'd tucked inside was still there. Something *would* be amiss, and soon.

"A son of mine can't renege on his promises," went on King George. "Besides, the ballroom's already decorated for a party—we'll have the wedding tomorrow! No, today!"

The king's inattention grated on Ferdinand.

Patience, he reminded himself. *Eliminate the root of the threat.*

"But I haven't finished," he said, waiting to reveal his trump card.

"What do you mean?"

"If only you'd listened to reason, sire," he lamented. "I knew the prince had fallen in love unnaturally quickly." Ferdinand leaned closer to the king's bedside. "The mystery maiden enchanted him, and that is why the poor young man hasn't been able to think straight since he met her. She cast a spell on him!"

"Oh, for heaven's sake, Ferdinand. This has gone on long enough." King George suppressed a cough. "I know you dislike the idea of Charles marrying a commoner, but these are modern times. This is hardly enough reason to wake me from my rest."

"It's true, Your Majesty. I heard it from the girl's lips myself." Ferdinand seized a nearby chair and shifted it close to the king's bed. He lowered his voice. "She admitted to having magic. That was why she left the ball so suddenly."

The king wasn't listening anymore. "Come, help me get dressed. Is she in the palace? Have someone fetch her."

"Listen to me, Your Majesty, you haven't even met the girl. She could be a—"

"A sorceress?" The king let out a shallow laugh. "If she's cast a spell over my son, then so be it. She can have him!"

"Sire!"

"Don't keep 'sire'-ing me." King George let out another cough and cleared his throat, looking aggravated.

"She could be practicing dark magic."

"If she were, you wouldn't bother telling me. She would be in the dungeon by now."

This was true, and Ferdinand cursed his luck that the king was in a mood of reason. Regrettably, it meant Ferdinand needed to resort to his backup scheme. "Are you quite well, Your Majesty?" he asked, putting on his most concerned voice. "Perhaps you should have some tonic for your cough."

"Bah, tonics are useless. Pass me my sleeping draught."

"Where is it?"

"Are you blind, Ferdinand? It's behind you—on my desk. Dribble a bit into my tea. Just a pinch now, I don't want to fall asleep immediately."

Surreptitiously, the Grand Duke turned his back to the king and reached into his pocket for a vial of his own: a little something he'd commissioned from a trusted pharmacist.

It was stronger than his past requests. Far stronger. But the pharmacist hadn't even asked what it was for. Everyone trusted Ferdinand. With good reason, too. Who had helped run Aurelais after the queen had passed, leaving King George overcome with grief? Who had attended every council meeting and kept the court together whenever the nobles quarreled?

Forcing his shaking hand to steady, he slipped a delicate dash of his vial's contents into the king's draught. Then a quick splash of the sleeping draught to mask the bitterness. An invisible thread of guilt tightened around his neck, and he tugged at his collar uncomfortably.

Sometimes a bit of unpleasantness was necessary—for the good of the kingdom.

If this business about His Majesty abdicating soon was true, Ferdinand would have to call upon a secret assembly of his most loyal supporters to propose the amendment to the law that he'd been working on. One that would place him in power, not Prince Charles. He'd have a few days at most—he would have to work quickly.

"Here you are, sire."

The king poured the mixture down his throat with a grumble. "Despicable stuff, I tell you. Couldn't they make this taste better?"

"Taste is insignificant if it'll improve your health, sire."

"Bah. What do these doctors know? They tell me what

I want to hear, that I'll be around to see my grandchildren, my great-grandchildren!" George snorted. "Quacks, the lot of them. I'll be lucky if I see the boy married at this point."

"You mustn't talk like that, Your Majesty."

"I will talk however I please!" the king roared, only to fall into another coughing fit. Once he recovered, he sighed. "This kingdom could use a little magic. *I* could use a little magic."

"Your Majesty, listen to yourself," pleaded the duke. "Magic has expressly been forbidden. That was my father's recommendation and your law. For good reason, too! Think of how dangerous it can be when wielded by someone with evil intentions."

"Yes, but maybe if we hadn't forbidden magic, we wouldn't have to worry about war with our neighbors. Or within our own country. Charles wouldn't even have to consider marrying a foreign princess."

At that, the duke hid a smile. He took out his monocle and pretended to clean it, a habit he was expressly aware he indulged in whenever he needed to deliberate before speaking.

He pulled his chair closer to the king's bedside, patiently waiting for his concoction to take effect.

"I was listening during the council," said George. "People are angry with me for not making Aurelais a fairer place for them to live. There isn't much I can do for them now, but Charles . . . Charles will right my wrongs."

"And I will help him, Your Majesty." A pause. "If he lets me."

The king trusted him. Depended on him. If Charles were to rise to the throne soon . . . The Grand Duke shuddered at the reality of it. He would lose years of hard work and decades of manipulating the king into depending on him for guidance on how to rule Aurelais. Ferdinand needed to strategize his next moves very carefully, and he'd begin with the secret assembly of his most trusted men.

Prince Charles certainly wouldn't listen to him the way his father did. At first, Ferdinand had resigned himself to the young prince going off to university. Maybe Charles would come back ready to listen to men with far more tact and experience at running a kingdom.

But alas, when the prince returned, full of ideas and disdain for Ferdinand, it became evident that things had changed at the Royal University; it had started accepting students based on merit rather than their upbringing, and engaging professors with "ideas." Why, he had even heard that Charles had studied under a false identity so he could experience his schooling like a commoner instead of the privileged royal that he was.

Ferdinand had suggested to George that his son return

home at once when word came that riots near the university had taken place.

"Let the boy be a boy," the king had said. "What are they rioting about, anyway?"

"Taxes," Ferdinand had responded automatically.

"Taxes?" The king frowned. "What about? Did we raise them recently?"

"No," the duke had lied. When, in fact, he *had* authorized a 20 percent increase in taxes, and during a particularly harsh winter at that. The people had been angry because there was no food. The new taxes were meant to discourage the people from rebelling against the kingdom, but they seemed to have had an opposite effect.

So while borrowing the king's royal seal to hide his error, the duke had sent a garrison of troops to quell the rebellion. How relieved he'd been when the entire catastrophe disappeared.

Until months later, when the prince—newly returned home after finally completing his studies—brought it up during the council meeting.

Charles's conduct had been a terrible surprise, the prince unwilling to listen to reason and logic. King George had immediately asked his son to join him in listening to the day's proceedings, but the first thing Charles did was criticize the council's composition.

"All of your advisers are lords," the prince had said, lashing out.

"They're men I've vouched for," replied the duke, keeping his temper in check. "Men who have served the council honorably since before you were born."

"They're men with only their best interests at heart. Men who are willing to extort the poor until they have nothing left. I was there during the riots when the new tax was imposed. I'll never forget them."

Confusion had etched itself on the king's features. "Ferdinand, you told me we hadn't raised taxes."

"Only by an insignificant amount," the Grand Duke blustered. Thank heavens at that moment he remembered the king's plans to throw a ball. "Perhaps we should discuss the ball tonight."

"The ball?" Charles asked, perplexed.

King George's expression brightened. "Yes, my boy. I'm throwing you a ball to celebrate your homecoming. Everyone will be talking about it for years!"

"That isn't necessary, Father. I'm sure I'll be able to greet everyone at court soon enough. Besides, should we even be throwing lavish parties when there is so much suffering outside the palace? "

"Everyone is invited," said the duke testily. "Not just the gentry."

"Everyone?"

"Yes, everyone."

Every eligible maiden, that was.

That had been enough to appease the prince. The duke had been naive to think that was the end of his troubles with Charles. That perhaps the king had been right—find a girl for the prince, and let him settle down.

But no! Then came this calamity of the runaway princess. If only he had been able to identify her earlier so he could send her off somewhere.

Then again, perhaps it wasn't too late for that.

"Ferdinand?" the king was saying. "Are you listening to me?"

The duke's head bobbed up. "Of course I am."

"I was saying," George said, his nose twitching as he absently held his side, "perhaps we should lift the ban on magic. Perhaps that was rash, motivated by grief and an attempt to control something we could not."

"B-b-but, Your Majesty, don't you remember what the fairies did? You cannot forgive and forget—the nation will think you weak, and—"

"You blamed the fairies, Ferdinand. You and your father. I was never convinced it was their fault. And now I wonder whether it's time to let bygones be bygones."

Ferdinand struggled to conceal his shock. Lift the ban on magic in Aurelais? He couldn't even fathom the chaos that would bring. Trying to hide his dismay, he cleared his throat again, loudly. "I'll add it to the list of items to discuss at the next council meeting, sire."

"Good. I know I can trust you." The king sniffled, grimacing at what must have been another pang in his side. "It's something I've been thinking about recently—after a long while of *not* thinking about it."

"Perhaps for the best, sire."

"But now that Genevieve is back . . . You know, she used to talk my ears off all the time about fairies and such, how she always wanted to meet one. Her husband—"

"Yes, I remember the Duke of Orlanne," Ferdinand cut in. "He was always a proponent of magic."

"Maybe he had a point. Maybe I was too hasty banishing—"

"Magic does not solve the problems of everyday life," Ferdinand said sensibly.

"Yes, yes, I know. But sometimes wonder brings happiness. I'd like to witness something wonderful before I go." He closed his eyes, his head sinking into his pillow.

He looks paler, and his eyes are sunken in, Ferdinand thought.

"Your Majesty, are you quite well?"

"Well? Of course I'm well." The king adjusted his sleeping cap to prevent it from falling off his head. "I would have been better if you hadn't interrupted my sleep."

The moonlight cast a ghostly light upon George's wan skin, and for a moment, seeing the king look so ill, Ferdinand felt a prickle of guilt. A *tiny* prickle.

The duke shrugged it away. Ruling a kingdom required a firm hand; guilt and regret were for the weak. "I thought the news of Charles's runaway princess would be important to you."

"Ha, backtracking already, aren't we? You used to be a better liar, Ferdinand."

Ferdinand did not reply. It was true; he had been a better liar. Now he was simply better at hiding his thoughts. A useful skill cultivated over many years, and one King George had never suspected.

"Fetch . . . a decree for me . . . Ferdinand."

"Which decree, Your Majesty?" The Grand Duke tapped the king's shoulder. "Your Majesty?"

George's hooded eyes blinked open. "It's inside my desk. Third drawer on the right. You'll see it right away."

The duke did as he was told.

A crisp piece of parchment slid out of the drawer. Ferdinand caught sight of the first line, and it was all he needed to see: *By royal decree, all magical persons are no longer expelled from Aurelais.*

"It's already been signed," continued George from the other side of the room. "I want you to give it to Charles before the next meeting with the council."

"Won't you be there?"

"I'll be in the back taking a nap." Another cough. "Let it be the first one he presides over."

Shouldn't I be the one to preside over the council in your absence? Ferdinand wanted to ask. It'd been *he* who had headed the council meetings for the past twenty years. The prince had only attended a handful, and maybe only one or two when he was actually old enough to understand what was going on.

But Ferdinand, again, wisely did not voice his thoughts. He crossed his hands behind his back. "I thought I should inform you, sire, your son is planning to hold a third ball this week, with the intent of proposing to the sorceress."

The king's eyelids drooped, and he began to snore.

"Did you hear me, sire?"

"What was that? Ah, yes. Another ball? Excellent." George wagged a warning finger at the duke. "If you do anything to ruin his chances with the girl, well . . . you know what will happen." He crossed his arms and tucked himself deeper into his sheets. "Now go away. It's the middle of the night and I need my rest."

The duke bowed, carefully maintaining his composure. "Then I take my leave, Your Majesty. Good night."

The king was already snoring. Ferdinand closed his eyes, envisioning what would happen the next morning. Dr. Coste would arrive just before breakfast, and His Majesty would learn that his illness had suddenly taken a turn for the worse. Ferdinand would be there to comfort him. His Majesty would reason that he should abdicate earlier than expected, and Ferdinand would smoothly convince him that he would aid the prince in ruling Aurelais. He'd even have the king put it down in writing. . . .

Such thoughts soothed his anxious mind as he exited the king's apartments. If things did not go as planned it could end up disastrous. First, King George didn't seem at all displeased that Charles was planning to wed a servant. And now he wanted to welcome magic back into Aurelais!

Indeed, something had to be done, and Ferdinand had an idea just where to begin. He crumpled the king's decree into his pocket.

Then he turned toward the south wing, headed for the servants' quarters.

Should there be any threat to the future of Aurelais, eliminate it immediately, his father had taught him. *Before it grows.*

He knew the root of his problem well enough, but eliminating it would be tricky.

Very tricky.

Ferdinand sniffed. Fortunately, he was up to the challenge.

He would find a way to get rid of Cinderella if it was the last thing he did.

Chapter Twenty-Seven

It was barely dawn when someone rapped on Cinderella's door, so loudly she shot up from her bed.

"Good morning, Madame Ir—"

"Get up and get dressed," Irmina said, cutting her off. Stray curls dangled over her face; for the first time, the mistress of the household's hair was not impeccably arranged.

"What's—"

"There's to be another ball tonight, and we need every pair of hands working. Don't stand there gaping—that includes you, Cinderella!"

Another ball!

Charles had been true to his word. He would announce his intention to marry her—tonight!

Cinderella dressed, her fingers shaking with excitement as she loosened her braids, pinned on her wig, and wrapped her lavender sash around her waist. A twinge of nervousness made her stomach flutter. After that night's ball, she would be . . . a princess.

I need to tell Louisa—before she hears it from someone else.

A distressed Madame Irmina surveyed the long line of young women under her supervision. Cinderella hurried to her place at the end, but not before waving to Louisa, who'd made it to the roll call just in time.

"Another party," Irmina grumbled. "Why do we even bother to take down the decorations?" She spun to face the girls. "When you have received your assignments, get to work immediately."

One by one, the girls received their duties. When it was Cinderella's turn, Madame Irmina crossed her arms.

"Why the smile? Are you actually *happy* that we all have to scrub the palace floors again, or are you simpering like a fool because you think you won't have to do your share of the cleaning?"

"N-n-no, ma'am," Cinderella stuttered.

"Then?"

"Nothing." Cinderella struggled to wipe the joy from her face. Failing miserably, her expression only brightened.

"It's just a beautiful day outside, isn't it? A wonderful day for dancing."

"All that perfumed air upstairs is addling your wits." Irmina narrowed her eyes. "The duchess asked me to give you the morning off, but it seems you need to learn your place. Your duty isn't only to the duchess—it's to me, too. Report to the kitchens. The maids need help with the dishes."

At the dismissal, Cinderella let out a great exhale, then hurried to change her uniform.

"Where were you last night?" Louisa asked, joining her by the cabinet. "I came by to pick up the gown, but you weren't in your room."

Cinderella swallowed. Where did she even begin? "I . . . I . . ."

Misreading her reaction, Louisa grinned. "Ah, you were with that boy from the masquerade, weren't you? I want to hear everything about it. Everything. But first, I have news."

"News?"

"I heard the prince has found the mystery princess," she said, lowering her voice as the two girls shuttled from the servants' quarters to their posts. "Everyone says he's going to propose to her at the ball. Figured the romantic in you might enjoy that."

Cinderella's heart thudded in her ears. "Where did you hear that?"

"For one, the glass slipper is not in its case outside the palace anymore. And"—Louisa waved an envelope in front of her face—"this! Didn't you get one of these?"

"No, what is that?"

"A letter from the prince himself! Everyone's to get an increase in wages after the ball, *and* a holiday. The royals don't just declare a holiday for no reason . . . it must be because there's going to be a royal wedding. Oh, you must have gotten one. Check your room."

But Cinderella was certain she hadn't gotten one, and it was time she told her friend why. "Louisa," she began.

She didn't get a chance to say more. Madame Irmina called for her in her strident voice, and Louisa's aunt inserted herself between the two girls.

"The duchess wishes to see you, Cinderella," she said, her brows furrowed with confusion. "She asks that you not wear your palace uniform, and that you meet her in her salon at once."

Dressed in the only clothes she owned—the shirt and skirt she had worn when she'd escaped her stepmother's home—Cinderella approached the duchess's chambers with trepidation. If Genevieve had given Cinderella the morning off, why would she summon her back to her room?

Well, in any case, this would be the perfect time to tell the duchess that she was the runaway girl from the ball and had accepted Prince Charles's proposal of marriage. She gathered her courage, rehearsing the words in her head.

Once the doors opened, an overjoyed Bruno barked, racing to greet Cinderella. Forgetting her restraint, she was bending down to massage his ears when a stern voice spoke over them.

"Bruno. That's enough."

The dog's ears lifted at the sound of the duchess's voice. He looked confused, his attention vacillating from Cinderella to Genevieve as if he were trying to decide who he was supposed to obey.

"It's all right, Bruno," whispered Cinderella. "Go on, now."

Hesitantly, her dog shuffled back toward the duchess.

Cinderella had had plenty of experience facing her stepmother when she was displeased. She'd gotten used to being punished for no good reason, and to having Lady Tremaine find fault with her work even when there was none to be had. But she had no idea what to expect from the duchess.

The older woman gestured at the empty chair opposite her. "Sit."

It was a command, not a request.

Swallowing the lump that had formed in her throat, Cinderella obeyed.

Genevieve reached for the teacup on her writing desk, indulging in a long, slow sip before speaking. "So." She returned the cup to its saucer, set it down, and dabbed the corners of her lips with a napkin. "*You* are the mystery girl he's been looking for all this time."

The swan mask Cinderella had worn rested on the table beside the duchess. Genevieve picked it up, tapping it against her shoulder as she pretended to wonder. "This was found in the gardens, and the guards said it belonged to the woman with Charles at the ball. I wonder who could have given it to her."

Cinderella's shoulders tensed. "I was just about to tell you—"

Genevieve raised a hand. "I trusted you. I treated you like one of my own. And you kept this from me."

Cinderella hung her head. "I know."

Genevieve's hand fell to her side. "And yet, I couldn't be more relieved."

Cinderella looked up, surprised to find the duchess smiling. "The two sudden disappearances from the balls certainly gave me reason for concern. I was worried that my nephew had fallen in love with some frivolous girl with an expensive dress and overdone hair—or worse, a pretty face

skilled at manipulating young princes into lovelorn states."
She tapped her cheek with her fingers. "But you . . . you'll
do nicely. Or so my gut tells me."

"Oh, I'm—I'm so glad you think so," Cinderella said in
surprise. "I was worried you wouldn't . . . that you might
not—approve."

"Well, I do. And if my brother doesn't, then I'll make
sure he knows what a fool he is." Something screeched
outside, and Genevieve winced, gesturing at the windows.
"Close them for me, will you? I have important things to tell
you, but who can concentrate with all that racket?"

That "racket" turned out to be because of flowers, hundreds of them, arriving by the cartful. Roses, orchids, lilies,
daffodils, irises, and a dozen other varieties that she could
not name. Heavy porcelain vases were mounted all around
the grand ballroom and the royal gardens, displaying the
arrangements in all their grandeur. But one arrangement
stood out from the rest.

From the duchess's window, Cinderella watched the
gardeners erect a trellis studded with roses. When the palace staff wheeled out a barrow of flowers, white pearlescent
roses intertwined with pink ones as flushed as the height of
sunrise, she nearly gasped.

Her parents' favorite flowers. White and pink roses,
with a touch of myrtle.

Charles *had* been listening.

"Are you paying attention to a word I'm saying?" Genevieve rapped Cinderella's shoulder with her fan. "A princess must be engaged and focused, not prone to daydreaming."

Cinderella jerked her head away from the window. "I'm sorry. I was looking at the flowers."

"Charles's doing, isn't it?" Genevieve clucked her tongue at the sight. "He's a romantic, like his father. Not all kings see the value of marrying for love, as my brother and nephew do. But sometimes love isn't enough. It'll take more, much more, for the court to accept you."

Now Genevieve had Cinderella's full attention. "Aurelais has never had a commoner for a princess. I know."

"That will not be your only challenge."

The heaviness in Genevieve's tone made Cinderella frown. "What do you mean?"

The duchess put on her tiara, and her voice turned grave. "This is between you and me, Cinderella, but the king is unwell. No one knows how ill—the blasted physicians here won't answer any of my questions directly. All they'll say is that he has taken a turn for the worse."

Cinderella's hand jumped to her mouth. She couldn't believe it. "But he seemed fine at the masquerade and at breakfast."

"Yes, I wasn't even aware myself that anything was wrong with him. But I suppose now it makes sense—his wanting to abdicate and everything."

Does it? Cinderella couldn't shake the feeling that something was not right, but maybe it was simply her surprise. "Will he recover?"

"I hope so, my dear. But Dr. Coste wants him to rest, and to steer clear of affairs that will strain him." Genevieve placed a gentle hand on Cinderella's arm. "You do realize what this means, don't you?" she said quietly. "My brother may step down sooner than anyone anticipated, meaning Charles will become king."

That meant if Cinderella married him, she would become—

She swallowed hard. *Queen.*

"I'm not even ready to become a princess," she said. "I can't even imagine—"

"I believe that's part of the reason my nephew chose you. Why he loves you." The duchess's voice remained gentle. "Few would even have second thoughts about becoming a princess, and that you do is a great sign of wisdom. The crown can be a heavy responsibility, but most girls won't understand that. They only see marrying the prince as an opportunity to wear pretty gowns, live in a palace, and become a member of the royal family."

Cinderella reflected on the duchess's words. She remembered how eager her stepsisters had been to go to the ball, how conniving her stepmother had been for them to get the prince's attention. She'd never stopped to consider *why* Lady Tremaine had been so ruthless.

You've never known hardship, Cinderella, her step-mother had told her once, years ago. *You had a roof over your head, food to eat at every meal. Your father spoiled you from the day you were born.*

A ragged breath caught in Cinderella's throat. "I do not wish to marry the prince as a way to better my status."

"I know, my dear. But others will not understand that. In fact, if you accept my nephew's proposal, you will face great opposition, particularly from the Grand Duke." Genevieve grimaced. "The question is, do you love Charles?"

"Yes," Cinderella said without hesitation. "Of course I do."

"And he loves you. I have no doubt that you are the right companion for him, and the right princess for Aurelais."

The duchess bestowed Cinderella with a rare smile. "Ruling Aurelais will not be easy for Charles. At times, it may even feel like a terrible burden, one that he should not have to bear alone. Now that he has you, I pray the two of you will help each other, and I will do what I can to help you feel at home with the role."

Genevieve continued, "You have only hours until you

go from palace servant to the future queen of Aurelais. Many will not take the news well, particularly not the blue-blooded young ladies who will resent the prince for rebuffing them for you."

Cinderella thought of her stepsisters, who'd reveled for years in tormenting her. "I can handle it."

When she did not elaborate, Genevieve appraised her. "When Charles declares that you are to be the princess of Aurelais, all attention will be on you. This is the first impression everyone will have of you.

"You have natural grace, which most princesses take decades to learn, but it won't be enough. Nothing would ever be enough, even if you had been born royal." The duchess lifted Cinderella's chin so their eyes were level. "In my time, we stood by the three Ps. I thought it was a bunch of hogwash, but I'll impart it to you anyway. It was essential that a princess be poised, pleasant, and—"

"Pretty?" Cinderella guessed.

"Presentable," corrected the duchess. "That's what all the wigs and powder and rouge were for. Nowadays, women are more after the natural look. Which, I suppose, isn't a problem for you." She hummed approvingly. "Now, what color gown should you like to wear tonight?"

"Something blue," replied Cinderella thoughtfully. "It was my mother's favorite color, and I wish with all my heart she could have met Charles and seen us together."

"That's a beautiful thought, Cindergirl." She patted Cinderella's shoulders. "Let it be one of several happy thoughts that hold you strong tonight."

"What do you mean?"

"Charles and I may not care that you're a servant in the palace, but the rest of the court will. We must give everyone as little opportunity as possible to find fault with you. The Grand Duke, especially."

It was the second time Genevieve had mentioned the duke. Cinderella decided it couldn't hurt to voice a question that had been nagging at her.

"When I went to the library last week, I came across an old page in a book. It was torn off from an adventure novel. I think it might have been one of yours, from your husband. . . . There was a message: 'We must bring magic back.'"

A note of surprise touched the duchess's features. "You found that?"

"I was curious about magic," Cinderella confessed at last. "You see, I have a fairy godmother, and I'm afraid she's gotten into some trouble for helping me go to the ball. Charles has promised to take me to the council to speak in her defense, but I worry that they won't listen to me."

"They won't," confirmed Genevieve, "not with Ferdinand there." She pressed her lips tightly. "Arthur used to leave me notes among the library's art books so Ferdinand wouldn't catch us trying to save as much of magic as we could: the art and the books and the gifts from the fairies. Alas, in the end we couldn't save the fairies themselves."

A cloud passed outside, darkening the duchess's expression. "In spite of the risks, my husband dedicated himself to reinstating magic into the kingdom. He actually had a bit of fairy blood in him—nothing that would amount to any power, per se—but it was something he was proud of.

"I believe Ferdinand saw him as a threat, as someone who might have more influence on my brother than he would like. It was looking more and more like George would turn to Arthur as his adviser instead of Ferdinand when the former Grand Duke passed. So Ferdinand accused my husband of treason for helping fairies hide in Aurelais, and for being magical—and therefore dangerous—himself. Arthur used the passageways in this very castle to get as many fairies out of Aurelais as he could. When he wouldn't give up their locations, Ferdinand further smeared his reputation. My brother listened, desperate to find some way to channel his grief, I suspect. And lo, we were banished."

A hard lump formed in Cinderella's throat, but she wasn't surprised. "That's . . . that's terrible."

"Ferdinand *is* terrible," Genevieve replied in a steely tone, "but Aurelais is the one that's suffered most without magic. Then again, I suppose you youngsters don't remember what it was like to have magic in the kingdom. It was like seeing sunshine on the other side of the storm or having a little extra wind beneath your feet as you ran home."

"I can imagine," Cinderella said softly. "When I had no hope left at all that things would get better, my fairy godmother came. I wonder now if hope is the most powerful magic of all."

"Hope, and I'd add a thick skin," said Genevieve sensibly. She touched Cinderella's shoulder. "I should have guessed that you have a fairy godmother. The fairies come to those with the heart to change the world around them. You are certainly no exception, Cindergirl."

The duchess inhaled deeply. "I'll do what I can to help her, but try not to worry about it tonight. Tonight marks a new beginning for you, and I have some words of advice: What friends you have now, you should treasure. Once you become royalty, people will only see what you can do for them. There's an unofficial last P my mother used to tell me."

"What is that?"

"A princess must know how to *pretend*—pretend that the jeers don't bother you, or that the whispers aren't about you." A sad smile touched the duchess's lips. "Now I'm not so sure it was the best advice."

Cinderella thought of how she'd sing to herself through

the chores for her stepmother, wearing a smile even when she was so exhausted and so frustrated with her life that all she wanted to do was sink into her bed and dream away her troubles. "I used to pretend quite a bit during the years with my stepmother. . . ." Her voice trailed off. "I pretended I was happy, but I wasn't. I was miserable." She swallowed. "I don't want to pretend anymore."

"Then don't," said Genevieve. "If it were up to me, the last P should have been for *punch*." The duchess chuckled. "Heaven knows I have a number of people I'd love to give a nice rap on the head. The duke being on the top of that list.

"*I* have faith you will make a fine princess. Charles does, too. And so will the rest of Aurelais, once they get to know you."

Cinderella drew a deep breath, trying to calm her nerves. "I hope so."

"You will. It begins tonight. Tonight, Aurelais will finally meet its runaway princess, the mysterious young lady who has captured Prince Charles's heart *and* the curiosity of the entire nation. Tonight, you'll show them you're as lovely as your name."

You're as lovely as your name, Cinderella echoed in her thoughts.

It was almost like something her father had said once, when Drizella and Anastasia first made fun of her name.

Your name is lovely, he'd chided her, *just like you. Do you want me to call you Ella?*

No, Papa. I like Cinderella.

Then ignore them. You're stronger than that, my darling.

"Thank you," she told the duchess. "Truly."

"Feel better?"

"Much."

The duchess clapped her hands. "Now let me show you the dress I've picked out for tonight. Oh, it'll go beautifully with those blue eyes of yours, Cindergirl! The court will titter-tatter what it wants to about your background, but I'm not going to give them anything to carp about when it comes to your wardrobe!"

Chapter Twenty-Eight

A princess must be poised, pleasant, and presentable, Cinderella repeated to herself. *When all else fails, pretending helps. Goodness, I hope I won't have to pretend tonight. Or punch anyone.*

Trying to calm the butterflies fluttering in her stomach, she smoothed her skirts with her hands. Her gown was azure blue, its ruffles accented with strands of pearls and delicate lace that gently tickled her ankles as she glided out of the duchess's apartments toward the Amber Room, the hall adjacent to the ballroom.

"I saw the flowers," she said softly, when Charles greeted her with his arm extended for her to take. "They're beautiful."

He lifted her hands to his lips, pressing a kiss on her

fingertips. "Now there's a piece of your home here—one of your happier memories—to make this your home, too."

Cinderella placed her hand on the prince's outstretched arm, and he guided her into an anteroom that overlooked the gardens. Outside, the arched trellis she had seen the gardeners begin to construct had been finished; now it was exquisitely braided with pink and white roses. As Cinderella gasped with delight, Charles reached for her fingers, gently pressing something into her hand.

On her palm was a ring, with a simple band of gold, slightly burnished with age, and a pale blue sapphire in the center that glittered like a star-filled midnight sky.

"This was my mother's," said Charles. "Nothing would have made her happier than for me to give it to you."

Cinderella was at a loss for words. "I've never seen anything so . . . so . . ."

"Do you like it?"

"I do." She blushed. "I mean, it's lovely."

Chuckling, Charles slipped it onto her finger. "A bit more comfortable than glass slippers, I hope."

"Yes." It was her turn to laugh. "Don't worry, I don't plan on running away."

Charles gazed at her tenderly, but he never got a chance to reply. Pierre found them. "They're waiting for you both to make the announcement."

Together, Cinderella and the prince stepped into the ballroom, hand in hand. No trumpets or royal heralds announced their entrance, and yet everyone in attendance turned to view them, their hushed anticipation almost palpable.

It wasn't the first time a thousand eyes had scrutinized Cinderella, but it was the first time she wasn't so wrapped up in the moment of being with Charles that she actually noticed it. As if he could read her mind, Charles gave her hand a reassuring squeeze, and she smiled at him. Then slowly, one step at a time, he escorted her down the staircase to the ballroom floor.

Immediately, moving like a flock of birds, the guests gathered for a closer view of them.

"Who is she?" their voices could be heard whispering.

"Could it be she? The girl with the glass slipper?"

Opera glasses and monocles flew up as the guests tried to catch a glimpse of her face, doing their best to identify her. At first, their attention unnerved Cinderella, but as she drew closer and closer to the king, it became easier to ignore the whispers and the gossip. What made her more nervous was her imminent introduction to King George.

As the music behind her swelled and ebbed, Cinderella's heart hammered. Seeing King George grimace at her made her anxiety multiply.

Wait, she realized, *he's not grimacing because he doesn't want to see me; he's in pain.*

How different he looked from the buoyant ruler at the masquerade, peering at the guests with his binoculars from his private balcony. Now he was shrunken and pale, his figure slouched against the throne. The king coughed, then straightened as best he could. At his side, the Grand Duke tried his hardest not to smirk.

Cinderella knew the smirk was meant for her, and yet something about the duke looking so smug beside the ailing king struck a wary chord in her. Something wasn't right.

She was barely listening to Charles's speech until she heard the words:

"This is the woman I have chosen to marry, Father."

At that, she perked up. A merry smile replaced the king's grim expression, and the prince held up the glass slipper she had left behind for all to see. It sparkled, catching the lights of the chandeliers, and Pierre brought a cushioned stool for Cinderella to sit on so that she could try the slipper before all the guests. But before she could sit, a woman's voice, low and malicious, rang out from the assembly:

"The prince cannot marry her!"

The music stopped abruptly, punctuated by the screech of a violin bow careening off the strings.

Cinderella felt her back go rigid. Even without turning

to look over her shoulder, she knew who had spoken. A hush came over the crowd, whispers buzzing.

"Guards, restrain her!" ordered one of the king's ministers.

At her side, Charles tensed, but the prince prodded Cinderella forward, urging her not to glance behind them and to continue walking toward his father. But she couldn't. Her legs were wooden, the blood in her veins ice. Besides, she didn't need to turn around. She knew exactly who had spoken, and it was time she faced her.

Turning on her heel, Cinderella rushed back into the ballroom to confront her stepmother.

"The prince cannot marry her!" Lady Tremaine repeated vehemently. She bowed low before the king. "Please, Your Majesty, listen to what I have to say."

"This is an outrage!" exclaimed the king. "My lady, you do us all a disservice with this spectacle. I will not hear any more. Guards, take this woman away."

"Sire," the Grand Duke spoke, "perhaps we should give the lady a chance to explain herself."

"Thank you, Your Grace," said Lady Tremaine. "Cinderella was under my care for many years."

Ferdinand frowned. "So she is your daughter?"

"No, she's a servant. A nobody."

"I'm not a nobody," Cinderella said firmly. If her

stepmother thought she would remain meek and silent as she had while under her care, she was wrong. Cinderella had changed, and she refused to let this woman ruin her dreams once again.

A sneer touched Lady Tremaine's mouth. "That is true—you're not a nobody. You're a thief." Without warning, she snatched Cinderella's necklace. "Ask her where she got these beads. They're my daughter's."

"No! They're—"

"And the glass slipper, and the dress. They were stolen. A girl like her could never have afforded such fine clothes. Why else did I dismiss her from my home? She's a thief and a liar!"

"No!" Cinderella exclaimed. "That isn't true."

"Then—how did you get this?" Lady Tremaine held up the green beads. "And the glass slippers? And the gown you wore? You have no friends, no family, no money."

"Yes, child," repeated the duke. "How *did* you get them?"

Cinderella was at a loss for words. Fearing for Lenore's safety, she couldn't very well reveal that it'd been her enchantments that had given her the dress and the glass slippers. Not when magic was forbidden in Aurelais.

"It doesn't matter." The prince's tone was cool, his dark brown eyes focused coldly on Cinderella's stepmother. "Lady Tremaine, you disrupt the happy occasion of my father meeting my future wife. Where Cinderella procured her garments is of no concern to you. As of tonight, she is no longer under your guardianship, and I would ask that you apologize to her for your accusations."

"Apologize?" Lady Tremaine spluttered.

"Yes, then kindly leave. My guards will escort you and your daughters out."

Anastasia and Drizella tugged on their mother's sleeves. "Mother! Do something, Mother."

Lady Tremaine gawked at the prince. "Your Highness," she began, "I'm merely trying to save you from making a terrible mistake. I've known Cinderella ever since she was a child. She is a manipulative, horrible little—"

"That is not true!" Cinderella cried again. Taking a breath to calm herself, she explained, "For nine years after my father died, I did all that my stepmother asked. I would never steal from her, or lie to her. She was the only family I had left, and I treated her and her daughters with respect."

"Even when Lady Tremaine made her a servant in her own father's home," added Charles, loud enough for all to hear.

A gasp came over the assembly, and Lady Tremaine whirled to deny the prince's accusation. "Her father placed her under my care—"

"My lady," interrupted the Grand Duke, his tone suddenly harsher than it'd been earlier. "I distinctly recall that when I visited your manor with the glass slipper, you said you only had two daughters. Where was Cinderella?"

Cinderella glanced at the duke, surprised he was taking her side.

Before them, Lady Tremaine pursed her lips into a thin line. "Come now, Your Grace, there must be a mistake. You cannot truly believe this—"

"There are records," Ferdinand interjected. "Your Highness, if you'd like to see—I have proof that Lady Tremaine has flagrantly disobeyed the king's proclamation to bring forth every eligible maiden in her household."

"I've heard enough," said the prince, raising a hand. "Guards, escort Lady Tremaine and her daughters from the palace. Come tomorrow morning, they are to leave Aurelais and never return."

Anastasia's and Drizella's faces went ashen, and they glanced nervously at the disapproving crowd around them. Their looks were met with narrowed eyes and lips curled in contempt.

A chord of pity struck Cinderella as she remembered how Lenore and her kind had been similarly exiled from Aurelais. She placed a hand on the prince's arm. "Don't banish them. They've been humiliated enough as it is. For me, please."

At her touch, Charles's expression softened, and he turned to her stepmother and stepsisters sternly. "By the grace of our future princess, you and your daughters may remain in Aurelais, but you are never to set foot in this court ever again."

"Guards!" called Ferdinand, motioning for them to resume escorting Cinderella's stepmother and stepsisters away, but Lady Tremaine raised her chin.

"My girls and I will see ourselves out," she declared to the guards, motioning for them to step aside. She lifted her skirts, and her daughters mimicked her, all three gathering their pride.

"Wait."

Cinderella barely recognized her own voice. She sounded strong, firm—nothing like the girl she'd once been.

"Stepmother. Anastasia. Drizella."

They halted in their step, turning slowly to face her. Cinderella caught her breath, not at all surprised by Lady Tremaine's upturned nose and lifted chin. She used to fear that expression, used to fear displeasing her stepmother.

She no longer had that fear.

The crowds had gone silent, but even if they hadn't, Cinderella wouldn't have noticed the dozens of onlookers in the chamber. A strange sense of calm had flooded her; the words she was about to say were ones she'd never dared before, but she'd dreamed of them for years. No longer would they be fantasy.

"I wish we could have been a family," she said, her voice strong yet quiet. "Ever since my father married you, it's what I wished for most. Instead, you neglected me, you made me serve you, and then you tried to sell me." She paused. "But I'm not angry with you."

Now she had Lady Tremaine's attention.

"I thought I would be," Cinderella admitted. "I *was*. But then I realized that it would only make me unhappy. And after being unhappy in your house for so long, I would never choose to feel that way again. I've accepted we aren't a family, and that we never will be. I've also accepted that I cannot forget those years that you were cruel to me."

The height of Lady Tremaine's chin wilted ever so slightly. She wouldn't look at Cinderella, but her stepsisters lowered their eyes, shame tingeing their cheeks.

"I forgive you, Stepmother, Anastasia, Drizella. I am not angry with you; if anything, I pity you. You can't know happiness if your life is built around resentment. For your sakes, I hope your hearts change."

There. That was all she wished to say, and a soft murmur swelled across the room. Their heads bowed, her stepmother and stepsisters hurried out of the palace, and Charles returned to her side. As conversation resumed among the court, the Grand Duke slithered toward Cinderella and the prince.

"Come now, Your Highness, you ought to take a moment

for the unrest from this unfortunate debacle to settle down before you introduce your bride to His Majesty."

Cinderella barely paid attention as the duke led the couple away from the ballroom and toward an anteroom blocked off by velvet curtains.

All her years with Lady Tremaine had come to an end, and she was free—for good. She'd never have to see the woman ever again if she didn't wish to. Cinderella sank onto one of the cushioned chairs, glad she had a moment to collect herself before going back out to meet the king.

"Are you all right?" said the prince, sitting beside her.

A mess of emotions tugged at Cinderella's thoughts— sadness, relief, pity. She wasn't sure how to sort them out yet, but one thing she was sure of was her love for Charles, and she managed a smile for him. "Thank you for letting her stay."

"Anything for you," said Charles. "Though I have to say, she's terrible, even more than you let on."

"Indeed," cut in the Grand Duke, reminding them both that he was there. Cinderella jumped in her chair.

"That was very elegantly done, Your Highness," Ferdinand said. "Imagine, the nerve of making a maid out of her own stepdaughter! Best to expel such ruffians from the future princess."

"Yes," replied the prince stiffly. "And thank you for your help, Ferdinand."

"It is my pleasure. I vividly recall visiting the Tremaine

household." He shuddered. "Who would have thought there was such a lovely maiden there?" He smiled widely at Cinderella. "Rest here now, and I will ensure that Pierre has retrieved the glass slipper for safekeeping. Allow me also to see to it that order in the ballroom has been restored, and then I will escort you both to His Majesty."

"It's unlike Ferdinand to be so helpful," murmured the prince when the duke had left. Charles stroked his chin. "The Tremaine household *was* on his list of homes to visit. I wonder why he couldn't find you."

"He couldn't find me because I was hidden away," said Cinderella softly. "My stepmother locked me in my room when he came to our estate with the glass slipper. I shattered the one I kept so my stepsisters couldn't use it to get you to marry one of them." She swallowed. Her mouth was dry, her chest still tight from the encounter with Lady Tremaine and her stepsisters. "Your father doesn't think I'm a thief, does he? I didn't steal the glass slippers—"

"I know that," replied Charles. "My father will understand once I explain it to him."

"But will you ask him about my fairy god—"

"Ahem," interrupted the Grand Duke from the doorway. He really had a knack for catching people unaware, and Cinderella wondered how much of their conversation he had heard. "Your father wishes to see you."

Charles sent her an apologetic look. "I'll tell Father everything, then send for you."

"Go," said Cinderella to the prince. "I'll wait here for you."

But as soon as the prince left with the Grand Duke, royal guards appeared out of nowhere, wearing dark and menacing glares.

Cinderella tensed, her thoughts sharpening with fear. They weren't the same men who often accompanied Prince Charles; Pierre wasn't among them. Cinderella was about to remark on it when one of the guards addressed her with a bow:

"For your safety, milady, we've come to escort you from the ball."

"From the ball?" Cinderella repeated. "I'm waiting for the prince. He's gone to see his father."

"Orders." The guard pushed her toward a side door that she'd never taken before.

"This way," he said gruffly, leading her into a dim, narrow hallway.

They're walking too fast, she thought, panicking. "I think I should wait for Charles." When she tried to turn back, the guards grabbed her shoulders.

"Wh-wh-where are we going?" she asked, her voice thick with apprehension.

"The Grand Duke will explain. He wishes to have a private word with you."

Cinderella frowned. "I thought he was with the prince."

The guard eyed her, but instead of responding, he tightened his grip on her shoulders and nudged her to walk faster. The music from the ballroom had grown so faint she couldn't even hear it anymore.

She bit her lip, unable to shake the feeling that something was terribly wrong. The windows seemed to be getting smaller, and the halls shorter. They'd made so many turns that she'd lost track of where they were in the palace.

She held her chin high. Whatever the Grand Duke meant to tell her, however he meant to humiliate her and taunt her that she wasn't good enough to become a princess, he wouldn't be able to change her mind about marrying Charles.

"The Grand Duke will see you here," said the guard, gesturing inside the room.

Someone closed the door behind her with a thud. Cinderella glanced back, but none of the guards had accompanied her inside, leaving her alone . . . with the Grand Duke.

A chill settled over her. The room she'd entered was sparsely furnished, with a square wooden table and two velvet-upholstered chairs that seemed out of place amidst the starkness of their surroundings. In the center of it all, framed by two tall candles and comfortably wreathed in shadow, sat the duke.

"My child," he said in greeting. Ferdinand set down his pen and folded in half the paper on which he had been writing. "Have a seat. I must apologize for taking you away from the ball tonight, but I have an urgent matter to discuss with you."

Cinderella glanced at the offered seat. "I'd prefer to remain standing, thank you."

"Very well, very well."

"You didn't take Charles to see the king," she said flatly. "You lied, didn't you?"

The duke took out his monocle and twirled the chain around his finger. Then he clasped it and curled his fist tight.

"My child," he repeated, "it is my misfortune to be the conveyor of bad news, but it is my duty to see to the future of this kingdom. You see, a nation is a fragile thing, and in these times . . ." He let his voice drift.

"What are you trying to say?"

"I am afraid there is no delicate way of putting this, but it has come to my attention that you have cast some dark and ancient enchantment upon His Royal Highness, our noble and beloved Prince Charles Maximilian Alexander, to make him fall in love with you."

Cinderella's hand shot to her mouth. "That's a lie. I—"

"Young lady, you may not have been aware of this, but magic is prohibited in Aurelais, and all magical persons are banished and expressly forbidden from practicing their craft. As such, your use of enchantment, and particularly upon a member of the royal family, is an act of high treason. Without further ado, you are under arrest."

The three guards that had brought her to meet the Grand Duke returned, this time with thick ropes slung over their shoulders.

Cinderella's eyes widened with alarm. She started for the door, but it was futile. The guards surrounded her. One muffled her mouth with a cloth, and the other two tied her wrists behind her back.

"A moment," said the duke, his voice cutting through her muffled cries.

Cinderella caught her breath. Maybe this was all a mistake.

But as the Grand Duke turned to address her, her heart sank. There was a gleam in his eye that suggested otherwise.

"Don't look at me like that, my dear," he said. "I wish it didn't have to be so. But the crown prince of Aurelais cannot marry a servant. Order would be disrupted, and centuries of tradition and propriety would be upended. It simply wouldn't do. You will come to understand in time."

It sounded like he was speaking more to himself than to her.

"I gather from your encounter with Lady Tremaine that you have not had an easy life," the duke went on, schooling his features into an expression that resembled sympathy. "I am not without pity, my child, and I certainly am not without reason. I am prepared to offer you a generous deal."

At the flick of his wrist, the guard closest to her pulled her toward the table and yanked off her gag and bindings.

Ferdinand touched his finger to his lips, warning her not to scream. "Listen to what I have to say first: I'd like you to pen a note to Prince Charles, informing him that you have had second thoughts about marrying him, and that you never loved him."

"Never." Cinderella squirmed, trying to escape the guard's hold, but he was too strong. "He wouldn't believe it even if I did."

"Young lady, you have known the prince for but a few days. I have known him all his life." The duke pushed a pen into her hands, but she flung it away. The guard tightened his hold on her shoulders.

"In exchange," he continued, ignoring her, "I will see to it that you are provided for. I will arrange for a generous estate in the southern region of Aurelais to be gifted to you, with a healthy annual reparation of ten thousand aurels. Surely, that would be more than enough to appease a young lady of your . . . upbringing."

"No amount of money or jewels or land will make me

change my mind. I don't care about any of that." Cinderella shook her head. "Go ahead and send me away. Charles will never stop looking for me."

"Oh, young love," said Ferdinand, shaking his head with a chuckle. "I take it you refuse my generous proposal?" He sighed. "Then we must move on to my alternative plan."

Ferdinand seized Cinderella's hand, and the guards held her firm so he could remove the ring that Charles had given her.

"A pretty bauble. Our beloved queen's, I presume? Bless her soul."

"Give that back!" cried Cinderella.

"Not another word," Ferdinand warned, and one of the guards immediately clamped a hand over her mouth, stifling her shouts.

The duke twirled the ring around his finger, watching the sapphire sparkle and catch the candlelight. "I think I shall include this with the message I have prepared for young Charles."

He reached into his jacket pocket, fishing out a neatly folded note. "I had a feeling you'd decline my offer, so I went through the trouble of already preparing one."

Alarm surged through Cinderella. "No!" she cried, but the sound was muffled. Desperately, she twisted and squirmed, trying to claw the guard's hands away from her mouth, but he only tightened his grip.

The duke waved the note before her. "Let's have this delivered to Prince Charles straightaway, shall we? Now I must hurry back to the ball before I am missed. Worry not, Cinderella, the prince will think of you fondly, though I regret that even he will forget you in time."

Without missing a beat, Ferdinand deliberately dropped the ring into the envelope.

Then someone threw a sack over Cinderella's head, and her world spiraled into darkness.

Chapter Twenty-Nine

My dearest Charles,

 I have had second thoughts about marrying you and becoming the princess of Aurelais. I must confess I only pretended to be in love with you to escape the dreary confines of my life with Lady Tremaine. Alas, I am overcome with guilt and cannot go on with the wedding. My mind will not be changed. Please don't look for me.

 Your Most Humble Servant,

 Cinderella

Charles read the letter again and again, trying to make sense of the puzzle it presented.

There was no puzzle, really. The message was quite clear.

She didn't love him. She didn't want to marry him.

He was a mess of emotions. Every other time he reread the letter, he believed it.

"I have no one to blame but myself," he murmured. He had told her, as honestly as he could, that life as the princess of Aurelais would not be easy. That if she changed her mind, he would respect it.

And yet . . . deep down, he couldn't believe she'd left him. Couldn't believe that this letter was from her. The words were formal and stilted, not at all like his beloved Cinderella.

But the greatest part of the puzzle was the ring. . . .

Tucked between the folds of the letter, it was the same ring he had given her the previous night. He rubbed the engraving inside the band, the one that proclaimed the love his father had had for his mother. *Equal in step, equal in heart. For always.*

So why did he refuse to believe it was from her?

Because if she truly left, then she isn't at all the girl I thought she was.

Clutching the letter tight, Charles rang for Pierre.

"There's still no word of her, Your Highness," said his attendant, responding before Charles even asked. It was the sixth time in half an hour that he'd rung for the man. Probably the hundredth time since the ball had abruptly ended the night before.

"Check everywhere. The servants' quarters, the stables, the coach house . . ."

"We are looking, Your Highness." Pierre bowed his head. "The Grand Duke has sent his entire staff in search of her. Unfortunately, so far, it appears she has vanished."

Vanished. For the third time.

Trying to sort out his thoughts, Charles clung to reason. The first time, she had fled at the stroke of midnight, fearing that the enchantment her fairy godmother had cast over her would expire. The second time, she had left the ball because she had feared an encounter with her stepmother and stepsisters.

This time?

I must confess I only pretended to be in love with you to escape the dreary confines of my life with Lady Tremaine.

Charles balled his fists at his side. He still refused to believe it.

"I should have gone after her last night," he mumbled to himself.

It would not do for you to chase after her, Ferdinand had said. *Especially with all the guests here, Your Highness, you must not appear distressed. It would only encourage rumors to spread, and given the uproar caused by Lady Tremaine's outcry, we must contain any possibility of scandal. Stay with your father; the strain of tonight's events is not sitting well with him. He has retired to his chambers to rest. Go to him, and allow me to search for the maiden.*

He'd been so stunned by Cinderella's disappearance and worried about his father that he had actually trusted Ferdinand.

This time, he wouldn't sit idly by. He grabbed his cloak. "Tell my father I won't be coming to breakfast, and please extend my apologies to my aunt."

"Wh-wh-where are you going?" Pierre blustered.

"To find her," replied Charles without stopping. "It's what I should have done the first time."

The prince cut through the gardens, headed for the hall where the seamstresses worked. Before he left the palace, there was one person he needed to see.

"Have you seen her?" he asked Louisa in lieu of a greeting. "Cinderella?"

The seamstress's brows leapt with shock, and she bent into a hasty curtsy. "No, Your Highness. Not since yesterday at the ball. It's not like her—she's usually so reliable."

Charles's shoulders slumped. He'd thought—he'd *hoped* that she would have given her friend a clue of where she'd gone. Cinderella had spoken so glowingly of Louisa.

She's the first friend I've had in years, aside from my dog, Bruno, and the mice in my stepmother's house.

"Louisa, isn't it?" he said quietly, only now becoming

aware that there were dozens of seamstresses trying their hardest to pretend they weren't listening. "Would you please let my attendant, Pierre, know immediately if you see her?"

"Yes, Your Highness. I will." Worry etched itself in Louisa's brow. "I didn't realize she was missing. You should look for her dog, Bruno—your aunt adopted him, and Cinderella wouldn't leave without him. If he's still here, he might be able to find her."

Bruno! Charles started. Why hadn't he thought of that?

He touched Louisa's shoulder, thanking her before he hastily left. "That's a brilliant idea. Thank you. Thank you, truly."

But when he reached the duchess's chamber, there was no sign of Bruno.

"Charles," Aunt Genevieve greeted him, looking grave. "I was about to send Pierre to look for you. Your father wishes to see you." She paused. "It's urgent."

It appeared Charles wasn't the only one who had received the king's summons. Armed with a fountain pen and a scroll, the Grand Duke was already present in King George's bedchamber. As usual, he looked like he was up to no good.

"In the event that the prince does not make a suitable match," said Ferdinand, "then I, Grand Duke Ferdinand de

Malloy, esteemed protector of Aurelais and trusted adviser to King George, will assume the duties of safeguarding the kingdom. By whatever means necessary."

"By whatever means necessary," echoed the king weakly.

"Thank you, sire," said the duke, taking a pen from the king's hand. An expression of smug glee grew on Ferdinand's face, one that Charles did not like at all.

"Stop!" cried Prince Charles. "Father, what are you doing?"

At the sound of his voice, the king's mouth bent into a feeble smile. "Charles, my boy. Is that you?"

The prince rushed to his father's bedside and tried to seize the scroll from the Grand Duke. "Father, did you sign—"

"Best not to upset your father," interrupted Ferdinand.

Charles glared at the Grand Duke. In his iciest tone, he said, "Get out."

Ferdinand blinked, pretending to look bewildered. "Your Highness, your manner is most uncouth, and certainly not befitting of—"

"Get out," repeated Charles. "I will not say it again. And give me that scroll."

The duke's smirk returned. "I'm afraid you do not have the privilege, Your Highness," he said calmly, tying the scroll with a green ribbon. "As your father's adviser, it is my duty to bring this to the council. Rest assured, I am merely trying to preserve the sanctity of this nation and protect—"

"You are *trying* to protect *your own* interests."

"He . . . he is not," wheezed the king. "Listen to what he has to say, Charles."

Startled, the prince knelt beside his father. "Aunt Genevieve said you called for me. That it was urgent."

"Your father is unwell." Ferdinand straightened his collar. "He has appointed me to discuss with you the kingdom's future. *Your* future."

Charles struggled to remain calm. He did not like the sound of this.

"It appears that the young maiden named Cinderella was seen leaving the palace yesterday evening, renouncing Your Royal Highness's admirable intention to marry her and publicly humiliating our noble prince before the entire court—"

"I don't need you to recount last night's events," said Charles through his teeth. "What is your point?"

"The point is, the lack of a bride also leaves in question Aurelais's line of succession," said Ferdinand. "His Majesty and I both agree that, as a matter of principle, Your Highness must consider an alliance with a princess from a neighboring kingdom."

"I have already made my choice."

"And your choice has abandoned you," rejoined the duke smoothly. "For the third time."

"I have kept an open mind regarding your choice of a bride, Charles," said the king. "But the girl . . . Cinderella is not suitable."

"Father . . ."

"Perhaps you should take your leave now, Ferdinand," said the king. "I'll continue this discussion alone with my son."

"As you wish, Your Majesty," said Ferdinand, hiding a smug smile.

When the door closed, Charles sat at the king's bedside. He couldn't believe how weak his father looked. His skin was sallow and his eyes bloodshot and sunken. Just yesterday, the king had seemed fine. What had happened?

"My boy, I know your heart was set on Cinderella. I wanted her to be the one for you. I wanted to live to see you two married, to bounce your child on my knee." The king's voice trembled. He sank deeper into his blankets, the bed's massive headboard dwarfing his shrunken frame.

"Unfortunately, given last night's events, I do not think she is right for you."

"Father, I know it looks like she fled the ball—"

"Not just one time, but three. The girl fled three times, and vanished three times." The king shook his head. "If she loved you, she wouldn't have left."

The words thudded in Charles's ears, and he swallowed, not wanting to believe them.

Please don't look for me, her note had ended.

No goodbye, no apology, no hint at all of where she was going or why she had suddenly changed her mind. That stung.

He'd seen how uncomfortable she'd looked being the center of attention. His aunt had told him how, when she'd asked Cinderella what she wished to wear for the ball, she'd replied, "Something blue. It was my mother's favorite color, and I wish with all my heart she could have met Charles and seen us together."

Other young women in the kingdom would have asked for a gown fit for a princess, for satin gloves rimmed with crystals, a tiara studded with rubies. Cinderella had asked for none of these things.

That was why he loved her. For the earnest way she thought of her words before she spoke, or how her eyebrows danced when she smiled, or how her voice became singsong when she teased him.

That was why he missed her.

His father reached for his hand. "I'm not well, my boy."

The prince's attention snapped to his father. "You will be. Dr. Coste will—"

"Dr. Coste can't figure out what's wrong with me. I don't know how much time I have, and there's no point in beating around the bush. I need you to promise me something."

The prince held his breath. He knew he wasn't going to like whatever his father was about to ask him, and yet he heard himself say, "Yes, Father. Anything."

"You are the future of Aurelais, Charles. Consider the duke's proposal and meet with the princesses. Secure peace for our country by choosing one to marry."

Softly, Charles replied, "What about love, Father? Didn't you say it was your love for my mother that made you a better ruler?"

A shadow fell over the king's face, and he grimaced. "Perhaps I was wrong," he said tightly. "Perhaps times were simpler then." He inhaled. "At least consider it, my son. For the good of the country."

Charles warmed his father's hand with his own. A hard lump formed in his throat, and each word crawled out of his chest, hurting more than the last. "Yes, Father."

Blinking away the moisture in his eyes, Charles slowly rose and kissed his father's forehead. "Rest well, Papa. I will come see you again soon."

George pulled on Charles's collar, drawing him close. He reached behind his pillow, pushing a scroll into Charles's arms. "You are king now," he rasped.

"What?"

His father coughed, his hands trembling as he let go of Charles. "I wanted to wait until you were married, but it was always the plan for you to take over. I'd only hoped I would live longer."

Charles wouldn't hear it. "You are not dying."

His father leaned back. "I certainly feel like it." His voice drifted. "You're young, Charles, but not as young as I was when I assumed the throne. You will be a good king. Ferdinand . . . Ferdinand will help you."

"Father?"

A soft wheeze escaped his father's lips, settling into a snore. After confirming that his father had fallen asleep, Charles sighed. He would try again later.

"Be well, Father," he said softly before exiting the king's bedchamber.

"Your Highness, are you . . . are you all right?" asked the royal chamberlain outside the door.

The prince drew a deep breath. What could he say to that? His father's health was rapidly deteriorating, and the only person he wanted to talk to about it—the only person left in the world whom he loved and who could possibly have made him feel better—had vanished without so much as a goodbye.

How could he be all right?

Yet he mustered the barest of nods. "Yes, thank you for your concern, Sir Chamberlain. Please see to it that I am not disturbed for the rest of the day."

"Yes, Your Highness . . . I mean, Your Majesty."

The words *Your Majesty* rang in Charles's ears. Without another word, he turned on his heel, feeling more lost and alone than he could remember ever feeling.

Chapter Thirty

Heavy strokes of pink brushed the dawn. Pink, like the ballet slippers worn by the dancers Charles had taken her to see only two evenings ago. A lifetime ago.

Chimes from the clock tower rattled Cinderella's nerves. Six o'clock. Just yesterday, she'd been in the duchess's chamber, preparing for her first introduction to the king and his court. Funny how much could change in half a day.

The clock tower went silent, and she wondered if that had been the last time she would ever hear its bells. Whether it would be the last time she ever saw Aurelais again.

She pressed her cheek against her cell's lone window, staring at the palace. How near it was, so near she could make out the colors of the curtains drawn against each window, but so far no one would hear her if she shouted for help.

"After I escaped Mr. Laverre, I'd promised I'd never feel so helpless again." Her fists clenched. "But what can I do?"

She'd tried everything: pleading with the guards outside, pulling at the bars on her window, kicking at the door—all to no avail. Her fairy godmother couldn't help her escape a locked cell, and calling for her would only incriminate Cinderella further. The only person who could do anything was Charles, but if he'd gotten the duke's falsified letter from her and believed it . . .

No. He wouldn't believe it. Cinderella clung to the hope that he was looking for her. He had to be.

But would he find her before the Grand Duke sent her away?

All night she'd dreaded the duke's return, feared being sent so far from Aurelais that Charles would never find her. Unable to sleep, she'd curled against the wall, squeezing the bars of her window as she waited for the outside world to wake. It was an ordinary day to everyone else.

Everyone but her.

Finally, she released the bars, her fingers so stiff it hurt to move them.

Three mice nipped at the frayed remains of a rope snaking across her cell. She knelt beside them, taking solace in their company. In the weeks since she'd fled her stepmother's house, Cinderella had tried to forget her past life, but she suddenly missed the little friends she'd left behind.

A faint but familiar pang of loneliness touched her heart, and Cinderella pulled her legs to her chest, hugging herself close. It was cold in her cell, the gossamer sleeves of her gown clinging to the goose bumps that'd risen on her arms.

Just as she closed her eyes, trying to summon a happy thought that might relieve the heaviness in her chest, the sound of a key turning in the prison door made her lurch.

She shot to her feet. Dared she hope it was Charles? Or the duchess, perhaps—

Alas, it was the duke. His tall, wiry figure emerged from behind the prison door, a frigid breeze accompanying him and jostling the blue tassels hanging from his shoulders.

"Get!" He stomped on the floor, trying to scare the mice away. When they disappeared into the holes of the walls, he exhaled with relief and finally greeted her.

"I thought you'd like to know that preparations are being made for your departure."

"I am not a sorceress," she said defiantly, "and you know it."

"I am quite aware of that. If you were, you would not still be in your prison cell, obviously, and we would have taken no chances with your punishment, which would have been far more severe."

His response surprised her. "Then why am I here?"

The duke heaved a sigh, the corners of his mouth turning downward. If not for the gleam in his eye he might have actually looked like he pitied her. "My role as adviser to the king is not an easy one. I take no joy in uprooting your life and causing the prince distress."

"Then let me go," Cinderella said. "There's still time for you to do the right thing—"

"You don't seem to understand. Anyhow, things are more complicated now. . . ." The duke paused deliberately. "Especially since the king is dying."

Cinderella stilled. Duchess Genevieve had mentioned the king taking a turn for the worse, but hearing it from the Grand Duke's lips confirmed her fear. "Dying?"

"Yes, he collapsed last night, not long after the ball ended. The physicians blame it on the stress caused by the scandal revolving around the true identity of a certain mystery princess."

"He collapsed?" Cinderella staggered back, putting space between herself and the duke. "How is he now? How is Charles?"

Ferdinand ignored her questions. "Imagine how aghast the king was when he learned that his son was planning to marry a maidservant! You, Cinderella—you're to blame for this."

"Me?" More than ever, Cinderella was certain something wasn't right here. The Grand Duke didn't seem to be worried at all about the king. But too much was happening at once, and Cinderella couldn't make sense of it all as her head swam with the duke's accusations and the news that the king was ill.

"In fact," he went on, "Charles has already conceded to the king's demand that he marry a princess of our neighboring kingdom."

"No," she whispered.

"Yes, I'm afraid it is so. You see, he chose duty over love, just as I expected."

"How is Charles?" she asked, her voice but a pale whisper. After four years, he had only just returned home. She couldn't imagine how distraught he must be to find his father gravely ill.

"The prince will be fine. No need for tears, my dear."

"And the king?" she whispered.

The duke leaned closer to her, and the smirk that had rested on his face in the ballroom returned. "His Majesty's health is none of your concern."

"How can you be so—" Her hands flew to her mouth as realization hit her. The vial she had found in the nobleman's pocket, the smirk the duke had been wearing as the king coughed. "The king isn't ill, is he?" Cinderella's distress over the king's health curdled into horror. "You . . . you poisoned him!"

A smile spread across Ferdinand's face. "*Poison* is such an unpleasant word. Indeed, I have been tipping the scales for months now. Only a little at first, mostly as a precaution, but once I realized my influence on the crown was, well, *waning*, something had to be done. But worry not. I will administer the antidote . . . once I am presented with my new title as Grand Overseer of the kingdom."

"How could you?"

Ferdinand sniffed, twirling the chain of his monocle flippantly around his finger. He seemed to revel in justifying his wicked deed. "His Majesty has become weak. Twenty years ago he would have never even *thought* about repealing the ban against magical beings. Yes, Cinderella, under King George's last decree, your precious fairy godmother would be allowed back into Aurelais." He sneered at her. "Don't look so surprised. Yes, I know it was she who helped you seduce the prince. Imagine, a doe-eyed young woman like you being a sorceress."

He laughed. "Your fairy godmother will never be safe in Aurelais, so long as I am in power. And as of noon today, I will be."

"Why . . ." She seethed. "I don't know how you live with yourself."

"Quite pleasantly, if you must know. Genevieve told you he means to pass on the throne to Charles, didn't she? At first, I was appalled by George's decision. Charles isn't ready to rule, and he knows it. Then I thought to myself . . . this is an opportunity to restructure the monarchy. Should Charles rise to the throne prematurely, he would naturally need someone by his side, guiding him."

Ferdinand tugged on the ends of his mustache. "Once the council meets today, it is *I* who will be safeguarding the kingdom, as Grand Overseer and Councilor Regent. That is, until Prince Charles is sufficiently prepared to be king—a determination that lies, naturally, with me."

"You lied to the king from the very beginning!"

"I *guided* him, young lady, as is my job . . . my duty! So you see, Cinderella, I cannot have you staying in the palace and knowing all my secrets. Especially not as princess of Aurelais. You will be brought to a proper dungeon, the location of which only *I* shall know. And there you shall end your days—"

"How could you do this to your prince?" Cinderella burst out, barely listening to the duke. "Your king? He trusted you."

Ferdinand scoffed. "I chose love for my country over love for my king."

"Why should they be different?"

"You think me without a heart, my child. But in time, you will see that all I have done is for the good of Aurelais."

"It sounds like all you have done is for the good of yourself," said Cinderella.

"A reputation takes a lifetime to build. I won't have mine fall to ruins because Prince Charles chooses an unsuitable girl to take as a wife, and the whole country falls to chaos as a result. Aurelais needs a traditional queen, one whose presence will not undermine the rigors of the monarchy."

"Maybe the people would welcome a queen like them," Cinderella countered.

"The people don't know what is best for them." The duke donned his hat, pushing the feather so it did not obscure his vision. "They complain that we nobles have all the power and all the gold, but if we were to allow peasants to make laws, then imagine the chaos that would unfold. If we were to give every commoner a hundred pieces of gold, then who would bother tilling the fields and working the land? Aurelais would fall into disarray. No, no, I shan't allow that to happen. Order must be upheld, above all."

"You think you're protecting this country," she said quietly, "but you're not. It's people like you who are hurting it."

"We shall see, Cinderella. We shall see. It is no longer your concern. Now I must go, for the council awaits my announcement of Charles's imminent marriage to the Princess of Lourdes. The guards will alert me when your fairy godmother arrives."

He bent, whispering conspiratorially, "You see, I'm quite confident she will come to your aid. And when she does . . . she'll regret she ever set foot in Aurelais."

He gave a dark chuckle, and Cinderella's insides clenched. "No!"

But he whirled away, and the door closed behind him, his steps clicking against the cold, dank stone. A plea for him to come back nearly crawled out of Cinderella's throat, but she closed her mouth, refusing to beg. She would find a way out of this herself.

Taking in her bleak surroundings, she swallowed. *Somehow.*

Doubt pricked at her insides. There was no Bruno to help her distract the guards, no Louisa to help her sneak out of the prison. And calling upon Lenore was out of the question. That was what the Grand Duke wanted.

She'd have to do this alone. But how?

Wringing her hands together, she leaned her head back against the wall, ignoring the mice skittering at her feet. Had it only been a few weeks ago that she'd been alone on the streets, promising herself she'd never feel this helpless again?

Think, Cinderella. She gritted her teeth. *Think.*

She only had until noon, when the guards would arrive to take her away from the palace. When the duke would meet with the council and become the Grand Overseer of the kingdom.

She needed to beat Ferdinand to the council.

Chapter Thirty-One

For the hundredth time, Cinderella kicked at her skirt, searching its silken layers for something, *anything* that could help her get out of there. Odds were slim an absent-minded seamstress might have left some pins or a needle in such a fine garment, but Cinderella was desperate.

She flipped the folds of her skirt back and forth and did the same with her sleeves, unrolling them. Nothing.

What was she hoping for—a needle, a button? None of it would be any good against the guards outside her cell.

It'd be better than nothing. And I have nothing.

Frustrated, she staggered back, resting her head against the brick wall. Her beads clattered against her neck, and Cinderella's hand went up to her mother's necklace.

More than once, it'd occurred to her that she could try to bribe the guards with it. But the beads were from her mother, and she would never give them away.

An idea came to her.

Her hands trembling, she reached for the loaf of bread a guard had tossed into her cell earlier.

"Breakfast," he'd barked at her. He'd shuddered at the sight of the mice nibbling at her ropes. "Better eat it before the rats get to it."

She'd ignored him, feeding the mice half her loaf while she brainstormed ways to escape. Word must have spread among the mice that there was food to be had—nearly a dozen now scurried about her cell, eagerly awaiting their meal.

Cinderella sprinkled a few crumbs on the ground, a plan slowly forming in her mind.

Outside her tiny window, the sun glimmered, nearly at the peak of its daily ascent. On the other side of the cell door, the guards started talking, and Cinderella stilled. Had the carriage arrived?

"His Grace wants to be sure no one notices the prisoner leaving."

"Go on ahead and fetch her. She was up all night scratching at the door, and I think she's at it again, the meek little mouse. I'll ready the carriage."

Cinderella clenched her fists. She'd show them just how "meek" she was.

I have to hurry, she thought. Carefully, she broke the remains of her loaf into the smallest chunks that she could and stuffed them into her pocket. Then she knelt, picking up five of the mice scurrying about her feet and tucking them into the folds of her skirt.

It felt like forever before she finally heard footsteps.

"Good morning, little mouse," the guard jeered. "You finish your breakfast?"

Open the door, Cinderella thought. *Hurry and open the door.*

"Is it time?" she asked, clutching her dress tightly. The mice inside wriggled, and she worried they'd scamper out before she could go through with her plan. "Have you come to take me away?"

With a laugh, the guard finally unlocked the door. He whipped out a long scarf, holding it toward her threateningly. "First I've got to make sure you don't make too much noise. Can't have you screaming the entire trip out of Valors."

He tried to seize her by the arm, and Cinderella sidestepped. Working as fast as she could, she reached into her pocket and threw the breadcrumbs into the guard's hair. Then she unclenched the folds of her skirt and let the mice go free.

They scurried after the guard, nibbling at his leather boots and climbing up his legs to his head. As he cried out in alarm, Cinderella stole out of the prison toward freedom.

A daunting hill separated the prison from the palace, the hundreds of steps no doubt designed to exhaust any captives who dared escape the Grand Duke's clutches. Hungry and tired, Cinderella could feel her muscles stiffening from the endless climb, but she pressed on.

Up and up the narrow steps she scrambled, keeping one hand against the hill's rough stone face to help her balance. There had to be a faster way to the palace.

Behind her, the two guards were catching up. She couldn't rest now.

Once she was halfway up the path, the stone behind her fingertips rumbled. A trapdoor behind the moss swung open, revealing quite possibly the last person Cinderella expected to run into.

The Duchess of Orlanne yanked her through the hidden door, shutting it behind them, and covered Cinderella's mouth with her hand.

"Quiet, Cindergirl. Louisa, blow out the candle."

A second surprise: Louisa, standing beside the duchess, her shaking hands clutching a candle that she immediately snuffed. And Bruno!

Her bloodhound looked fiercely proud of himself, and

Cinderella knelt to hug him. "Were you the one who found me?" she whispered. "Dear, brave Bruno. Thank you."

In the darkness the four waited, Cinderella's heart hammering through the silence.

"Where did she go?" the guards asked each other.

"I saw her disappear around here."

Outside, leaves rustled.

"Nothing but moss and ivy. She couldn't have gone missing like that."

"Why not? The Grand Duke said she was a sorceress, didn't he? Maybe she's evaporated into the air, or turned into one of these birds squawking everywhere."

When the voices faded, Louisa relit the candle and the duchess ushered Cinderella into a dimly lit tunnel.

"What is this place?" Cinderella asked.

"You didn't think the servants' tunnels were the only secret passageways in the palace, did you?" Genevieve harrumphed. "I know all the service entrances and exits, most of them so well hidden you wouldn't think to notice them. *These* were built during darker times, in case the royal family ever needed to escape. These are the ones Arthur used to help the fairies all those years ago. There are two paths: one back to the palace, and one into Valors."

Right as she said it, they approached the fork. "The choice is yours, Cindergirl. You've seen what dangers come with being a princess, and this is only the beginning. Take the left and it will bring you to Valors. Or the right—"

"I'm going back to Charles," Cinderella said immediately. There was no hesitation in her tone; she knew her choice.

The duchess smiled, taking the candle to lead the way. "Then right we go."

Cinderella fell in step with Louisa. "I wanted to tell you, but I didn't . . . I didn't know how."

"You don't need to apologize," Louisa said, threading her arm through Cinderella's. "I understand."

"Friends?"

"Always," replied Louisa. She winked. "I got to meet the prince this morning, thanks to you."

Cinderella's pulse quickened. "He was looking for me?"

"Yes, and I had no idea where you were. That didn't sit well with me, so I sent him to find Bruno. But—"

"But he never got a chance to look for you," Genevieve interrupted. "The king sent for him, and now he's stuck in a council meeting. Fortunately, Bruno here knew something was amiss. All day the mutt was whimpering, and when I took him on a walk he raced out of the palace—nearly gave me a stroke, I tell you! But he kept running and barking, and I put two and two together and figured that it was because of you. Didn't take a genius to figure out that Ferdinand, the snake, had you taken away." Genevieve picked a piece of straw from Cinderella's hair. "And I was entirely right."

Louisa pushed open another trapdoor, this one leading into the palace. Once Cinderella was inside, Genevieve started leading them toward the royal audience chamber—to find the prince and stop his betrothal ceremony to the Princess of Lourdes. But halfway down the hall, Cinderella stopped. There was something else she had to do.

"Your Highness, Louisa," she said, "you must find Charles, and hurry. Interrupt the ceremony if you have to."

"Where are you going?"

"The Grand Duke . . . I have to stop him. He's been poisoning the king."

"What?"

"And lying to him—to engineer his own rise to power. I have to prove that he's a traitor to Aurelais."

"You can't go snooping around the duke's offices looking like that," Louisa said, eyeing her torn gown and bruised arms. "Not when the guards are looking for you. Here, take this."

The seamstress reached into her basket and passed Cinderella a pile of garments. "These are yours. After we found out *you* were the runaway princess, Aunt Irmina asked me to take them back to the sewing hall. I'm glad I kept them."

Hurriedly, Cinderella changed into her old work uniform. Then the four parted ways, with Cinderella and Bruno heading for the Grand Duke's office.

She didn't know what she was looking for. Her pulse thundering in her ears, she rifled through his drawers. There were maps, charts of the lineages of the noble families of Aurelais, tax reports, and letters from various members of the council, but nothing that suggested he'd been lying to the king. Nothing about burying King George's wish to permit magical persons back into Aurelais, or about poisoning his own sovereign.

But as Cinderella looked through the papers, she stopped. She had never seen the duke's handwriting before, yet it looked familiar. Neat with a careful flourish—and the seal he used on his documents looked like something she *had* seen before.

She frowned, searching her memory. Where, oh, where had she seen it before? She'd been with Louisa, sewing—ah!

Digging into her apron, she fumbled for the scraps of paper she had found while helping Louisa mend clothing in the seamstress room. She'd forgotten to toss them away.

The seal was the same. The handwriting the same.

But where was the rest?

"Can you help me find this?" she asked Bruno, letting him sniff the scrap she'd found. After a moment, his nose twitched. Then, nose to the ground, he quickly edged out of the duke's office toward the bedchambers, where he stopped in front of a wide wooden closet.

"In here?"

The dog's grunt confirmed the answer to her question.

She swung open the duke's armoire, scouring his clothes until she found a row of hanging trousers, each with identical satin stripes. She started searching through their pockets, but Bruno was faster. He bobbed his nose at a pair at the end of the row, and Cinderella unhooked it from the rack.

There.

Something crinkled against her fingers. Daring to hope, she pulled it out, and there it was! The rest of the missing page. Piecing the scraps together, she held the papers against the window. "'I have a need for a concoction that will cause grievous pain—enough to make one consider stepping down from his responsibilities,'" she read aloud. She gasped. This was it—proof that Ferdinand had been poisoning the king!

The front door to the duke's chambers creaked open, and Cinderella quickly stuffed the pages into her pockets.

"What do you think you're doing, young lady?"

Under the glare of the duke's attendant, Cinderella shot to her feet, hiding the document behind her back. "I'm . . . I'm cleaning His Grace's—"

"What's that in your hand?"

"It's . . . n-nothing."

"You . . . you look familiar. You're—" Before the attendant's suspicion could grow any further, Cinderella dashed out of the duke's chambers into the hall. She was in such a hurry she didn't look ahead . . .

And ran straight into the arms of the Grand Duke himself.

Chapter Thirty-Two

"You're a clever one, escaping the royal prison—I'll give you credit for that," said Ferdinand. "But you've made a great mistake returning to the palace. Your time is up, my child."

He clapped, and the guards rounded on Cinderella.

She twisted away from them, holding up the papers she had taken from the duke's office. "These! These are proof that the duke is a traitor!"

The guards hesitated, glancing at the duke with uncertainty.

"You would listen to her lies?" Ferdinand lashed out. "Useless, all of you." He seized her arm, snatching at the papers she'd found, but Bruno snarled, pouncing on the duke and gnashing ferociously at his legs.

The duke kicked Bruno aside, pushing him toward the guards. He tugged at the collar of his shirt, looking flustered. "Get those papers!" he barked at the guards. "And arrest her!"

Reluctantly, the guards advanced, but Cinderella dug her heels into the carpet, her eyes steely and cool and daring them to come for her. She held up the papers she'd found, reading as loudly as she could, "'I have a need for a concoction that will cause grievous pain—enough to make one consider—'"

"Stop her!" Ferdinand shouted.

The guards tried to seize her arms, and Cinderella twisted away, bolting for the royal audience chamber. She'd gotten as far as across the portrait gallery when, suddenly, Duchess Genevieve appeared on the other side of the hall.

"What is the meaning of this?"

Immediately, the guards halted, and the Grand Duke recoiled at the sight of the king's sister. "Stay out of this, Genevieve," he warned her. "The girl is under arrest."

"For what crime?" entered a new voice.

Charles! Cinderella's heart swelled when she saw him emerge beside his aunt.

"For what crime, you ask?" Ferdinand blustered. "She's a sorceress, Your Highness, a danger to the kingdom—"

"Enough," commanded Charles. "The only danger to the kingdom is you."

"Come to your senses, Your Highness. She's cast a spell on you. Y-y-you aren't yourself."

The prince wasn't listening anymore. He turned to Cinderella, relief flooding his eyes as he took her hands in his own. "I knew that letter wasn't you. But when I saw the ring inside . . ."

"I wouldn't leave you," she said, her fingers tracing along his palm. "I thought you were at the council to announce your betrothal—"

"I couldn't go through with it. Then Aunt Genevieve found me and explained everything." Charles broke his gaze from Cinderella to glare at the duke. "After what you've done to Cinderella, you're a brave man to dare remain in the palace, Ferdinand."

To the duke's credit, he maintained his composure. "Magic is forbidden. You know the law, and *I* know the girl used magic to attend the first ball."

"Then it's time the law changed," replied the prince.

"Unfortunately, that is not your decision to make." The Grand Duke waved a familiar scroll, tied with a green ribbon. "Your father made me Grand Overseer of Aurelais."

"I would check that decree again if I were you," said the duchess. "You'll find that it hasn't been properly signed."

Ferdinand frowned as he fumbled at the scroll. "H-h-he signed the declaration. I saw it with my own eyes!"

"Look again. *I* convinced George to go along with the plan to bring out your true colors. It wasn't easy, given how much he trusts you. Luckily, even after all these years, he still trusts *me* more."

The duke's eyes bulged, and he looked like he was about to faint. "Why you . . . you conniving old witch!"

"I learned from the best, Ferdinand," said Genevieve cheerily. "I couldn't very well counsel my brother to entrust the kingdom to *you*, now could I?"

Cinderella caught the scroll as it slipped from his fingers. "'By royal decree, I hereby declare Ferdinand, the Grand Duke of Malloy, Grand Overseer and Councilor Regent of the kingdom of Aurelais, until he should see fit to grant full power to my son and heir, Prince Charles.' Signed—" Cinderella laughed softly. "Signed, Grinning Ginny."

Ferdinand made a choking sound.

"I hereby strip you of your lands and title," said Charles coldly. "Ferdinand, you are banished from Aurelais, never to return."

"B-b-but, Your Highness, Your *Majesty*—you simply don't understand. I was just—"

"Trying to protect the kingdom?" Charles finished for

him. "By going behind my father's back to seize more power for yourself?"

Spinning for the door, the duke tried to flee, but the guards grabbed him by the arms so forcefully that his monocle fell out of his pocket, swinging back and forth.

"You were about to make a mistake," Ferdinand said pleadingly. "By marrying a servant, you invite war to Aurelais. The people will never understand. They will never accept her."

"Cinderella may be a commoner," spoke up the duchess, "but I have no doubt she will make a queen far more worthy and beloved than any you might have chosen."

Cinderella stepped forward. "I know not everyone will accept me," she said quietly, "but I've learned that life isn't perfect. You can't be happy all the time, and I can't expect everyone to love me. But the people are our future. If we don't realize that, if we keep clinging to the past, then Aurelais *will* crumble."

The doors behind her burst open, and in stormed the king, still in his pajamas.

"Where is the traitor?" he rasped. Shadows hooded King George's eyes, and his voice was barely louder than a whisper. In spite of it all, his energy had not dimmed, and as he shook his fists at the Grand Duke, two attendants scurried after him.

"Father, what are you doing here? You should rest."

"Bah, rest? When my sister tells me that this *scoundrel* has been poisoning me?" King George ignored his son's entreaties and set his gaze on the duke. "How could you, Ferdinand? Poison, really?"

The Grand Duke cringed. "Your Majesty, there, there— allow me to explain."

"What is there to explain?" Charles seethed, clenching his fists. "You tried to kill the king. There had better be an antidote."

The king's guards began to search the duke, but he twisted in their grasp.

"I-I-I can obtain the antidote for you," he stuttered. "But perhaps an act of clemency might be in order first, sire— a-a-after all, it was all in good measure, and n-n-o one was harmed—"

Bruno pounced on the duke, tearing at his pockets. A vial tumbled out, landing on the soft carpet, along with a crumpled piece of parchment.

"That's it, sire! The antidote. You see, it was harmless. Truly. I didn't mean for it to go so far."

"Lock him up," King George ordered the guards. "I never want to see him again."

"B-b-but, sire!"

"And throw away the key." The king turned his back to

Ferdinand, a deep frown setting on his face until the guards dragged the Grand Duke out of sight. Then King George sniffled, blowing his nose into a handkerchief. "I thought of him as a friend, you know. He wasn't always so terrible."

"People change," said Genevieve, patting her brother's shoulder. "Sometimes for the better, sometimes not."

"He wanted to protect the kingdom," added Cinderella gently. She picked up the vial along with the parchment that had slipped out of the duke's pocket, and handed them both to the king. "Sometimes even the wickedest deeds begin with good intentions."

Could the same be said about her stepmother? Cinderella realized she no longer needed to find out, and that was probably for the best.

Still clenching the antidote tight in his fists, the king drank it all in one gulp and made a face.

Cinderella wasn't the only one holding her breath as she watched the king. Slowly but surely, the pallor in his skin faded, and a slight flush returned to his cheeks.

He let out a deep breath. "And you, young lady—" He gestured to Cinderella. "It's high time we were properly introduced."

"Meeting your future daughter-in-law while still in your sleeping clothes, George?" said Genevieve. "And in the presence of a traitor? How unceremonious."

"Better here than risk her running away again. No glass slippers on you this time, eh?"

Cinderella couldn't help laughing. "No, Your Majesty, I won't run away. Not ever again."

"Glad to hear it. It's an unbecoming trait in anyone, let alone a princess, having the entire kingdom search for you with nothing other than a glass shoe." The king chuckled. "That will be a story for the ages."

At the mention of magic, Cinderella's laughter faded. "The Grand Duke was right about me using magic, sire. I'm not a sorceress, but my fairy godmother gave me the dress and the glass slippers to attend the ball. She's the kindest person, and it would mean the world to her—and to me—if you would allow magic in Aurelais again."

Bewilderment came over the king's face. "Allow magic? I already cleared this up with Ferdinand. . . ."

His voice drifted as he unfurled the crumpled paper. "My proclamation! I . . . I gave this to Ferdinand this morning to present to the council."

"It looks like he never intended to share it," said Genevieve.

"Remind me to add another twenty years to the duke's time in prison," mumbled King George. He cleared his throat, turning to Charles. "I believe I left Aurelais in your charge. It's up to you, my boy."

Charles took Cinderella's hand. "It's up to *us*," he said. "By royal decree, all persons of magical talent are hereby welcomed once more in Aurelais."

As soon as the words left his lips, a halo of glittering lights appeared in the hall. All present watched in amazement as Lenore materialized before them, her hands clasped at her chest and her dark eyes glittering with tears.

She wasn't the only one. The duchess's eyes were misty, too, and it took Cinderella a moment to realize why.

"Your Majesty, Your Highness, Charles"—Cinderella gestured—"allow me to introduce you to my fairy godmother."

"It is our good fortune to finally meet you." The duchess spoke first. Her words came out thick and hoarse, and she sniffed before clearing her throat. "My husband would have been happy to see this day."

Lenore clasped the duchess's hands. "I remember your husband well, Genevieve. I wish I could have thanked him for his many kindnesses to my friends. And for the sacrifices he made so this day could finally come."

"I wish we could have done more. For too long, Aurelais cast your people away. Magic has nearly been forgotten, and for that, I am truly sorry."

"Now, that isn't true," soothed the fairy godmother, letting go of Genevieve's hands to circle the small crowd. "What is magic if not a little miracle? Those come in all shapes and sizes every day, with or without my help. In the form of love and joy, most often, but in other forms, too. Magic only makes the miracles come faster."

Lenore placed her hand on Cinderella's arm. "And what a miracle you've fashioned for us all, my dear child. I wanted to help you find your happily ever after, but it is you who has helped me."

"I'll never be able to thank you enough for everything you have done for me," replied Cinderella. "Magic is welcome again in Aurelais, and it always will be."

Wiping away her tears with her sleeve, the fairy godmother bounced back onto her heels, then gave Prince Charles a stern look. "Well, young man, are you going to hold the slipper all day long?"

"Pardon?" Startled, Charles looked down and found Cinderella's glass slipper on his palm.

"If I recall, you were going to give it back to her at the ball. This is as good a time as any, after all!"

Extending his arm to help Cinderella keep her balance, Charles knelt, tilting the slipper toward her foot.

It was a perfect fit.

"But where is the other slipper?" asked the king.

"It's gone," said Cinderella softly. "I had to—"

"Say no more." Lenore winked. At the wave of her wand, the missing slipper appeared on Cinderella's foot, and a gentle rush of wind swept across the palace.

When Cinderella blinked next, pink and white roses

decorated the hall on white trellises. And not just inside the palace, but outside as well! Everywhere she looked, pink and white roses bloomed across the kingdom.

"An early wedding present," said the fairy godmother triumphantly.

The king leaned out the window, inhaling the fresh air. With a happy sigh, he looked up at his sister. "Seems like I've left the kingdom in good hands, doesn't it? It's high time I retired to the country, or—what do you say to a visit in Orlanne?"

"I'll give you three weeks before you come running back to Valors," said Genevieve. "I know you, George. You won't be able to stay away from the palace, especially if there are grandchildren in your future."

A deep blush reddened Cinderella's and the prince's cheeks.

"You're in the business of granting wishes, aren't you?" the king asked, nudging Lenore, a joking gleam in his eye. "Make sure these two continue the royal line! There's plenty of space on the palace walls for portraits of ten grandchildren. Or more!"

"For goodness' sake, George," scolded Genevieve, "let's get on with the wedding first. At this rate, you're going to frighten the poor girl away."

"No, she's here to stay. I can tell." The king cocked his

head at his son and Cinderella, who were by the window murmuring with their heads close.

Oblivious, the couple shared a tender kiss. As Cinderella's heart swelled with happiness, a burst of rose petals swelled up from the gardens and danced into the sky: a celebration of magic, love, and hope.

She touched her forehead to Charles's, both of them smiling at the sight.

By the end of the day, all of Aurelais would know that the prince had finally found his princess, and that magic had returned to the country.

The next week, Cinderella and Prince Charles were married. It was a magnificent affair: Cinderella wore a lustrous white gown—sewn by none other than Louisa and her mother—that went beautifully with her sparkling glass slippers. Duchess Genevieve walked her down the aisle, and Bruno proudly bore the ring—balancing it on a velvet cushion on his head.

Out of the goodness of her heart, Cinderella even invited Lady Tremaine and her stepsisters to the wedding. She didn't want the happiest day of her life to be marred by any bitter feelings toward her stepmother. Though Lady Tremaine did not attend, Anastasia and Drizella did, and over the years, Cinderella and her stepsisters developed a civil if not warm relationship.

The king never did retire to his estate in the country-side, but instead, he relished his new freedom by visiting Genevieve in Orlanne and traveling to Aurelais incognito, often borrowing his son's university jacket during his stolen evenings out even though it was far too large for him.

Magic returned to Aurelais, fairy godparents bringing hope and little miracles to those in need of it, and the Grand Duke of Malloy was exiled far from the kingdom, never to be seen again. King George and Genevieve took over the duke's former quarters, using it as an office to help newly reinstated magical beings return to Aurelais, while Cinderella and Charles dismantled the council, putting in its place an assembly of forward-thinking men and women, regardless of rank or wealth, to advise them as they ruled the country.

The story of Cinderella and her glass slipper had spread far and wide, and many wished to hear it from her own lips. But as she and the prince traveled the far corners of the world, recounting how they'd met and come to fall in love, they emphasized that their story didn't end with the glass slipper being found and returned to Cinderella. No, their fairy tale continued on, with each day together and later with their children.

As for the glass slippers, Cinderella and Charles kept them displayed in the garden for all to see—as a reminder that magic, as wonderful as it could be, was never the key to making one's dreams come true or making one happy. After all, spells were fragile, hopes could shatter, and dreams could stay dreams, never given a chance to take wing.

If one looked very carefully, sewn onto the cushion upon which the slippers stood was the word for what Cinderella and the prince found to be even greater than magic, than dreams, than happily ever afters, than even hope—

It was love.